YELLING AT THE STARS

MICHAEL HERTZOG

Fresh Prints Publishing
Seattle, WA

Content editing by Fran Lebowitz
Copyediting by Rebecca Behrens
Cover design by Youness El Hindami
Layout by Paul Baillie-Lane / www.pblpublishing.co.uk

Hardback ISBN: 979-8-9871289-0-9
Paperback ISBN: 979-8-9871289-3-0
Ebook ISBN: 979-8-9871289-2-3

Visit my website here:

HOME IS WHERE THE HURT IS

"What?" I shout, sounding similar to Grandpa's screaming goats. "Why do we have to move?"

"It's a good opportunity," Mom assures me. "Your grandpa left us the farm."

"A good opportunity for who?" I look at Dad to see if that crossed the line.

"Asher!" he roars. "Watch it!"

Yep. Crossed it.

He jabs his finger at me from his side of the table. I can almost feel the thump, thump, thump of his fingertip on my chest.

Rory buries her head between my back and the couch cushion, probably wishing this would all just go away. The problems aren't going anywhere, but apparently we are.

"But what about my friends?" I argue. "I just leave them?"

"I'm so sorry, sweetheart," Mom says. "I know this is hard. We can come back and visit. We'll only be forty-five minutes down the road, and you can talk with your friends on the phone whenever you want."

"Are you serious? I don't talk to my friends. We play outside."

"You could play games on video chats," says Rory, the words somehow escaping her pillow-muffled mouth.

"Would you want to do that?" I ask.

"No," she says. "Probably not."

"And you're forgetting that the farm doesn't even have Internet. You have to go to the library to use it. I'm not going to the library to talk to my friends."

Mom chimes in. "We'll make it work."

"Why can't we make it work here?"

"Listen!" Dad barks. "We're not asking for your permission. We're telling you that we're moving."

I've always considered myself a polite kid, but Dad is making it nearly impossible lately. It's hard to respect someone that doesn't deserve it.

"Now quit the whining," he commands. "End of discussion."

"That was a discussion?" I ask, accidentally out loud.

SLAM!

Dad hits the table, which makes me jump. Mom's glass tumbles over, spilling water all over Rory's art. The colors bleed together, trickle off the table, and pool on the floor.

Rory yanks her head out from behind me, flings herself over the back of the couch, and crawl-sprints down the hallway.

"Mac," Mom whispers, as she puts her hand on his knee.

"Don't *Mac* me," he orders.

Then he pushes her hand away and turns to me with a look that dares me to keep talking.

"What more do you want to discuss?" he asks.

He doesn't really want to know. His face isn't inviting me to share. It's threatening me if I do. It's like the time he asked, *"Do you have a problem with that?"* after he told us he quit his job. The only correct answer was *no*.

I muster up my calmest response.

"I'm just wondering why."

"Why?" he scoffs, as if the word itself is offensive. "Life sucks sometimes. That's why."

This year has proven that already. I didn't need a reminder.

"We don't have a choice," he continues. "We're losing the house."

It takes a second for the words to set in.

We're losing our house?

"You happy now?" he says. "Is that a good enough reason?"

How do you lose a house? I thought we owned it.

"Great," he says sarcastically. "If there aren't any more questions, I have work to do."

"What work?" I ask, then instantly regret it.

"Work!" he says. "Somebody needs to hold the government accountable. I can't let them win."

I know better than to discuss the government with Dad. It's like he bottles up all his anger toward "the man" and dumps it on Mom, Rory, and me. If this is what he's been wasting his time on instead of finding a job, then I'm the one who should be angry, since *He's* letting the government ruin my life.

There are no words for moments like these. Anything I say would just make things worse.

"Great," he says. "Now go find your sister and start packing. We leave in a week."

WE'RE FARMERS NOW

"Rory!" I yell. "Stay on your own side of the car!" I draw an imaginary line down the middle of the back seat.

Dad offers the response fathers have given since the invention of cars. "Zip it! Don't make me come back there!"

The drive to the farm has never felt so long. Maybe it's because there's a lot on my mind. Maybe it's because I won't be returning home this time. Or maybe it's just because of Rory. So annoying.

Dad named her Aurora; after the aurora borealis. He said it's because she danced every night before she was born and was stunning when she entered this world. I think it's because her head's a hundred miles from Earth. Dad got to choose her name because Mom chose mine. Asher is from the Bible and means happy. The woman in the Bible named her son Asher because she was so happy he was born. The weird thing, though, is that he wasn't really her baby. Her slave had the baby for her. It's a messed-up story. I'm changing my name the day I turn eighteen, which is still six torturous years away.

The road straightens, and I see their mailbox up ahead. I guess it's our mailbox now.

I've been here plenty of times, but this time isn't like the others. Usually, it's just a few days, or maybe a week at most, but this time we're here to stay.

Rory taps on my shoulder like she's a woodpecker. "Look, look, look, look, look! Look Asher! Look at the fish!"

"I see it. I see it. It looks the same as last time, and the time before that, and the time before that." Except everything has changed.

The number 6629 is stenciled on the side of a fish-shaped contraption, mounted on some weathered two-by-fours. A while back, Grandpa saw this mailbox on TV that looked like a giant bass. To get your mail, you pulled down the lower lip, reached deep into its belly, and plucked it out. But of course Grandpa didn't want to buy one off the TV.

"Four easy payments of $19.95?" he complained. "Do they really expect people to fall for that hogwash?"

This was one of the rhetorical questions he liked to ask.

"*Rhetorical* means that you're not supposed to answer it," he informed me. "You're just supposed to think about it."

Since Grandpa wasn't the type to spend his hard-earned money on hogwash, he made his own bass mailbox, and let me just say that he was a great fisherman; not really a great artist. It was such a pain to open and close the dang thing that he eventually just put the original mailbox next to it. He left the fish as a reference for visitors, though. "Turn right at the bass," he used to say, and he'd leave it at that.

Turning right at the bass, we rumble up the long, gravel driveway, between two seemingly empty fields, to Grandma and Grandpa's old farmhouse. I press my forehead against the window, watching the line where the gravel road and the dirt field meet as it dances back and forth.

Even after Grandma passed away a couple years ago, we

still called it Grandma and Grandpa's farm. Anything else just sounded wrong. But now that Grandpa's gone, what do we call it?

"Are we going to give the farm an official name?" I ask.

"No," says Dad, glancing back in the rearview mirror. "It's just the farm."

Mom tries the less bitter approach. "Oh, Mac. Can't we just let them have a little fun?"

She turns her attention toward us. "You guys can let us know if you come up with some creative ideas, okay?"

"Rory's farm!" squeals Rory.

"She said creative," I point out. "Rory's farm isn't creative, and it's only about you. Why would we name it after you?"

"Asher," Dad says sharply, "don't be a punk."

Again, Mom's words soften dad's harsh edge. "Sweetheart. Your sister's only eight. Extend some grace, please."

I want to tell Dad he's a hypocrite, but I don't, of course. Angry fathers frown upon talking back. No need to make things harder on myself. Instead, I rest my head on the window, let the drama fade away, and picture Grandpa and me out in the field.

Grandpa loved asparagus more than anyone should love a vegetable. He valued the dirt it grew in, the water he shared with it, and the sweat it took from him. Grandpa refused to leave the farm when Grandma died. As he said, "I will not be put in a home." That didn't make sense to me, since he was already in a home, but Mom explained that it meant he didn't want to be put in an "old folks' home." I get that. How depressing would it be to be stuck with a bunch of other old, dying people? You meet them, and everyone is so nice, then you watch as your new friends die off, one by one. That's kind of messed up.

Mom says that his home is in heaven now, which is great for him. And it apparently leaves the farm to our family at a very convenient time since Dad just lost our house. But is there really a convenient time to leave all your friends behind?

Moving sucks, but it's not like life has been great up until this point. Dad hasn't really been himself for almost a year now.

Our last few "good" times together consisted of Dad inviting me on errands. They were attempts at father-son time, but he was really just squeezing me into what he was already doing. We'd walk around Home Depot, and he'd pretend like he wasn't lost. We'd run into his work on the weekend to grab something his boss needed him to fix. I'd make prints of my face on the copier and eat candy from the jar on the receptionist's desk. He'd ask me to work in the yard with him on nice days, probably because I was free labor. The best was when he would ask me to watch a show with him. That was the easy, low-risk way to spend time together.

Things went from bad to worse a few months ago. As the autumn leaves lost their color, the rest of Dad's joy faded. A bone-chilling winter took hold of Central Washington. Its bite turned my dad to ice. Mom said it was just because of the weather and that sometimes things like that happen to people when the days are dark and dreary, so I tried not to worry about it too much. But, as winter pushed through, Dad didn't bounce back. He stayed cold, an iceberg refusing to melt. We started doing less and less together. The cold made it too hard to be near him.

ANOTHER REASON TO WHINE

A pothole in the driveway jolts me back to the present. My seat belt locks, pinning me to the seat. It brings a brief panic, but I calm myself with deep breaths, then pull on it slowly until it lets go.

If I were an optimist, I might say that this move could be our chance at a fresh start. Maybe we can get back to life like it was two years ago, when we had season tickets to the Bears' games. The Bears are the Yakima Valley minor-league baseball team. They've had a few successful seasons, but I'm not really sure how well they did this last year.

I know Rory needs the old dad back. He used to build Popsicle-stick houses with her and teach her the fundamentals of engineering. And every Valentine's Day, they'd get dressed up and go to the daddy-daughter dance.

Needless to say, it's been tough on her. Going from being treated like a princess to being treated like a pain in the butt has to be tough.

Still bouncing up the never-ending driveway, I stare out my window and try to catch a glimpse of the river. Rory stares out my window too.

"Look at the dirt on your own side," I tell her.

She doesn't budge.

"Rory!"

Still nothing.

Fine.

I rotate so I'm blocking most of my window.

"Dad! Asher's blocking his window!"

"Who cares?" he responds. "There are five other windows in this car. Pick one of those."

I can't help but send a smirk her way.

"I saw that," Dad barks.

Stupid rearview mirror.

"Being a jerk isn't helping," he continues. "Why are you blocking your window? Do we really need to give your sister *another* reason to whine?"

He's got a good point there. Harsh, but a good point.

———

I tune back in to the world outside the car. All around us, there are fields that appear empty. Ten acres on Rory's side, ten acres on mine. I don't know how much that is in normal-people measurements, but it seems like it goes on forever. The whole thing is loaded with life. Grandpa's asparagus fields are already planted and ready to go. They'll be sending up stalks in just a couple weeks.

Rolling up to the barn, it glows bright white, except where it doesn't. In all of its ancient glory, the faded and chipped paint gives way to the old, weathered wood. None of the animals are out to welcome us, sadly. Not even Winston: Grandma and Grandpa's donkey.

Maybe I can call him my *donkey now.*

In front of the house, Grandma's gardens look like they've been well taken care of. It was probably Manny, or I guess it could be Mari or Julia, his daughters. They came here from Mexico a few years ago, and Manny has been Grandpa's right-hand man ever since. When Manny needed a job to get into the country, and Grandma and Grandpa heard he was raising two girls by himself, nothing more needed to be said. "We needed them, and they needed us," Grandma told me. I'm glad they're here, because if there was no Mari, I'd be stuck with just the animals as friends.

Every time I come to the farm, Mari and I pick up right where we left off. We jump back into farm life, playing with the animals and running over to the grove to climb trees. We spend hours down by the river with our lines in the water, staring at the patterns in the ripples and pointing out deformed animals in the clouds. After years of fishing, I'm pretty dang good at it. Mari's decent, but I've got the McCovey magic. Grandpa could catch fish with a baitless hook. I wouldn't believe it unless I saw it with my own eyes, but it happened.

——

Dad pulls up next to Grandpa's baby-blue Ford . . . the truck that Grandpa said would be mine someday. While I appreciate the sentiment, I'm not sure I want it. I have four years to decide . . . if it even lasts that long.

Dad turns off the engine. We sit silently, taking in the moment. I don't know what to say, and clearly no one else does, either. It's a life-changing event, a defining moment for our family, and maybe that's why no one speaks. No one can think of just the right words.

"Gosh darn it!" Mom exclaims.

The words are especially shocking coming from her, since those are near-cuss words.

"What?" Dad explodes. "Why are you yelling?"

Ironic much?

"I just realized Grandpa may not have seen the pictures I sent him."

"What pictures?"

"He asked for some digital pictures of the family, and I kept putting it off. I finally picked the perfect ones and sent them, right before he died."

"Then he probably didn't see them," says Dad, "since he had to go to the library to use the Internet."

"Yes, Mac. I'm aware. That's not exactly the supportive response I was hoping for."

"Sorry!" he responds sarcastically. "If you didn't want help, why did you tell me your problem?"

"I was just looking for a little empathy."

"I'm all out," he says.

"I see that."

Dad changes the topic. "All right. Here we are. Everybody out. And make sure you take something inside."

"Okay," Mom says, steering the conversation in a different direction. "Welcome to our new home. I know this is a big change for all of us, but we can do this. God has given us a chance at a fresh start."

I want to say, *"God could have gotten rid of Grandpa's cancer instead of forcing me to move away from my friends. God could have let Dad keep his job. Why would God suddenly help us now?"*

Instead, I open the door without a word, stand up, stretch, and take a big breath of fresh air . . . with a little manure mixed in. I grab a pillow so Dad can't say I didn't help, and fling the door shut behind me strong enough to make a statement.

Then I make a beeline to the barn. If I'm going to be here for who-knows-how long, I should start by reconnecting with a good friend.

"Hey, Winston!" I yell. "I'm hooooome! Hee-haw, hee-haw!"

NICE RUNNING INTO YOU

After spending some quality time with my donkey, I give in to my conscience and decide to help unpack, but before I make it out of the barn, I notice Grandpa's quad.

Now, I'm not sure if my parents ever gave Grandpa permission to let me drive it, but I drove it plenty, and I'm not about to stop. As they say, *It's easier to ask for forgiveness than permission.*

I take some old tools off the seat and toss them onto the ground. Then I throw one leg over, plop my butt on the not-so-soft cushion, and situate myself as comfortably as can be expected. Finally, I turn the key that's always in the ignition.

It takes a few attempts, but the engine soon roars to life. As I squeeze the throttle a little too tightly, rocks shoot from the spinning wheels, pelting the side of the barn, sending the chickens running and clucking.

"Sorry, chickens!" I yell, and I'm on my way to Mari's.

To get to her house, you have to go all the way back down the driveway, hook a right, and go a little farther down the main road. They're still on Grandma and Grandpa's land, which is our land now, I guess.

Grandpa let Manny live there rent free as part of an agreement they made. Manny said he'd at least stay until Grandpa died.

I hope he doesn't leave. This farm wouldn't exist without him.

While zipping down the driveway, I stand up halfway, with my hands firmly on the handlebars. The wind seems to lift me, and I feel free.

It's short-lived though, since the main road is quickly approaching. With just a few seconds left until I reach the end of the driveway, I plop down on the seat and squeeze the brakes. Instead of slowing down, I hear metal-on-metal screeching.

Oh God! What's wrong? Manny must have been working on it!

Out of the corner of my eye, a flash of red catches my attention. It's a pickup truck a couple hundred feet to my left.

My instincts take over and I dig my feet into the gravel. I push as hard as I can and lose a shoe for it.

Still going too fast to stop in time, I hold on for dear life and pray to any gods that might be watching.

The loose gravel beneath me steals any hope that I might survive. I skid, and skid, and skid, and when I finally come to a stop, I'm in the middle of the southbound lane.

Before I have a chance to inhale, the truck is skidding toward me. I squeeze my eyes shut and brace for impact. It skids, and skids, and skids for what feels like forever, and when it finally comes to a stop, its bumper is pressed up against my wheels, forcing the quad to tilt to the side. My leg dangles in a perfect little pocket between the truck and the quad. A leg-saving pocket.

I hang my head in exhaustion, feeling like I might pass out. After a few seconds, I raise my face to the sky; take a deep breath of sweet, fresh air; and thank every god I can think of.

Then I remember I'm not alone. I glance over, ready to apologize to the poor soul that nearly witnessed my demise, and a familiar face stares back at me. It's a confused face, a scared face, and an angry face, all wrapped into one contorted look. It's Manny. Of course it's Manny. It couldn't just be a stranger that checks to see if I'm okay and then goes on his merry way.

"Hi," I say, giving a timid wave. "New truck?" Then, realizing he probably can't hear me, I yell, "Thanks for not killing me!" and give him a sheepish smile.

He lets his head fall hard onto his crossed arms, which lie resting on the steering wheel.

"De nada," he yells back, and then he adds a few more Spanish words I haven't heard before. I'll have to ask Mari what they mean.

A WARMISH WELCOME

"Hey, Mari."

I walk through the door, trying to shake off my near-death experience.

"Asher! You're here!"

"Yes, I am. Just barely."

"You look all here to me," she says.

"I'm just happy to be alive."

"That's great! I know how hard it is to lose somebody you love. I've been sad too, but it's good to know that you're focusing on life instead of death."

"Did someone say death?" asks Manny, after walking up behind me silently. His words cause a vivid flashback. "Was Asher telling you about how he tried to kill himself in front of a speeding truck? My truck!"

"You almost killed Asher?" cries Mari.

"No! He almost killed himself!"

"In front of you?"

He stares at us, shakes his head, then heads over to the couch.

Mari turns to me. "Why did you try to kill yourself in front of Papi?"

"I didn't try to kill myself in front of Papi! I mean, your papi." *How do I explain this one?*

"Do you want the truth?" I ask. "I was stupid and ended up driving the quad into the road, right in front of his truck. He stopped right before hitting me, though . . . and I'm alive!"

"Estúpido!" says Mari, clearly not holding back her true feelings.

"Hey!" I argue. "I may not know a lot of Spanish, but I know that one."

"I'm glad you know what that means! Your abuelo dies, and then you almost kill yourself your first day here? You need to be safer, amigocho, or else I'll kick your butt!"

I almost laugh but hold it in. "What? That doesn't make any sense," I point out. "You'll hurt me if I hurt myself?"

"*You* don't make sense!"

"You're missing one major detail," I remind her. "I'm alive!"

"You're lucky you're alive! You're lucky Papi didn't turn you into roadkill!"

She turns abruptly and speed-walks back to her room. I'm left standing there awkwardly.

On the table next to me, I notice a black-and-white picture of Grandpa. It's among half a dozen similar images in the local newspaper: *The Prosser Post*. Each portrait has its own paragraph of tiny words below it. The title at the top of the page reads: OBITUARIES.

After inching a bit closer, I still can't read the fine print.

"Can I sit down?" I ask Manny.

"Of course. You don't have to ask."

I know that. I just want to look overly polite while I intrude.

I sit on the edge of the chair and pore over the words under

Grandpa's picture. They read:

William F. McCovey, of Prosser, WA, passed away due to complications from thyroid cancer, brought on from his childhood as a Downwinder. Bill, as his friends and family called him, was born on July 26, 1942, in Hanford, WA. When the government chose his family's land as the location for the new Hanford plant later that year, young William and his parents, Frederick and Irma (deceased), were displaced. The family moved to Kennewick, WA, to begin a new life. When William graduated from Kennewick High School, he married his high-school sweetheart, Judith Downing, and they moved a short way up the road to Prosser, WA, where they bought twenty acres on the Yakima River and started a successful asparagus farm, still in operation today. After years of farming and being active in the community, Bill was diagnosed with cancer, believed to be connected to the Hanford site fallout. He was preceded in death by his wife, Judy McCovey, and his son, Gabriel McCovey. He leaves behind a son, Mac McCovey (m. Sarah Brown), and two grandchildren, Asher McCovey and Aurora McCovey. Instead of sending flowers, please donate to the American Immigration Council. In honor of his sense of humor, his memorial service was held on April 1st, at the Desert Rose Memorial Home.

This paragraph packs a punch, full of disturbing new details of Grandpa's life.

Three questions now live in my head: Who is Uncle Gabriel? What's a Downwinder? And what is a Hanford plant?

Before I can begin obsessing over this new information, Mari shows up in her bedroom doorway. She props herself up against the frame, where she inhales slowly through her nose and exhales slowly out of her mouth.

"The last couple weeks have been really hard," she says. "Ever since Grandpa died, I can't stop thinking about my mom and how I'll never get to know her."

Oh crap. How did I not think about that? I'm such an idiot.

"I'm sorry," I say humbly. "I'm so sorry."

"Thank you."

Quick. Say something less stupid.

"Tell me more about your mom."

"I feel like I should know more, but I don't really remember a lot. And I'm worried the details I do have are just from pictures or Papi's stories. I'm not even sure I have my own memories of her."

"What's something you think you might remember?"

"I think I remember being with her right before Julia was born, but then I had to leave the room." She fiddles with her fingers, and her head hangs low, like a thirsty flower. "And that was the last time I saw her alive."

"I'm sorry," I tell her yet again. "I didn't mean to bring up more sad stuff."

"It's okay," she assures me. "It's sad to remember, but it's also good. I like trying to picture her."

"What did she look like?"

"Usually when I picture her, she's putting me to bed. She's so beautiful. Her skin is dark. Her hair is dark. Her eyes are dark. But her smile is super bright, like her teeth are glowing."

"So like a bigger you?"

"I guess," she says, with a kind-of-confused look.

"I'm sorry," I tell her. "Was that rude? I didn't mean anything by it."

"It's fine," she says. "It was nice."

"Oh. Okay, then. Glad I could be of service."

She laughs and gives me a little shove.

"Do you want to talk about her more?" I ask. "We can. I didn't mean to stop you."

"It's fine," she says. "It was a sweet way to ruin it."

"So we're good?"

"Better than good. Just be safe, please."

"I will. I promise. Pinkie swear."

We hold out our pinkies and interlock them in a sort of pinkie hug.

"Is there anything I can do to make it up to you?" I ask.

"Don't die," she says with a small smile. "You can get hurt, but don't die."

"Okay. I think I can do that. Anything else?"

"Un abrazo!" yells Julia from their shared bedroom.

"What's a 'brazo'?"

As if on cue, Julia runs full speed and plasters herself to me. She throws her arms around my waist and squeezes me tight.

"Un abrazo!" she yells. "A hug!"

I want to say, "No thank you. I'm not really the hugging type," but I hold my tongue, because I'm not rude . . . usually.

Mari walks over and doubles up on the hug. It's not as bad as I would have imagined.

Eventually, Mari frees me from her grasp, and Julia follows. I turn my attention to Manny.

"I don't think I've ever told you how much I appreciate everything you do around the farm," I tell him.

"I still have to let your parents know what happened," he says, as he puts some things into a bag.

"What? Why?"

"Because I'm an adult and it's my job to do the right thing, even when kids don't. Especially when kids don't, actually. And I don't want to be on your dad's bad side."

I want to warn him about what's coming his way, but maybe it's best that Dad starts with a clean slate.

Manny continues, "Hopefully, we'll be working together for a long time."

"So you're not leaving?" I ask.

"No! Of course not. Why would you think that?"

"Because Grandpa died?"

"No way! We have a good thing going here. I'm not leaving unless somebody makes me or I'm dead."

What is it with all the death talk?

"Then, unless you have powerful enemies or a major medical condition, it sounds like you'll be around for a long time!"

"That's the plan," he says. "I'd love for the girls to grow up here."

I knock on wood, just to make sure we don't jinx it, then turn my attention back to Mari.

"I hope so too. What would I do without Mari here?"

"What am I?" asks Julia. "Dropped liver?"

"Chopped liver," I tell her, hesitant to correct her since "dropped liver" is pretty cute.

"How ruuude!" she exclaims. "That's even worse! And after I gave you a hug!"

"No, I didn't mean it like that." I try to explain myself, but I get nowhere.

"Well, how's this," she says. "I'm rubber and you're glue. Words bounce off me and stick to you."

I didn't see that one coming. She brought it old-school. I look at Mari, hoping she'll jump in to help, but she just shrugs and laughs. My only options are to argue with a six year old or go along with it.

"You got me, kiddo. I am chopped liver. How will I live with myself, knowing that I'm just a diced-up part of the digestive system? I'm ruined."

"Yes!" she exclaims. "I knew it would work one of these days."

All I can do is laugh. That girl is so stinkin' funny.

I turn to Mari once again. "So, you wanna hang out with some chopped liver?"

MY SHADOW SELF

"I really would love to hang out," says Mari, "but I can't right now. I have to finish my homework, and it's my week to keep the house clean."

"Homework? On the weekend?" I exclaim, hoping it isn't true.

"She doesn't normally give us homework on Fridays," Mari assures me, "but I'm a little behind. Ms. Sprunger, my ESL teacher, helped me figure out how to do it, and now I just need to finish it. Whoever started the English language is not a good person. None of it makes sense. They teach us 'rules,' and then they change the rules all the time. How can you call it a rule if it changes?"

"Yeah. English doesn't make a whole lot of sense."

We sit there for a few awkward seconds before I excuse myself. I want her to have time to catch up on her work. "Well. I'm gonna head out. Let me know if you have time to hang out tomorrow. If I don't see you then, I guess I'll see you at the bus stop Monday morning."

"They just pick you up at the end of your driveway out here," she informs me. "Since people are kind of far apart."

"Oh. Okay then. Well, I guess I'll see you on the bus."

"Okay," she says. "Sorry I can't hang out. I really would if I could."

"No problem. We'll have lots of time since we're neighbors now."

"You're right!" she says, as if she just realized it.

I walk to the door, then glance back. "I'm glad you're here," I say, hoping it doesn't sound too weird. "Not sure what I'd do if you weren't."

"Ditto," she says.

"Ditto? Did you make up a new word?"

"I learned it at school. It's a little like the rubber-and-glue thing. If someone says something to you, and you say *ditto*, it means you say the same thing back to them. If someone says, 'I love you,' and you say *ditto*, it means you love them too."

"Interesting. You learn something new every day."

As my hand takes hold of the doorknob, Mari squeezes in one more thought.

"Asher . . ." She pauses.

"Yeah?"

"I think my dad just got in his truck, so be careful."

I shake my head. "Ha, ha. Muy funny."

"I thought it was," she says with a teasing smile.

I give a small wave with my free hand and add my best, "Adios, amiga."

"Hasta luego, muchacho."

I open the door, step out, and close it quietly behind me.

Not wanting to catch Dad at a terrible time, like right after Manny tells him about the almost-accident, I decide to lie low for a while. Leaving the quad where it sits seems like the best option right now. Walking back to the house will give me some time to think, and it'll also make it so there's no roar of the engine to draw attention to my return.

After walking for a minute, my mind begins racing. When I worry, there are so many things that try to piggyback their way into my brain. Like, if Dad yells at me, my mind will quickly sift through this last year's memories and show me the many times that I've made him angry. There's a mounting collection of evidence that suggests he would rather suck on a sea urchin than deal with me.

I drag my feet across the rocks just to break the silence. It's the time of evening when the sun is low and the shadows are long. I turn around and walk backward, picturing the steps I've taken. My shadow stretches out far in front of me.

Although it's intriguing, this flat, dark "me" isn't anything like me; it's all stretched thin. But, whether I want it to or not, it follows me wherever I go. And whatever I do, it does with me. I move left, and it follows me. I run to the right, and it chases me. I jump as high as I can to break free of it, but even then, it's short-lived. I make it small by lying down on the sharp rocks of the road, like I'm dead. This just makes me an idiot, lying in the driveway. But at the very least, with this new perspective, I can look up at the sky, with its scattered clouds, burning red, orange, and pink, then fading to yellow.

Why does the setting sun cast long, dark shadows down here, but in the sky, the same sun sends colors spilling across the clouds?

HERE, FISHY FISHY

I roll over and open my eyes.

"Oh jeez!" I say to my room full of boxes. "Too bright!"

I snap my eyelids closed again.

Maybe I shouldn't have moved the head of my bed right next to the window.

I rub my eyes for a few seconds, then try opening them again.

Good enough.

Dragging my forearm across my face, it catches some drool from the corners of my mouth. I roll out of bed, change into my lucky fishing underwear, then slip on my jeans and my favorite fish-catching T-shirt that says GRANDPA'S FISHING BUDDY. It's a little tight since Grandpa gave it to me when I was eight, but I'll wear it until the day I can't fit it over my head.

Slowly opening my bedroom door, I question the silent house.

"Hello? Anybody here?"

Nothing.

Dad is hopefully somewhere attempting to be a farmer.

Last night at dinner, Mom said she and Rory were going to try one of the churches around town. She invited me, of course, but that's not really my thing. They must be gone already, leaving me here in peace. Despite the evidence of an empty house, I can still feel Grandpa here. It seems like I could turn the corner and run into him.

In the kitchen, the only sign of life is Rory's bowl by the sink; still half full of milk with a few store-brand Frosted Mini Wheats floating on top.

I grab a banana off the counter and a muffin out of the fridge. Then I cram five granola bars into my pocket and fill up two water bottles in preparation for a long day of fishing.

I head out to the small shed next to the back steps, where I grab my tackle box along with the pole that Grandpa gave me when I turned eight. It had been his since he was a teenager. Apparently I always asked him if we could trade poles when we were fishing, since I thought his was lucky, so he eventually just gave it to me. Now that I'm almost a teenager, reason tells me that poles aren't lucky, but a part of me still thinks that Grandpa's has a bit of magic.

My boots fit snugger than I remember, but that's not going to stop me.

As soon as I round the corner of the house, I hear the gentle rumble of the river. It's calling me. Not in a weird way. Just in the way nature sometimes reminds you she still exists, and she's waiting for you to visit.

I almost feel bad about not going to church. I feel like I should, but ever since I went with Mom on Mother's Day, I haven't been back. The children's pastor asked the class if we knew what love was, so I raised my hand and, when he called on me, I said, "I love the river."

He laughed and responded, "No, I mean genuine love." He continued to chuckle.

I didn't get what was so funny, so I asked him what he was laughing at. Apparently that caught him off guard, as he stopped laughing and explained, "I mean love as in you would do almost anything to be with them."

"Yep, that's me and the river, all right," I replied.

"Your love doesn't change, even if you've had a bad day."

"Correct."

"Okay, okay," he said, "but can the river love you back?"

"I don't have any reason to believe it doesn't. I feel happier when I'm around it."

"How can a river love? Can you even get to know it?"

"I get to know it better every time I'm near it. I could point out a hundred things you've probably never taken the time to notice."

"Fine," he said, looking somewhat dejected. "I'm trying to get at the idea that Jesus died for you because he loves you. That is the ultimate love. A river can't do that. Get it?"

Well, that's a weird way to go about it.

"No. I don't think I do," I said. "If you have to die to show someone you love them, then I think there's something wrong with that. I'd rather have somebody *live* for me." There was a long pause, and I thought maybe he was actually considering what I said.

"Moving on," he announced.

I thought I had a good point. I'm not sure why I keep hoping adults might think what I have to say is important when I'm constantly being reminded that they don't like to be questioned.

But I'm going fishing to get my mind off of these things. No serious thoughts allowed from here on out.

As I get closer to its banks and more of the river is revealed, my heart hurries in excitement. Then, as I finally sit down next to its waters, my body calms. Perched on *my* rock, I open my tackle box, trying to decide what type of fish to go for and what type of gear to use. I see that this pole has the thirty-pound leader on it with the size-two hook, so I guess that means I'm going for the big ones today; meaning, it's time to catch some catfish.

After setting up my gear, I walk down to the catfish pool. There's a tree that fell into the river and created a sort of wall, leaving a calm pool behind it. Rather than being out in the middle of the river, swimming against the current, the lazy whisker-fish like to hang out here and let the food come to them . . . and I am more than happy to send some their way.

I open the bail and give a small wrist-cast, plopping my bait right on the line between the calm water and the current. Then I let out a little extra line, walk back a dozen steps, and lean up against the catfish tree. Not that it looks like a catfish or anything. It's just the best spot to sit while catching them.

I close my eyes and try to take in all that my senses can absorb, hoping to replace the thoughts that aren't welcome. I start by focusing on the more obvious sensations, like the sound of the water and the feeling of the river-born breeze on my face. When I tune in more, I can hear the leaves rubbing against each other and feel the bark imprinting on my back. I try to ignore the bump under my left butt cheek and the bug crawling up my arm.

After a few minutes, I'm snapped out of my trance when I feel a tug on my line. Yanking the tip up, I attempt to set the hook, but the line goes slack.

Dang it! I must have pulled up too quickly.

Within a couple minutes, I get another bite. This time, I wait a split second longer to make sure the bait's in his mouth, then I rocket my tip up in the air, bending my pole in a massive arch and setting the hook into the beast's lip.

The fish runs a bit, which is fine by me, because he'll soon tire himself out.

I want to put this guy back, since I'm not in the mood for gutting a fish. I eventually get him up to the bank, grab the pliers out of my back pocket, and pop the hook out of its fat, slimy lip. I wonder what evolutionary purpose their ugliness plays. They have nasty skin tags hanging off their heads. It looks like their grandmas pinched and pulled their cheeks so hard that they left long strings of skin hanging from their ugly faces.

I don't think Mr. Catfish will mind the hole in his lip since he's already ugly, and the alternative was being dinner. Besides, he can use the piercing as a reminder of my grace.

I push him back into the water. He must be exhausted because he just floats there, looking lifeless.

"Are you dead, fishy?"

Then, as if my words are magical, he takes hold of his second chance at life. He shoots off like a rocket, ready to make the most of this generous opportunity. He's probably racing off to tell his family how much he loves them and share his story of the human who offered him mercy. Then he'll spend some time planning healthier life decisions and setting goals for himself . . . like not eating everything put in front of him.

I hope he realizes how valuable second chances are.

FATHER-SON TIME

After getting my first fish pretty quickly, I only have a couple bites over the next four hours. The fish I spared must have gone and warned all his friends. That ungrateful mud sucker.

After my fifth granola bar, and almost to the end of my water, Dad shows up out of nowhere. I'm not sure how he found me, or if he was even trying to, but here we are.

I wanted a peaceful day to myself, but if he's going to make a rare attempt at being a dad, I feel like I should give him a shot.

"How's the fishing?" he asks.

"It sucks," I tell him, slightly shocked at the boldness of my words. "How's the farm work?"

"That's a sore subject," he says. "I've been focused on a few other things. I'll get to it."

Great. New pile, same crap. I wonder which rabbit hole he stuck his head in this time.

He eases himself to the ground, and we sit for a bit, with our lines in the water. We don't say anything at all. Maybe that's for the best, though. Who knows what words could come flying out if he attempts a conversation.

Unfortunately, I soon find out.

"Why did you drive the quad without my permission?" he asks.

So that's why he's here? To lecture me?

"Grandpa always let me drive it."

"Oh really? Into the street?"

"Well, no. Not that part."

"What other kinds of things were going on here?" he asks.

"Nothing?"

"Is that an answer or a question?"

"An answer?" I don't do so well being interrogated. I wonder if I can plead the fifth amendment. "I've driven it lots of times, and I'm a good driver . . . except yesterday, I guess. But that wasn't my fault. The brakes weren't working. Besides, I was just going by what Grandpa said, and you can't get mad at Grandpa because he's not here anymore."

"You're right. He's not here, but *you* are."

That sounds like a threat.

"Did you have to ask Grandpa to use it when you wanted to?"

"No."

"Seriously?" he questions me.

"Seriously."

"Asher."

"Dad."

"I don't need the attitude right now."

"All I did was answer your question."

"Sure you did," he says. "Just leave out the snark, will ya? I've got enough crap going on. I don't need my son trying to make things worse."

"I wasn't trying—"

Just then, there's a strong tug on my pole. My attention turns to the tight, thin line darting back and forth across the surface of the water.

I can't put my finger on the exact reason, but I get wildly excited every time a fish bites. It somehow sucks me out of every problem in life and focuses me on one attempt at temporary greatness. I've felt it hundreds of times, but it feels like the first time, every time. Anyone who has felt "the tug" and experienced the epic battle between man and fish—or boy and fish, in my case—knows it never gets old.

As I fight the fish, Dad stands there, staring at the water, like he's picturing the fight beneath the surface. If you're not the one struggling with the beast, it's easy to just see the relatively calm water and not understand the battle for life and death going on underneath.

I try to get his attention.

"Dad! A little help here? Can you get the net?"

The old man groans, like a weak tree in a strong wind, as he bends down to pick it up and then makes his way over to me . . . clearly in no hurry. He takes a few steps into the water and squats down in preparation for netting the fish. Slowly, he dips the net and his hand into the cold Yakima River waters.

I reel the last few feet of line in until the ugly-as-all-get-out catfish is just about resting on top of the net.

Dad is obviously thinking about other things, as he sits there and stares at it.

"Dad!"

He quickly lifts the net, capturing the exhausted fish.

I grab the pliers out of my pocket and bend down to take the hook out of its fat lip.

"You're going to keep it, right?" asks Dad.

"I wasn't planning on it. I don't really want to clean it."

"What? That's like two dinners! I'm not sure if you noticed, but we're not rich."

I noticed, but I wasn't aware we were relying on my fishing skills to provide for the family.

"Well, it sounds like this is important to you," I tell him. "You're welcome to it if you want to gut it and cook it."

"It's not a matter of wanting to," he says. "It's more of a need to at this point. Your mom's freaking out about the budget, so I have to do something so she'll stop being mad at me. "

I just stare at the water, not sure how to respond.

Dad takes the silence as an opportunity to change the subject and get all philosophical, as he sometimes does when he's trying to appear wise.

"You know, time spent fishing is never wasted, even if you don't catch anything."

"But we did," I point out.

"Well, yeah but . . ."

I resist the urge to roll my eyes. "Never mind. Go ahead."

"Time spent fishing is never wasted."

"You already said that."

"I know, for God's sake! I'm starting over since you interrupted me!"

"Okay. Jeez."

He starts again. "Time spent fishing is never wasted. The catching part is great, but the quiet times between the catching really heighten the value of the experience."

I hate that he makes even the slightest bit of sense.

"That's deep, Dad. A little time between catches does make it sweeter, but it's also true that if you go too long without success, it's hard to want to keep trying. If you spend all your time hoping and wishing and nothing comes of it, everything within you says to give up. It's hard to hold out hope."

"Are we still talking about fishing?" he asks.

"I don't know. Are we?"

He's silent. I wish this were the case more often.

SLIVER OF THE RIVER

"**H**ave fun," I tell him. "Don't hurt yourself."

He stands there, holding his slightly-rusted fillet knife, staring down at the fish.

I hustle up to the house, drop my muddy boots on the back steps, and mentally prepare myself to rush inside. My goal is to pass Mom before she gets a chance to say anything. I know she's probably in the kitchen by this point in the day, so I have an emergency statement planned out. Something that requires no response from her.

Three, two, one, go!

I send the door flying open, and there she is: messy apron, messy hair, and messy counter to make a matching set. I pretend like I'm panting from the long run and slam the door behind me for an added, startling effect.

"Hi, Mom! Bye, Mom! Dad's got a fish for dinner."

I take a few more deep breaths as I rush over to the stairs, making sure they're fast enough and loud enough to fill any air space Mom might want to fill with her words. I execute it perfectly and, before she knows it, I'm thumping up the stairs, rounding the corner into my room, and shutting the door behind me.

Standing with my back to it all, I draw in a slow breath and let it out just as steadily.

I lie down on my bed and allow myself to relax. My attic room at the farmhouse has always been my place to rest. I stare at the wood-planked ceiling, creating dot-to-dot patterns out of the dark knots while pondering deep thoughts.

Next to my bed, my window is nature's perfect picture frame. If I ever have mysteries that can't be solved by staring at the ceiling, I look out the window and soak in the view. Off to the right is the barn, faded white with red trim. Cut into the side of it, there's one square opening where Winston's little gray donkey head often pokes out. He's my best friend of the animal variety. I also have other friends that live there: two pigs, Pumba and Ms. Piggy, six goats, and of course many, many chickens. The chickens are Rory's friends now, I guess. She has them all named, and it's only our second day here.

Whenever I get lonely, I visit Winston. Since he always looks sad, I figure we can cheer each other up.

Beyond the barn, the southern field rolls slightly. It doesn't have much natural appeal to it. The important part about the southern field is that Mari's house sits just beyond the border. I can't actually see it from here because of the hill, but it's nice to know she's there.

And of course, whenever I need it, I look past the northern fields and see my sliver of the river. To find peace, I picture myself there, sitting next to certain trees that mark specific spots and special memories. It's always there for me; it always comes through, even on my worst days.

SUPPERTIME

Mom yells up the stairs, "Asher, please go let your father know it's time for supper!"

"It's not polite to yell in the house, Mom!" I respond, with more than a hint of attitude. A few seconds later, the steps creak one by one, announcing her approach. She arrives outside my door and stops. The pause is too much.

"Hello?" I say, just to break the silence.

The handle turns, and the door opens, leaving just enough room for her head to fit through.

"Would you please let your father know it's time for supper?" she asks calmly.

"Um. Sure."

She pulls her head back out of the opening but stops midway to add one more thought. "I love you. Please try to be kind. We're all going through a lot right now."

Ugh.

"Sorry. It just comes out lately."

"I understand," she says. "It makes sense, but that doesn't make it okay."

"I know," I admit. "Sorry."

"Thank you." She closes the door behind her and starts down the stairs.

"Wait a second," I call out.

She stops and turns around as I poke my head out my door.

"Where's Dad? I thought he was cooking dinner."

"Your father?" She laughs. "Cooking dinner?"

"Yeah, I caught the catfish, and he said he was going to—" I pause, not sure what to say. I don't need to create more drama. "Huh." I fake confusion. "I must have misunderstood him."

"Well, thank you for catching the fish, sweetheart. Your dad asked me to prepare and cook it for dinner. It'll be on the table soon."

He didn't even gut it himself? What the heck, Dad?

Mom continues, "He said he had something to take care of in the barn."

"Okay. I'll head over there." Then I decide to verify something else Dad said. "Are you mad at Dad?"

"Mad? No. I don't think that's the right word."

"Then what is?"

"Well, we have our fair share of disagreements, and we both have our things to work on."

"That's more than one word," I say pointedly, wanting a direct answer for once.

"Asher," she says, "I can tell you're looking for something specific, but do we really have to do this right now?"

"Can you please just finish the sentence: I'm not mad, I'm . . . ?"

She pauses long enough that I almost give up.

"I'm not mad," she says. "I'm praying."

"Mom. Seriously? Is that your answer for everything?"

"Sometimes prayer is the only answer."

I throw my hands up in disbelief. "Is anybody around here

going to DO SOMETHING? Like ACTUALLY DO SOME-
THING to fix this family?"

"Asher," she says, with as much warmth as she can muster.
"This isn't easy for me, either."

"Fine," I say. "Forget I said anything."

I rush to change the subject. "You said Dad's out in the
barn?"

She stares at me, knowing there are no words that will make
things right. "Yes, the barn."

I slide past her and take the stairs two at a time. After grabbing a piece of cornbread and shoving it into my mouth, I
shoot out the back door and almost trip over my boots.

Mental note: Bad idea to leave your boots out.

I slow down and take my time walking to the barn. Step-
ping through the doorway, I see Dad on the far side, underneath the tractor, possibly attempting to fix it.

"Dad?" I say quietly, trying to not spook him.

Please don't freak out.

When Dad freaks out, I freak out, and then he freaks out
more, and things just go downhill faster than an avalanche.

He sticks a wrench up into the belly of the beast.

After waiting a few seconds, I call his name again, just a bit
louder.

Still no response.

I take one more step, and then **CLAANNG!** . . . **THUNK!**
Silence.

What the heck was that?

The stillness lasts too long.

Then I watch as Dad slowly rolls out from under the tractor. He lies there for a few seconds, staring at the rafters.
Then he reaches up, grasps the seat, and pulls himself to his
feet. He stands there with one hand on the tractor, propping

himself up. His head hangs, and he rests for a bit.

It seems like he's recovered, as he stands up straight and walks a few steps. But then, in a hot flash, he grabs an old broomstick by one end, lifts it high in the air, and takes out every single ounce of his stored-up rage on that old-as-dirt, broke-down, good-for-nothing tractor. All I can do is stand and stare.

WOOSH! BANG! WHACK! CLANG!

Swear words flow from his mouth as fast as the river exits the mountains, his gritted teeth doing little to stop them. Random gibberish and loud grunts make up the rest of his explosion. He's covered in sweat and dirt, with accents of blood on his knuckles.

The hits continue. Hit after hit after hit . . . until the broomstick snaps.

My dad has snapped.

I can't move. I can't speak. There's nothing to say even if I could, but I quickly realize that I don't need to say anything. Dad doesn't know I'm here. For all he knows, I haven't seen anything . . . and life will be much easier if it stays that way.

I back away slowly until I'm out of sight. Then I take a deep breath, turn toward the house, and run.

TGIF

The first week of school went by without a hitch. I don't actually mind being stuck inside a building half the day. It's a small price to pay for the privilege of being somewhere other than home.

I do mind being stuck on the bus, though, especially when the driver's tiny bladder is holding things up. Her job is only two hours at a time. Why does she have to pee every single time she gets to school? Plan ahead, lady.

The first morning, we caught the bus without any problems. Rory stuck by my side the whole way. I'm not the best big brother, but I show up when it's needed. Apparently, the elementary school is only five blocks away from the middle school, so our bus driver drops Rory and the other little kids off first and then takes us to our school down the street.

Mari has been there for me all week, whenever I've needed her. She showed me where our classroom is and introduced me to the no-homework-on-the-weekend teacher. Her name is Ms. Mitchell. Rory brought her new teacher an apple. I did not. Why do kids always give teachers apples? My fourth grade teacher, Mr. Pierce, gave us a list of things he liked, and apples weren't on it. Now that's a smart man. He turned those apples into gift cards and Starbursts. My dad used to joke that he was going to buy our teachers alcohol, but luckily he hasn't. I wouldn't put it past him, though.

My favorite part about Ms. Mitchell's class is that we're learning things I already learned at my old school. I could tell her this tidbit of information and get some different work, but I think there's enough going on in my life right now that I might keep that to myself.

Mari invited me to sit with her at lunch on Monday, which brought on a few looks from the tables around us, so we decided I should find a few guys to sit with. The group I found doesn't talk much, which is fine by me. If I had to give them a group title, like jocks or nerds, I'd say they're the fast eaters who wonder why there's so much time left until recess.

I didn't really make any new friends, but I didn't make any enemies, either, so that's a win. Most of the kids in my class seem okay. There are a couple guys that aren't very nice, but I feel bad for them more than anything, since they aren't the sharpest pitchforks in the barn. I bet their dogs teach them new tricks. But it looks like if you leave them alone, they'll leave you alone. So, I think I'll be fine.

I already have Mari, so unless I run into a specific issue where I need a guy friend, I think I'm good.

Our driver finally walks out of the school and notices that all the other buses are gone. She jogs for two seconds to fake some effort, then goes back to a walk once she realizes nobody important is watching.

It looks like she made a detour. She didn't have that coffee and donut when she went in there.

I get a sinking feeling in my stomach.

Maybe it's the hot-lunch burrito and corn dog combo.

I stare at the school and reflect on my first week, but then I get distracted by the raindrops racing down the window. I watch to see if any of them will make it to the bottom without being sucked into the big blobs along the way. Two small drops begin their battle. First one takes the lead, then the other. A ways down, they cut toward each other and team up, becoming one super-drop. Together, they're pretty much unstoppable and cut straight through everything on their way to the finish line.

The bus jerks and then rolls. The raindrops on the window go back to being invisible, and the school disappears as we turn onto Market Street.

The shops are becoming familiar now. There's Bonnie's Board Games, Gid & Lil's Pint-size Apparel, Karen's Koffee Korner, and a couple dozen other little stores.

We soon leave the shops behind and fly by fields and farmhouses. Then I realize what that sinking feeling is. It's not the burrito and corn dog. It's worse.

Until recently, weekends meant basketball in our driveway, chalk drawings on the street, setting up jumps for our bikes, and countless other neighborhood activities. I'm just now realizing that weekends aren't going to be the same; not even close. In a weird turn of events, it's like school became the place to relax and be safe while our house is now the home of useless work, boring lectures, and a big, unhinged bully. Since there's not a lot to do around town, weekends will pretty much be two days of dodging Dad so I don't tick him off.

The bus hauls down the long straightaway right before our farm. As it slows to a halt at Mari's stop, I hop up, dragging Rory behind, and follow Mari up the aisle. When we get to the front, the bus driver stops us.

"Hey, guys. You're not allowed to get off the bus at a differ-ent stop unless you have a TTP," she informs us.

"What's a TTP?" I ask.

"Temporary Transportation Pass. Your parents have to send a note in with you saying where you're gonna get off, and when you turn it into the office, they'll give you a TTP."

"So if I don't have one of those, I have to get off at my stop and then walk back to Mari's house?"

"Yes. It's for your own safety."

That's one of the stupidest things I've ever heard.

"So backtracking on a road that doesn't have a sidewalk, in the rain, when I could have just gotten off right where I needed to, is for my safety?"

"Yes," she says, with zero expression on her face.

My muscles tense. My breathing quickens. I notice the broom behind her seat, and a vision plays in my head, in which I go Dad-crazy on this bus until I snap the broom in half.

Don't do anything stupid.

Mari, now standing on the side of the road, speaks up. "It's okay, Asher. I have to get my work done, anyway. Go find something useful to do for a few hours and call me tonight. Comprendo?"

I'm not happy that I have to give up the argument. The woman is nuts, and she needs to know it, but I give in for Mari's sake.

"Sí. I comprehendo."

"Nerd," she says. "Hasta la noche."

"Okay. Talk to you tonight."

The old hand-powered, bifold door shuts quickly and, before I know it, the bus is moving. I fall backward and almost land on top of Rory.

Okay. I'm done with this.

"Jeez, lady!" I yell. "Aren't you supposed to wait until we're sitting down?"

"Excuse me?" she shoots back. "You weren't even supposed to be up here in the first place!"

"But we were! All you had to do was wait a second! Your sign right there says safety first."

I point to the bright yellow sign above her head, next to the fire extinguisher and medical supplies box. "How was that safe?"

"Son, there's no point in gettin' your britches in a bundle. You're fine. Just stay seated next time, and we won't have any more problems."

"I will," I tell her, "but you better watch it. I'll report you if you do anything like that again."

"You do that," she says.

BAGGAGE

You would think, with this long driveway, somebody could meet us at the bus. The hike only takes ten minutes, but when it's pouring buckets, it seems ridiculous to walk. I mean, we have plenty of wheels around here. When I asked Mom to give us a ride, she said it was good exercise. That's a parent answer for way too many things. They don't exercise, so I'm not sure why they get to tell us we should.

We finally arrive at the house, drenched, and make our way around the back. Leaving our muddy boots by the back door, we drag our tired feet into the kitchen and let our bags fall to the floor. I feel lighter for a second as the load leaves my shoulders. My body adjusts as I survey the room. When I take in the house full of memories, an even heavier weight falls on me, as I'm blasted with a series of quick, painful reminders of everything that's not here. Grandpa, gone. Grandma, gone. Old friends, gone. Old school, gone. Old house, gone. Dad?

I feel like I've been patient for a long time, maybe too long. Part of me feels like I need to speak up for myself, and for Mom and Rory. I know Dad's under a lot of stress, but ever since he raged on the tractor, it's hard to convince myself that he's even the same person. Memories of playing board games at coffee shops and going on family walks almost seem like a dream. Now, it's like he has a grudge against the world and, just by living on the same planet, you're fair game.

Mom's still here, but she's kind of in her own world. All of her time seems to be taken up by prayer and God. Her sit-back-and-take-it method of dealing with Dad doesn't seem to be helping a whole lot, but her long-term plan of praying for him is . . . well . . . I don't know, cause it's a long-term plan, and you never really know if those are working.

Rory's plan is to be cute and rely on her heart-melting expressions when Dad's heart turns to ice, but that's becoming less and less effective.

She's a good sister. Annoying at times, but good. I wouldn't consider her a friend though. She can't be my friend because it breaks my friendship selection guidelines. I've always had two rules for being my friend: One, you can't be more than two years younger than me, and two, you can't be a girl. When I met Mari, I made it a little easier to become my friend. Now you only have to meet one of the two requirements. Unfortunately for Rory, she still doesn't qualify, so she's solidly stuck in the sister category.

Mari is the solo bright spot of having to move here. She's an exception to the no-girl rule, obviously, since she's a friend who's a girl.

Since Mari's busy, I decide to see what Rory's up to. If my dad starts to dislike us even more than he already does, Rory and I will probably have to hang out more just to stay sane. I should probably start being a better big brother to prepare.

"Hey, Rory."

"What? Are you gonna share the money from the couch with me?"

"What? No. I was just going to ask you something."

"Oh. Sad. Okay."

"If you're Russian when you go into the bathroom and Finnish when you come out, what are you when you're in there?"

"Peeing? Pooping? I don't know. Is this a trick question? I'm American."

"European!"

The look on her face tells me her brain's not running at full capacity.

I try to explain it to her. "Get it? You're 'a peein'"!"

"That's what I said," she argues.

"No, you said, 'peeing and pooping.'"

"Right, peeing."

"No, it's European." I slowly lay it out for her. "You're 'a peein'.'"

"I think we're saying the same thing. Can we stop now?"

"But you don't get it!"

"Does it really matter?"

"Yes!"

"Why?"

"Because it's annoying that you don't get it! It's obvious!"

"I don't get it, okay! I'm stupid! I know!" yells Rory.

Dad immediately takes his cue and begins yelling about how we shouldn't be yelling because he needs peace and quiet. He sits in his recliner, head cocked toward us, and fires his bullets. "Knock it off! Just . . . stop! I'm trying to relax for a few measly minutes. Can ya just shut it?"

I want to say, "You're the one yelling! Why are you telling us to be quiet when you're the loudest one here?" But "Sorry, I didn't see you there" is all that comes out.

He continues, for some inexplicable reason. "You know how much I hate it when you two fight. There's more on my plate right now than you will ever know. I just need a few minutes to relax, and ya can't even do that for me."

I continue to be stuck on the very clear contrast between his words and his actions.

I repeat myself, "I said I was sorry."

"You did. I know." He acknowledges it, but doesn't accept it. "I know I sound angry . . ."

Ya think?

Then he triples down on the same complaint. "But it just . . . never . . . ends. So much yelling and whining. I can only be patient for so long . . ."

More like NOT so long.

". . . cause then it overflows like it's doing now," he adds.

I love when he blames us for his freak-outs. God forbid we act like kids.

"I need less sorries and more silence."

I want to yell at the top of my lungs, *"I said I was sorry! I'm sorry! I'm sorry! I'm sorry!"*

I want to scream, *"Where's the quiet we need from you?"*

I want to say, *"You're the loudest one here! Where's your sorry?"*

But all that comes out is, "Sorry. We'll try harder next time."

The room goes silent. I guess that must have made things good enough. But good enough is never good, and it's definitely not enough.

Dad's explosion has exposed him as a volcano, temporarily back to dormant but never safe. His boiling lava spewed out, covering everything and everyone close to him. As his molten rock slowly cools, it hardens, turning everything it's engulfed to stone.

I feel my heart hardening.

FRAGILE

Rory's head hangs low; chin-to-chest low. She's clearly not okay. None of us are.

I walk over and place my hand at the top of her back, between her shoulder blades. Her body is pulsing. It isn't the beat of life. It's a pain from deep down, trying to escape. Tiny convulsions of choked-back tears jolt her body. She's been broken and left to clean up her own tiny pieces.

I wonder how long it took her to master crying silently. Does he seriously not notice her?

"It's gonna be okay, Rory." I do my best to comfort her.

When I was younger, Mom used to rub my back, and within seconds, I'd feel better. I attempt to do the same for Rory, and her body calms quickly. Then I whisper to her, "Hey, do you want to go do some exploring?"

"Really?" she says, a little too loudly. Dad squirms in his chair and takes a deep breath, exhaling as loudly as he can so we know we've disturbed him.

"Psst. Let's go out to the barn. There's a trunk in the loft that Grandpa said I could look in when I was older. I wanna see what's in there."

"Is that okay to do?" she asks timidly.

"Grandpa's gone. We're going to have to go through his stuff, anyway, to figure out what to keep. We might as well get started."

The look on her face is *skeptical.* Then it changes from *skeptical* to *considering,* and finally from *considering* to *approving.*

"Okay. Let's do it! But first, can you get me a tissue? I have cry boogers."

"Sure, kiddo."

"And a glass of water, please?" she adds.

"No prob."

I hand her a paper towel, hoping that's good enough.

"Do you want a plastic cup or an actual glass?"

"Real glass, please."

"Real glass it is."

I walk over to the cupboard and swing it wide open. Every one of Grandma and Grandpa's glasses has its own unique shape and design. I wonder if that was on purpose or out of necessity since glasses break all the time.

I spot one that I think Rory will like. It's covered in detailed, etched flowers.

Standing on my tippy-toes, I wrap a couple fingers around the bottom. As I pull it over the edge, my grip slips. I squeeze harder, but instead of clinching it, the pressure forces it to fly out of my grasp.

Time slows as the glass falls. I watch helplessly, unable to move. Knowing this isn't going to end well, I prepare an exit strategy.

The glass hits the floor with a gut-wrenching sound, exploding into pieces, shattering my hopes for a peaceful rest of the night.

Dad whips his head around and unleashes his volcanic rage. Burning words spew from his mouth like lava.

I turn to Rory and have to yell so she can hear me. "Watch out for the glass!" Then I point toward the door and tell her to run.

I follow right behind her, but for some reason, I pause. I want to say something magical to fix things, so I turn around, grasping for something meaningful, powerful, and inspiring to say. But when I open my mouth, my emotions take over. "Stop it! Look at yourself! What's wrong with you?"

Then I slam the door behind me and run for it.

HIDE-AND-SEEK

"**A**sher! Over here!" Rory says in a loud whisper. My head whips around, and the rest of my body follows.

"Where are you?" I ask.

"Behind the woodpile." She lifts her hand and waves. "Over here."

I sprint over to her and jump behind the stack, squishing Rory in the process.

"Do you think this is a good-enough spot?" I ask.

"Maybe not," she says quietly, "since I can't really breathe."

"My bad," I apologize, as I give her a little space. "We should probably find a better spot. Something more out of the way and comfortable if we're going to be hiding for a while."

"That sounds good," she agrees. "Maybe somewhere with cushions and snacks."

I stare at her, wondering if she's serious. All I can do is laugh and move on. "When we're sure the coast is clear," I tell her, "let's run to the barn."

"Aye, aye, captain," she agrees. "Thar she blows."

A laugh forces its way out, then I quickly regain my composure. We pause for a few seconds, straining our ears to hear any sign of Dad.

"Are you ready?" I ask.

She sighs. "Do I have any choice?"

"You always have a choice," I tell her, "but sometimes none of the options are that great."

"Well, I don't want to stay here alone."

"Sounds like you've made your choice, then. Ready . . . set . . . go!"

We take off like we're stealing second base. When we're only a few steps away from the woodpile, Dad's voice comes booming from the other side of the house. "Asher!"

We run faster.

He keeps yelling. "You're not making things any better!"

We make it into the barn and press our backs against the wall, catching our breath before we climb to the loft.

"Asher!" he shouts again.

That one sounded really close.

I peek out the door and see him checking behind the woodpile.

"Oh jeez. Up the ladder. Go, go, go!" The fierce whisper rockets out of my throat. We scramble up to the loft like squirrels up a tree. Rory climbs over the top ledge and scoots out of the way. I pull myself up and we sit in silence until there's no sign of Dad. Then Rory asks a quiet question.

"You think we can wait here until he forgets about it?"

Sometimes, I wish I was as naïve as she is.

"He won't forget," I say. "He's got the mind of an elephant."

"That's not very nice," Rory chastises me. "He's still our dad."

"It's not an insult," I explain. "Elephants have amazing memories."

"Oh, I'll have to remember that."

"Ha. Nice pun."

"What pun?"

"Never mind. It's more likely that he'll get mad about something else, and *it* will become the new focus of his rage. A newer, more important thing to be angry about."

"Do you think we can fix it?" asks Rory.

"He doesn't even accept apologies anymore," I remind her. "What chance do we really have of fixing anything?"

"Well, maybe if we show him we learned our lesson. Parents like it when you learn your lesson. What do you think we're supposed to learn this time?"

"Don't drop stuff?" I say sarcastically.

"Does he think you did it on purpose?"

"I don't know what's going on in his head, but I'm sure he knows it wasn't on purpose. He's not an idiot. A jerk maybe, but not an idiot."

"Then why would he get mad at us for an accident?"

I shake my head. "I don't know. It doesn't surprise me, though. He just keeps getting worse."

She lays her head gently on my shoulder, and we sit in temporary peace.

SEEK AND FIND

Turning my attention to the task at hand, I take in my surroundings. I see what I've come for: the trunk that Grandpa and I talked about a few years ago. It's dark green with brass buckles and leather handles. No locks.

When we talked about it, Grandpa said, "It's not the right time. Maybe when you're older."

Well, now I'm older, and the time seems as right as any.

"Over there," I say to Rory, pointing toward the chest. "Grandpa said I could open it."

"Are you sure?" she asks.

"As sure as sure can be," I tell her, with more confidence than is actually inside me.

When I need Rory to go along with something, the best method is to confuse her and then pretend like everything is as clear as blue skies, when it's really as clear as mud.

"Okay," she finally says. "If you're sure."

"I am," I assure her.

I walk over to the old trunk and pull the buckles up. It pops open and seems to inhale the fresh air, savoring it after years of holding its breath, its secrets.

I lift the lid. Its hinges moan, and a musty smell invades my nostrils. I whip my head around and take a deep breath behind me, then turn back toward the chest and peer in.

Paper? A bunch of paper?

I don't know exactly what I was expecting, but I was hoping for something more interesting than paper. There are newspapers, typed papers, and handwritten notes.

"Hey! Pictures!" Rory points to a short stack of photos poking out of an old red-and-yellow envelope.

I reach in and pull it out, then slide the photos into my hand. They're a bunch of random images: some are photos, probably taken by Grandpa. Others are printed diagrams or maps. But mostly, it's a lot of old newspaper clippings.

I hand the stack to Rory and grab some other papers out of the trunk.

"What are we looking for?" she asks.

"I'm not sure. Anything that looks interesting, I guess."

She flips through a few pictures. "Is a picture of a bomb interesting?"

"I'd say so. You don't see those very often . . . if you're lucky. Does it say anything?"

"It says FAT MAN."

"Fat man? Are you sure?"

"They're only three-letter words," she points out. "I'm not stupid."

"Well, that is interesting," I admit after taking a look. "I don't know what the heck it means, though. Let's keep searching."

I shuffle through some more papers and see a word that I recognize: *Hanford.*

"Hey, Rory. I saw this same word in Grandpa's obituary."

"Grandpa's what?"

"Obituary. It's the thing in the newspaper with the dead people and . . . You know what? Never mind. Just look for more papers with Hanford on them, okay?"

She stares down at her stack.

"Please?" I ask, doing my best to be polite.

She doesn't budge.

"Rory!"

"Huh? Oh," she says softly. "What did you say?"

"Why don't you listen?" I scold her.

Her head droops.

"Sorry," I say, knowing exactly how she feels.

"It's okay," she says. "I'm used to it."

Oh man. That's not something anyone should be used to.

"I found one," she says. "H-A-N-F-O-R-D. Hanford."

"Already? Let me look," I say, as I grab the picture from her.

"Hey! Don't you know how to ask?"

"Sorry. Can I see it?"

"Well, you already have it, so I guess so."

"Thanks."

I hold the picture close to my face and angle it so a stream of light, cascading through a crack in the wallboards, hits it just right, giving it a slight glow in the dim, dusty loft. It's a flimsy black-and-white newspaper photo of a boxy gray building with a smokestack rising up from it. The words underneath the photo say HANFORD NUCLEAR REACTOR B.

"Hanford is a nuclear reactor?" I wonder out loud.

"What's a nuke-you-larry actor?" asks Rory.

"I think it's where they make bombs."

Her face contorts. "Did Grandpa go there? Is that from a trip?"

"I don't think so. It's just a newspaper clipping."

"Do you think Grandpa made bombs?" Her eyes widen as she stares at the photo.

"Don't be ridiculous. He was a farmer."

"Then how does a bomb kill Grandpa? Was he in one piece at the hospital?"

"Yes, Rory. He was in one piece. We know for sure that Grandpa didn't die from a bomb explosion. He died of cancer. But the real question is, if Hanford was involved somehow, and we know a bomb didn't blow him up, then how else would it kill him?"

"Falling on him?" she says. "I don't know." As if I actually expected her to answer.

"Let's look through more papers and see if we can figure anything else out."

"Got another one," says Rory, almost immediately.

"Okay then. It looks like we might end up finding a lot of information. Let's just make a pile of papers that say Hanford. Then we'll go from there."

"Okay. Got it," she says.

"You're doing great," I tell her, partially to encourage her, and partially to convince myself I'm better than Dad.

"Thanks!" she says in a chipper voice with a big grin on her face. "You haven't found anything yet."

I can't help but laugh a little.

"I guess you're right. I'll get on that."

"Okay. Good," she says. "Try to catch up."

INFORMATION OVERLOAD

"**D**ude! Are we keeping *all* of these?" I ask.

"I'm not a dude, dude," says Rory. "And yes, there were lots of HANFORDS, okay?"

"I believe you. It's just . . . it's a lot."

"Yeah," she says, "but we can do it a little at a time."

"I guess. We probably have more than we need at this point. Now we just have to read them."

"Let me know when you're done with that," she tells me.

I'm not sure if she's joking or not, so I ignore it.

"Hey. Do you want to be my official sidekick and solve this mystery together?" I say cheerfully, needing her to buy in to keep this all a secret. She can't go around telling everybody. I still have a million details to figure out.

"What's a sidekick, exactly?" she asks.

"Like Flounder in *The Little Mermaid* or the genie in *Aladdin*. A sidekick is a partner who is brave, dedicated to the mission, and maybe sometimes a little sneaky."

"Ooh, I can be that!" she says, quickly turning her frown upside down.

"I knew I had the right person!"

"What do I do first?"

Good question.

"Uh, first we have to get these important documents to a safer place, like my bedroom."

"Okay," she says. Then her eyebrows furrow. "How do we do that?"

Another good question.

"Since you're my sidekick, I'd like you to have a say. Do you have any ideas?"

"Well, we can't carry them down the ladder 'cause we'll need both hands."

"True," I confirm.

"So, we have to get them down some way without using our hands."

"Also true. You're good at this."

"So, what other kind of thing can we use to get them down?"

"That is the question, yes."

She thinks for a few seconds. "Do you know how they got this stuff up here?"

I do, but now I feel dumb for not thinking of it myself.

"Um, probably with the hoist they use for the hay bales."

"Can it make things go down or just up?"

"Both."

"Okay then," she says. "So let's wrap up the important papers and lower them with the hoist."

"We could wrap them up in that tarp," I say, pointing to one on the other side of the loft.

"Good job, Asher! You helped solve the problem!"

When did I become the sidekick?

Her smile touches both ears.

Oh well. I'll swallow my pride this time. For the sake of the mission.

"Rory! You're the best partner ever!"

"Thanks!" she says, beaming.

I head over to the hay door and open it, prepared to grab the hoist rope, but it isn't there.

"There isn't a hoist anymore," I call back to her.

"What's that thing above your head?" she asks.

I look up, and at first, I don't recognize it. It's orange and gray with a motor and a . . . rope with a hook. The words on it literally say MINI ELECTRIC HOIST. Duh. I'm thinking that I have severely underestimated my little sister's abilities or extremely overestimated my own. Or both. Sure, she forgets a few things, but she clearly has some great ideas.

I wrap the papers up in the tarp and tie a loop to slip over the hook. I secure it, check for witnesses, and push the button.

That really couldn't have been any easier.

Now the hard part: getting it past Mom and Dad. Dinner should be ready soon, which means Mom will more than likely be cooking. Dad's probably in front of the TV, hopefully zoned out enough that he won't notice us.

After climbing down and retrieving our tarp-bag, we tiptoe over to the house and peek through the window to see if Mom and Dad are in their normal spots. We look at the recliner. No Dad. We can see the whole kitchen. It's empty. Things seem to be going our way.

We quietly slide through the back door. On the stove, a chicken carcass is boiling. Mom's making broth again.

I make my way past the couch and over to Dad's chair to feel if the backrest is still warm. It is, which means he hasn't been gone long, and he could be close. I hope Dad's not "having a word" with Mom. For him, that means he says lots of words really loud, and then Mom might get to have *a* word before she gets interrupted again.

We head over to the stairs, trying to silence the tarp's crackling noises before they give us away. Rory starts up first. I stop her to explain a spy trick.

"If you walk with your feet on the outside edge of each step," I whisper, "they don't creak as much because that's where the beams are."

She stretches her legs wide, making her walk like a city slicker fresh off her first horseback ride. It physically hurts to hold back my laughter.

We make it to the top of the steps without drawing attention to ourselves, slip into my room, and quietly shut the door.

I burst into laughter and fall on the floor.

She stares at me for a second, not sure what's so funny. Then, apparently not needing any reason to join in, she giggles and grins, then falls on the floor next to me. Pretty soon, she's progressed to hoots and hollers, then she moves on to squirms and snorts.

Right now, being sane is more important than being silent, so we both let loose.

After a few minutes of this, she massages her cheeks.

"My face hurts," she says.

"A good problem to have. What better thing to use your face for than laughing? The sore muscles just mean we haven't been using them enough."

I contemplate that thought for a minute, then decide to make her smile some more.

"Good work, partner!" I tell her. "I couldn't have done it without you!"

"Thanks, partner!"

She glows and gives me a sweet smile.

I give her a cheesy grin.

"So what else do we have to do besides read?" she asks.

"Well, after we figure out more about Hanford, we have another mystery to solve."

"Ooooh! Exciting!" she squeals. "What's this one about?"

"It's about your secret, dead uncle."

"I don't have a secret, dead uncle. Do I?"

"I found out that Dad had a brother."

"And you're just telling me now? How come we never met him?"

"I said *had* a brother, genius."

Her head droops a little as my tone pierces her, deflating her spirit. I scramble to repair the damage.

"Sorry. I mean, all I know is that he's not alive anymore. I don't know when he died or how he died."

Her head rises, her face still somber. "Maybe that's why Dad is so sad. He lost his brother, and now his mom and dad are gone too."

"Not to mention his job and our house," I point out. "But Dad isn't sad. He's mad. He's angry and mean."

She looks at me as though she feels sorry for me.

"Maybe he's sad about so many things that, when he was filled to the tippy top, it turned to mad."

I don't know how to respond to that, so I don't.

WINNER, WINNER

"I'll be out in the barn!" Dad thunders.

SLAM!

Even though it's muffled by the floorboards, the crashing door, the reverberation of his words throughout the house, and the bitterness in his voice tell me there will be dinner for three tonight. Dad will eat leftovers, alone.

Rory and I look at each other. The joy is gone. Our sore cheeks will get their rest.

We take deep breaths. On the bright side, we dodged a bullet by not running into Dad. And, now that he's gone, we'll have a peaceful dinner.

"Let's wait a few minutes to go downstairs," I say. "Mom might want some time to herself."

"Aye, aye, captain!"

"And let's try to be extra nice to her tonight, okay?"

I know Rory's going to freak out when she realizes what's for dinner. When we hurried through the house, somehow she missed the boiling pot and smell of chicken broth in the air, but there will be no missing it once we open my door. It's creeping through the cracks already. She's had chicken plenty of times, but not since we moved to a farm. If she realizes that this chicken had a name, a name she gave it, and that we're eating her friend for dinner, she's going to lose it.

"Okay. Deal," she says and holds out her pinkie. "Pinkie promise."

Sweet. She even added a pinkie promise. Maybe she can pull this off.

After a few restful minutes, I pose a question: "Should we head downstairs for dinner now or wait until she calls us?"

"Let's go!" she says. "Maybe we can make her feel better!"

I don't think it's going to be that easy.

"Okay," I say. "Just remember your promise."

"I will. I always keep my promises."

I open the door and look back at her. She inhales deeply through her nose.

"Mmm. That smells yummy!"

Oh no. This is hard to watch.

She continues. "We haven't had chick—"

Her eyes go wide, and her lips wilt at the edges.

"Rory, you promised."

"But. But. But."

"That's a lot of butts," I joke, trying to break the tension, but she's clearly not in the mood.

"Sorry?" is really all I can say.

"I can't eat one of my chickens!" she says, her volume quickly rising. "I cuddle with them! You can't eat things you cuddle with!"

I want to tell her to stop cuddling with chickens so it won't be an issue, but I attempt to comfort her instead. "What if they bought one from the store?" It's highly unlikely, but there's not much else to say.

Rory storms out of my room and stomps down the stairs.

"Rory! You promised!"

"NO CHICKEN!" I hear her yell. "Chickens are friends! Not food!"

Oh, Lord. Pinkie promises don't mean what they used to.

I start down the stairs and hear another door slam.

Was that Rory leaving or Dad coming back?

I pause.

It's silent, which means Dad and Rory are gone.

I continue my way downstairs.

"Hi, Mom," I say, attempting a positive tone. "What's for dinner?"

Dumb question.

"Hi, sweetheart. It's raspberry-thyme chicken with pickled asparagus and crescent rolls."

"That sounds great!" I lie. We've had asparagus every day for the last week. We must be on a tight budget, considering our only vegetable is asparagus, and we're eating Rory's friends.

The door rockets open and slams against the wall.

"You killed Sunshine! Sunshine was my favorite!"

"I'm sorry, sweetie. We didn't know they meant *that* much to you."

"Did Dad do it?" Rory demands an answer. "Did Dad kill Sunshine?"

Mom pauses. "Well, sweetheart . . ."

Mom is pretty big on the Ten Commandments, and one says she can't lie.

"It was just her time," she says, not actually answering the question.

"Her time for what?" asks Rory.

"Her time . . ." Mom pauses. "Time for . . . " She pauses again. "I'm sorry dear. I just know she was very lucky to have you as a friend while she was here."

She's still here, just with added flavor.

"One thing I do know," Mom continues, "is that it's time for dinner. Can you please wash up, sweetheart? Asher, will you set the table? Four spots in case your father decides to join us."

Don't jinx it.

"Mom!" yells Rory.

"Sweetheart, you can just have some extra asparagus and another roll if you'd like, instead of . . . the protein."

The protein who shall remain nameless.

"Fine!" says Rory. "But don't kill any more of my chickens!"

"I'm sorry, sweetheart. I can't promise that, but I'll do my best."

Mom clearly needs some backup here. "Hey, Rory, do you like fish better?"

"Fish is gross!" she says as she makes a vomiting sound.

"Well, would you rather eat fish than . . . What's your second-favorite chicken's name?"

"I'll never tell you!"

"Would you rather eat fish than your new best friend?"

"Obviously!" she says, with more than a hint of attitude.

"Okay, then how about I keep a bunch of fish, and we have those for dinner more often, so we don't have to eat as many chickens?"

"As many?" she yells.

I don't think I'm actually helping.

"Or any? I don't know."

I look over at Mom and shrug my shoulders. She looks back with an exhausted smile and simply mouths, "Thank you."

"More fish. Fine," says Rory. "Feed us the donkey if you have to, just don't touch the chickens!"

"Hey!" I argue back. "Leave the donkey out of this!"

"All right, all right," Mom says. "Let's just have dinner, okay?"

"Fine," says Rory, slumping into her chair.

"Fine by me," I add.

I finish setting the table, and Mom brings over the food. She sets the hot pans on Grandma's old trivets to protect the table made by Grandpa's hands. We sit there in silence, waiting for Mom to pray for our meal, but she doesn't. Her head is bowed, but it's just resting on her folded hands.

Things stay like this for a bit before I say something.

"Mom?"

She lifts her head. Her eyes are red.

"Sorry. I'm just tired."

Again, with the partial truths. I'm sure she's exhausted, but those are cry eyes. I should know. She can try to hold the tears back, but sometimes they force their way through.

"I'll pray," I say, catching myself off guard.

Not being much of a religious person, that's a big offer and one that I didn't expect myself to put out there. It seems easy enough when she does it, though.

We bow our heads and close our eyes. Or at least I assume they do it with me, since my eyes are shut tight.

"Dear God," I begin. "Bless this food to our bodies. Thank you for Rory and Mom and please help Dad to not be so angry all the time. Say hi to Grandma, Grandpa, Gabriel, and all our other dead relatives for us. Oh . . . and Sunshine too, if that's a thing. Amen."

"Asher!" cries Rory.

"Sorry! I thought you would like the Sunshine part."

"Not that!" she says, looking at me like I'm a complete moron.

"Then what?"

"Asher," Mom says. "Would you mind sharing what you know about Gabriel?"

A CUSS WORD

I want to share a few cuss words, but I don't think that's what Mom has in mind.

My mouth shoots out disconnected thoughts. "Did I say something about a Gabriel? Dad has a Gabriel? What does that even mean? That's cool. Um, I don't know anything about a brother. What do you know about a brother?"

"I didn't mention a brother," says Mom. "So far, I believe you've done all the sharing."

"Oh cool. Tell me more."

"Asher, can you start by telling me what you know? I won't get mad."

It's not her I'm worried about.

"I know it too!" says Rory, not wanting to be left out.

"Okay. Well. I know he died," I tell her.

I pause, but nothing else comes to mind.

"Is that it?" she asks patiently.

"Um." I look at Rory. She shrugs her shoulders. "Yes?"

"Okay. Well, that's definitely a big part Gabe's story."

"There's a story?" Rory asks excitedly.

"Yes, but unfortunately, it's a short story."

"Oh."

"And a sad one."

"Ohhh."

"I just saw his name in Grandpa's obituary," I explain. "It just said that he died."

"We were going to tell you guys when you got older. It's difficult for your father to talk about. He was three when his brother was born too early. His body hadn't grown enough for him to stay alive on his own. He only survived at all because he was hooked up to machines . . . and that's the only time your father got to be with him. He lived for less than a day.

"Your father wasn't able to understand everything that was happening since he was so young. All he knew was that he had a brother, and then he didn't.

"After you were born, Asher, these memories of Gabriel kept coming up, so I encouraged him to see a counselor and talk about it, but he said he could handle it on his own."

"So did he?" asks Rory.

"Well. He handled it in his own way."

"What did he do?" I ask.

"He left the faith."

"Faith?" Rory and I say at nearly the same time.

"Dad believed in God?" I ask.

"He realized he had been blaming God for Gabe's death . . . and all the other horrible things in the world. He decided that the answer to it all was to stop believing in God. That way, he reasoned, there was nobody to blame when bad things happen. They just happen. And from his perspective, the plan worked."

"I think he should go back to church," adds Rory.

"I don't think that's going to happen anytime soon. Grandpa's death is entirely different than what your father had previously considered, so it's proving to be quite diffi-cult for him."

"How is it different?" I ask.

"Yeah, how?" adds Rory.

"I don't want to get into details without your father here, but as you've noticed, things are piling up on his shoulders. With God's grace, I'm just doing my best to support him." Mom looks around the table; not at our eyes but at our plates. She takes a deep breath.

"The food I worked so hard to make for you is getting cold. Eat up."

I want to blurt, *"I know about Hanford and the bombs,"* but I don't really know anything, so I decide it's best to keep quiet.

"Sure, Mom," I say.

I stab my fork through a piece of asparagus and then a piece of chicken to cover the taste.

Rory just stares at her plate. I clear my throat to get her attention and then use a precise head nod, aimed at her food, to get her to eat. When that doesn't work, I add some facial expressions to make it more clear. To me, the message was obvious, but to Rory, it was not.

"Asher, what's wrong with your face?" she says. "Are you having a seizure? I told you that you shouldn't have eaten Sunshine. That's what you get."

WHO'S READY FOR SECRETS?

"**H**ey, Rory! You almost done?" I yell across the yard.

"Yeah. I'm just spending some quality time with Buttercup."

I can't say I blame her. It's tough to get quality time with folks around here. Why not a chicken?

"We're almost done with chores, and it's not even lunchtime! Then we can get to what Saturdays are really for!"

"What are they for?"

"Anything but chores," I tell her. "Well, not anything, I guess. Anything that doesn't have to do with Dad, preferably."

I look around to make sure he didn't hear that.

"Have you seen him?" I ask, hoping to confirm his absence.

"Nope!"

"He could be out in the field, I guess, but he's probably doing 'important work' at the library. I'll bet you five bucks he's using their free Internet to do research on the government."

"I'm not old enough to gamble," she says. "And if I were, even I know that would be a dumb bet."

Rory finishes collecting the eggs, and I rinse the soap off the car.

What's the point in washing your car when you live on a farm? It's going to get dirty as soon as you drive it.

I look down the driveway, and Mari and Julia are coming. Rory notices them and begins jumping up and down, waving.

Pretty soon, they're within shouting distance. "Hi, Asher! Hi, Rory!" yells Mari.

"Yeah, hi!" adds Julia.

We yell back, urging them to hurry up.

When they arrive, I fill them in on what's been happening. "We're just finishing up our chores, and then Rory and I have something to talk to you about."

"We do?" asks Rory.

"Yes. We do."

"What is it?"

"She's great at keeping secrets," I tell them, as I put the supplies in the shed.

"Good job, Rory," says Mari. "I'm a good secret-keeper too. Speaking of, Asher, I have something important to tell *you,* but it's not for little ears."

"I don't have little ears!" says Rory. "My ears are just the right size for my head."

I'm so tempted to say, *"It's your mouth that's too big,"* but I don't. I'm such a good brother.

"Unfortunately, you have to be over ten for this one," adds Mari. She looks at me and winks. Since I can only wink with two eyes, also known as blinking, I don't return the gesture.

"Oh, sorry girls," I say. "You'll have to sit this one out."

Rory crosses her arms and makes her pouting sound, *humph,* as a quick exhale shoots out her nostrils.

Julia tries to mimic her but shoots boogers onto her coat. Then she opts for the classic stick-your-tongue-out-while-making-the-raspberry-sound, showering my face with spit.

After I wipe off her saliva with my sleeve and successfully hold in a near puke, I'm not exactly Julia's biggest fan, but her "oops" grin makes it hard to stay mad for long.

"Thanks for the shower," I tell her, trying to laugh it off.

"You're welcome?" she answers, not sure how to respond. "Do you need a towel?"

LITTLE AGENTS

"Shut the door," I say, sounding ruder than I intend. "It's actually really tight in here with all the boxes and the four of us. We're going to have to split up. Rory, I have an important job for you. I need you to be a leader. Can you do that for me? For us?"

"No prob, Bob!" She gives me a big thumbs-up.

"Okay, here's what I need you to do. We're going to split up into two groups. You and Julia are going to go in your room to do your secret task, and Mari and I are going to stay here to work on our part. I need you guys to look through your stack of top-secret documents and—"

"Top-secret documents?" Julia blurts out.

"Shhhhhhh!" Rory and I say in unison.

"We want them to stay top-secret!" I add.

"Sorry," she says, with embarrassment in her voice. "I won't do it again."

"I need you to look through the documents and tally any words that you see lots of. Do you know what a tally mark is?"

"I do!" says Rory. "I learned it from Mrs. Evans in kindergarten. Four tall lines, then make a slide from left to right."

"Very good," says Mari.

Rory grins, showing off her teeth.

"Let's look at a couple articles together before we split into teams."

I grab a random paper out of the box.

"First, we have one titled 'US Knew of Hanford Risks from Radiation. Government Refuses to Start Cancer Studies.'"

Slightly stunned, I glance over at Mari. "Wow. Okay then."

She raises her eyebrows.

"Let's look at another one. 'Hanford Likely Caused Cancer Downwind, Jury Decides.'"

"Okay, uh, maybe this is too much for little eyes."

"I don't have little eyes!" cries Rory. "My eyes are very normal!"

"Me too!" says Julia.

"You have to let us help! Remember? We're a team!"

Mari jumps in. "Okay, okay." She directs her attention toward me. "Where did you say you found these?"

"In a trunk in the loft."

She hesitates before continuing. "I don't know if we want to get into this. If this is Grandpa's research, there might be stuff in here we don't want to know."

I pretend like I don't hear her and quickly devise a plan to ease some of her concerns.

I turn to Rory and Julia. "Let's just have you two stick to the titles, then. Okay? Those should give us enough information for now."

"More than enough, for sure," says Mari. "I really don't like this."

"What harm can come out of reading a few articles? We're educating ourselves. Surely you're not against education."

Ooh. That was a good point.

"Besides," I continue, "don't we deserve to know about our family history?"

"What makes you think anything in there will be helpful? Maybe there was a reason Grandpa hid it. "

"Wouldn't he have thrown them away if he didn't want us to see them? And besides, he said I could look when I was old enough."

She pauses.

"And you're old enough now?"

"Well, since Grandpa's gone, there's no for-sure way to know."

"So you're going to do this having no way of knowing, for sure, that it's a good idea."

"Right," I confirm. "They're just articles."

"Top-secret articles," she reminds me.

"Right. Just top-secret articles."

She sighs and then gives in, kind of.

"I just need to make it clear that I'm fully against this. I'll stay and make sure you don't do anything stupid, but I'm not helping you do anything stupid."

"Fair enough," I tell her, before turning my attention to the girls.

"You see, Rory? Julia? In these two titles, you can mark down the important words to see what they have in common. So, put down two tally marks for *Hanford*, one for *radiation*, one for *government*, one for *downwind*, and two for *cancer*. Does that make sense?"

"Yes. Yes, yes, yes," agrees Rory. "Titles. Words. Tally marks. Check, check, and check. I'm on it! I mean, we're on it! Right, Julia?"

"Right, Rory! We're on it!"

"Okay, come on, partner!" Rory signals her. "Let's find some clues!"

Rory grabs a handful of papers from my top-secret card-board box. She walks over to the door, cracks it slightly, and peers out. She presses her ear against the opening to see if she can hear anything.

"The coast is clear," she whispers back to Julia, then she opens the door wide and motions her forward. "Follow me."

Rory gets down on all fours. Then, unexpectedly, her butt goes up in the air, and her head rests on the floor. She kicks her feet up, then flops like a flipped pancake. She lies there for a second, stunned, then realizes that somersaults aren't the best idea when you're holding on to top-secret documents.

Julia jumps into action, cleaning up the papers. Mari and I can't help but crack up as we watch her scramble to collect everything.

Rory picks herself up, and the two of them run into her room, ready to take on their challenge. They shut the door behind them, and I shut mine.

"So," I say, turning to Mari, "What's your top-secret infor-mation?"

SECRETS MAKE FRIENDS

Mari pulls a folded-up piece of paper out of her pocket and sits down on the edge of my bed.

"What's that?" I ask, wondering if this secret could be any bigger than mine.

"I found a letter that Papi left on the table. I thought it might be from one of my aunties in Mexico, so I opened it. It's been a long time since we've heard from them. I wanted to see how they were."

"And?"

"It wasn't from them."

"Well, who was it from, then?"

"I should have put it down," she says. Her nervous look tells me she didn't.

I sit next to her on the bed. "But you read it?"

"I did."

She pulls at the edges of the paper as if she could stretch it.

"So? Who was it from?"

"It was from one of our friends in Mexico; one of the men that helps on the farm during harvest. We have four that come every year."

"Are they legal?"

"Yes," she tells me, with a bit of scorn on her face. "There are some workers that come to America illegally, but like most immigrants, they follow the law. Although, this time, doing the right thing might ruin everything."

"What do you mean?"

"After three years, every worker has to go back to their own country for ninety days."

"Okay, so they'll be back in time, right?"

"No. They won't."

"What do you mean? Why not? Is it money?"

"It's not about that. The government won't let them back in."

"What? Why?"

"The government is too far behind on processing their piles of paperwork; there's no way they'll approve our friends in time for them to come this year. The letter says they are very sorry, they did their best, and they will miss us."

"Okay, well, there are plenty of people around here that we can pay, right?"

"I don't think so. I think that's the only reason that the men can come from Mexico. Nobody here wants to do the work."

"What is it with people? Lazy bums!"

I flop back on to my bed, but the twin-size mattress doesn't leave enough room for a smooth landing, causing my head to slam against the wall.

"Owww! Fudge! That hurt."

Mari sticks her elbow into the bed to prop herself up as she reclines next to me. "Are you okay?"

"Mentally or physically?" I ask, half joking, and then realize that NO is the correct answer either way.

"Both?" she says, not sure how to respond.

"I'll be fine. I'm a quick healer."

"Mentally or physically," she asks, smiling at me.

I'm not sure how to respond, so I roll over and bury my face in my blanket.

I feel a soft touch on the back of my head, and instantly, my breathing stops.

"Where does it hurt?" she asks tenderly.

"Pretty much everywhere," I say, still holding my breath.

Why would I exaggerate like that? It's just one little spot.

She searches for a bump, running her fingers through my hair.

"No blood," she says.

Something inside me considers asking her to check again, but I shake my head to reset things and pull myself back together, wondering what the heck just happened.

The door handle jiggles, and in comes Rory, looking concerned.

"What happened?" she asks. "It sounded like you might be hurt, and since I'm your sidekick, I thought I should check on you. Are you dead?"

I roll over to show her I'm still alive.

"I'm fine, sidekick. Thanks for checking on me. You've always got my back."

"No, I don't. How would I have your back?" she asks.

"Never mind."

"Okay," she says, chipper as can be. Then, she claps twice and shouts, "Chop, chop, people! This mystery ain't gonna solve itself!"

She flings her body around, rotating one hundred eighty degrees, and then soldier-marches over to her bedroom, leaving my door wide open.

"Back to work, Agent Julia. No time to dillydally."

"I guess we should probably get to the research too, huh?"
I tell Mari.

"What should we do about the letter?" she asks.

"You should put it back and let our dads figure it out. I mean, we're not even supposed to know about it! Besides, I've got a lot on my plate already."

"I just thought maybe we could come up with some ideas to help," she suggests.

"And maybe we can, but let's give the old people a shot at it first."

She gives me a concerned look.

I hold up a pile of articles. "I mean, look at this."

I flip through the stack, showing her just how many pages there are.

She sighs deep and long.

"And this isn't even half of it," I tell her. "There's a ton more in the loft."

"Aren't you worried about what's in there?"

I toss the pile onto the bed and fan them out, trying to take in as much information as I can all at once.

Mari pulls one out of the pile and takes a long look at it.

Attempting to read the title upside down, I think it says, *Lawyers Say Hanford Lawsuit Is Too Late*. I cock my head to the side a bit to verify.

As soon as I confirm it, Mari pulls it away.

"Hey! I wanted to read that!"

"Do you really, though?" she says.

"Yes," I tell her, as I reach for it.

She reluctantly hands it over.

TRUTH BOMB

THE SPOKESMAN-REVIEW

Spokane, Washington   Est. May 19, 1883

Lawyers Say Hanford Lawsuit Is Too Late
By Karen Dorn Steele
Friday, July 16, 2004
(Adapted)

The expiration date of a . . . deadline to file suit is a question being raised by the defendants in the Hanford Downwinders' lawsuit scheduled for trial in March 2005. Lawyers for . . . Hanford . . . are pointing to the newspaper publicity in an effort to oust many plaintiffs . . . who claim their health was harmed by emissions of radioactive iodine-131 during plutonium production at Hanford . . .

Iodine-131, a byproduct of plutonium separation, lodges in the human thyroid where, in sufficient doses, it can cause cancer and other illnesses. It is most damaging to the tiny thyroid glands of infants and small children . . .

Farmers living eleven miles east of Hanford across the Columbia River were keeping a detailed map of a "Death

Mile" near Ringold where all the residents got cancer, and most suspected their nuclear neighbor was the cause . . .

A three-judge panel tossed out two lawsuits brought by plaintiffs living near the government's Oak Ridge, Tennessee, weapons complex who alleged they were exposed to radiation and other toxic emissions and developed health problems, including thyroid cancer. In their July 15 decision, the judges said the plaintiffs waited too long to file their lawsuit.

[Their] study said local children drinking milk from a backyard cow or goat in the early 1950s and women carrying fetuses in the 1950s and 1960s who ate fish from nearby streams were at elevated risk from the toxic emissions.

EXPLOSIVE NEWS

"**W**hat the heck?" The words explode out of my mouth.

"This is how Grandpa got cancer?" asks Mari. "Fifty years ago?"

"They have to be connected, don't they? His obituary talked about Hanford and said he was a 'Downwinder.'"

"No wonder he was so mad when he found out," she says. Then she points out a part that doesn't fit. "But it says the death mile was in Ringold. That's over an hour away. Didn't he grow up here?"

"Yeah. He always talked about growing up on the farm."

"And it was this farm?" she asks.

"Yes! No? I don't know! He just said 'farm'!"

"Sorry," she says. "I'm only trying to help."

"Thank you," I say, as I take a deep breath. "I know. I'm just sick of being kept in the dark."

"Asher. You know your grandpa loved you. You have to trust that he kept this from you for a reason."

"Yeah, but now he's gone, and I can't even ask him about it."

"That's true, but he said he would tell you when the time was right. He wasn't really hiding it. He was just being cautious.

Would it have changed anything if he showed you earlier?"

"Yes!"

"Really?"

"I don't know. Maybe?"

"I guess you just have to trust that he wanted what's best for you."

"And that's supposed to be good enough?"

"Yes. You need to look at it the way Grandpa would. Remember that everything he did for you was because he loved you; maybe even keeping this information from you."

"That's a ridiculously optimistic outlook, and I don't know if I can commit to that."

"Well, at least you're honest," she says, trying to keep things positive. "Now, are you sure you want to keep digging into this?"

There's a knock on my door.

"Who is it?" I ask.

"It's Julia. Can I come in?"

"Just go in," I hear, as Rory flings the door open and pushes Julia forward.

"We're done with finding the big words. Here's the list."

nuclear |||| |||
Manhattan Project ||||
Hanford |||| |||| |||| ||
Cancer |||| |
Contamination |||| |||
Government |||
Nagasaki |||
Bomb |||| |||| |||
Plutonium ||||
radio active |||| |
uranium ||
cleanuP ||||
Downwinders ||||
iodine-131 ||||
thyroid ||||
milk |||

"Milk? Why did you write milk?"

"You said to write words we saw more than once."

"Ya, but just the big words."

"I know. They were BIG MILKS."

"And Nagasaki?"

"It's a word!" Rory cries out.

"An Asian word," I say.

"An Asian word?" asks Julia. "I don't think Asian is a language."

"I know that! I was just saying that it was probably from an Asian country."

"Do you also think that Julia and I speak Mexican?" Mari hassles me.

"No! You speak Spanish! I'm not an idiot or a racist or anything. I love Mexicans!"

"You love Mexicans?" laughs Mari.

"Of course! You're Mexican!" I point out.

The next few seconds go by so slowly, they would lose a race with a sloth.

"And Julia . . . and your dad! I love you guys!"

"Anybody else?" Mari eggs me on.

"Selena Gomez?"

"She's not even Mexican."

"She's not? Dang it! I was so sure about that one!"

"I'm kidding. Of course she is."

"Why would you do that to me? I'm emotionally fragile!"

Mari laughs. Not exactly what I was going for.

"I'm sorry," she says. "I couldn't help it. We Mexicans love you too."

We sit in silence for a few seconds. There's so much stuff racing through my mind, I decide to change the subject.

"So, sidekick," I look at Rory. "What should we do next?"

"I know exactly what we should do!" she says.
This girl just keeps surprising me with her good ideas.
"All right! Great!" I encourage her. "What is it?"
"Dinner!"

MR. NICE GUY

"**A**sher! Rory! Dinner!"

Dad has such a way with words.

"I guess that means we should go home," says Mari.

I'm glad we have the same idea, because the last thing I want is for her to stay for dinner. Not because of her. Because of Dad.

"Good work today, team. I'll work on this more tonight, and we'll get together again soon. I'll walk you guys out."

I lead the crew downstairs, through the kitchen, and to the door; a knob turn away from a smooth exit.

Then, in the blink of an eye, my worst nightmare comes true.

"Do you have to get home for dinner?" Dad says. "You're welcome to eat with us if you'd like."

Wait, what? Oh no. No. No. No. No. No. No.

"They were just leaving," I say, trying to cut this off before it starts. "I think they have to help cook, right?"

"We're just having leftovers," blabs Julia, smiling innocently.

I try again.

"Are you sure your dad will be okay with it?"

"I can give him a call," offers Dad. "I'm sure it won't be a problem."

"Asher," Mari whispers as she leans toward me, "we don't have to stay if you don't want us to."

"No. I like being with you," I whisper back.

How the heck do I get out of this?

I turn to Mom. "Is there enough food?"

Please say no. Please say no.

"Well. We have plenty of asparagus," she says with a chuckle, "and I made extra rolls."

I don't like where this is going.

"Ooh! I know! We can split the sausages, fry up some eggs, add a little cheese, and have farmhand breakfast sandwiches. How does that sound?"

It sounds like this is happening whether I like it or not.

"Sounds great," I lie, without even attempting a fake smile.

"Mrs. McCovey, can I help with anything?" asks Mari.

"You could fry up the eggs if you'd like."

"I can do that."

"I'll cut the cheese!" yells Rory.

"What's new?" I blurt out.

"Ha, ha," she says. "Very funny."

"Well, thank you. You're too kind."

She sticks out her tongue and scrunches up her nose. Then she whips herself around and heads over to the fridge. Mari's already in there grabbing some eggs.

"Asher, could you grab another jar of asparagus out of the pantry?" asks Mom.

"Um, yeah. Sure," I say, glad that I got the easy job so I can keep an eye on Dad.

I have to make sure he doesn't talk to Mari while I'm not looking. He's so unpredictable that I can't risk it. If he can ruin relationships with his own kids, I'm sure he can ruin other people's relationships too.

I can't just sit around and let this happen.

I grab the asparagus, put it on the table, then make my way over to the end of the couch next to the recliner.

"Hey, Dad?"

"Yeah?" he says, as if nothing were out of the ordinary.

"What are you doing?"

"I'm watching the Mariners and Yankees," he says, his eyes fixed on a Taco Bell commercial telling him to "Live Life Outside the Bun."

"That's not what I mean. Why are you acting like this in front of our friends?"

"What do you mean? Isn't this how I'm supposed to act?"

"No! I mean, yes! But you're supposed to be like this every day, not just invite them to dinner so you can put on a show, pretending like you're . . . normal."

"Ouch." His head falls back like I landed a punch.

"You know what I mean."

"I don't think normal even exists," he says, "but I'm trying my best."

"If you've been trying your best, I'd hate to see your worst."

I'm not sure where the words came from or how they made it past my lips, but now they're out there.

"Hey!" he yells, then tries to rein himself back in. "Sometimes things are out of my control. I didn't want to lose my job . . .or our house . . . or Grandpa."

"Ya. It must suck to lose your dad!" I tell him, unable to stop myself. This clearly isn't going to help anything, but telling him what I've been dying to say is, in some odd way, the best feeling ever.

"You think I want it like this?" he yells. "You think I wake up every day and shoot for this? This isn't what I want, either! This isn't what any of us want!"

The kitchen sounds stop, except for the sizzling eggs.

Mom takes the frying pan off the stove and sets it on a hot pad.

"We'll give you guys some time to talk. I'll take the girls on a walk down to the river. Just ring the dinner bell when you're ready for us to come back. Let's go, girls." Mom ushers them toward the door and then out. She closes it quietly behind her.

"Nice one," we say in near unison, agreeing that the other is at fault.

"Me?" he argues. "I was fine until you came over and trash-talked me!"

"They're not scared of me," I protest. "Everybody's scared of you!"

"Did you not hear yourself? I realize some of this is my fault—"

"Some of it?"

"Yes! Some of it. Maybe you can't see it because you're so focused on being angry at me that you can't even see how angry you are!"

"I don't have to be focused in order to be angry at you. It comes naturally."

"You think I don't know that?" he says. "Anger comes very easily. THAT'S! THE! PROBLEM!"

"Then do something about it!"

"I'm trying!" he roars.

"It's not enough!" I shoot back.

"I know!"

Silence.

A few seconds pass as we both let our words soak in.

"Finally!" I blurt out. "Something we agree on!"

I walk to the door and fling it open, grab the rope hanging from the dinner bell, and whip it back and forth. It rings loudly, announcing that this conversation is over.

WHATEVER

Stupid Dad. Stupid bell. Stupid night. Stupid steps. Stupid stars. Stupid moon. Stupid freezing cold. Stupid everything.

I ring the bell for the fifth time. Still no one comes. It's dark now, but there's no way I'm going back in.

The sound of an engine roars up the driveway, and two headlights bounce in unison. The lights are too close together to be a car. It has to be the quad.

When it gets closer, I see that there are two people on it.

They pull into the barn; the engine shuts off, and the lights go out. A few seconds pass, and two shadows exit the barn, walking toward me. As they get closer, the porch light gradually illuminates their faces.

"Mom? Rory? How did you fix the quad? Where are Mari and Julia? Where have you been? I've been waiting forever!"

"Not forever," Mom corrects me, "and Manny just had to tighten a couple cables."

"Urgghh!" I roar. "I'm so stupid!"

"No. You're not, sweetheart. Please don't say that. I'm sorry you had to wait for us, though. When we heard the bell after just a few minutes, I knew things couldn't have gone well, so

I walked the girls home. I'm sorry it took so long."

She turns to Rory. "Sweetheart, can you head inside and make yourself a sandwich? I want to talk with Asher for a few minutes."

My head drops back as I look to the stars and release an exhausted groan. "Oh great. What now?"

She ignores my question. "Thank you, Rory. I'll be right in."

Rory walks up the steps and bumps my elbow.

"Watch it, lady!"

"It was an accident!" she says. "Jeez. You don't have to be mad at everyone! Mom and I didn't do anything!"

I want to say, *"You're right, Mom didn't do anything at all. If she would step up and do something, anything, maybe we wouldn't be stuck in this mess."* But all I can say is, "Leave me alone."

Rory opens the door slowly, peeking in to see if Dad is still there. He's either gone or he's fallen asleep in his recliner, because she steps in and quietly closes the door behind her.

"Asher, what's going on?" Mom crosses her arms. I'm unsure if she's frustrated or just trying to stay warm.

"If you were paying attention at all, it would be pretty obvious."

"Asher. You don't have to be mean. You have the right to be upset, but you don't have the right to be unkind."

"You wanna know what's going on? I'm sick of this! I'm sick of Dad being a jerk. I'm sick of you just praying and nothing happening. I'm sick of more problems popping up every day. I'm sick of not being able to do anything to fix them." By this point, my volume is just below yelling. "I'm even getting sick of myself!"

Mom softens her voice even more. "It's okay for you to feel all these things, sweetheart."

"Yeah, but it doesn't do any good! Feelings don't do any

good! Feelings don't fix things."

I look at the ground, and I can feel Mom staring at the top of my head, trying to read my mind.

"Nothing is getting better!" I yell at the floor. "Everything is piling up and up and up. I can't fix any of it! Everything just keeps getting worse!" My voice breaks. I won't let myself cry.

"I know your father has changed a lot, and that has to be so hard for you. I'm sorry, dear."

I look her in the eyes. "Hard for me? Hard for me? That's the understatement of the century. You wouldn't understand anything I'm going through."

"Can I try?"

"You could start by not keeping secrets. I know all the stuff you guys have been hiding from me, pretending like every-thing is okay."

"Asher." She looks at me with concern in her eyes.

"Don't 'Asher' me. I know way more than you think. I know Dad lost his job because he didn't actually do any work, and I found out about Gabe, no thanks to you. And you know what else? I know that Grandpa died from cancer that he got because of the Hanford nuclear plant. I even know that the workers from Mexico can't come, so we probably won't be able to sell the asparagus or keep the farm!"

Mom looks stunned. I can't blame her.

"My dad's crazy and hates me, and my mom's trusting a mythical being to magically change things, so it's pretty much up to me to make something happen."

"That's not your job," she says.

"Then who's going to do it?"

"Your father and I."

"Yeah? Like you've been doing so well already?"

"Asher," she says in a desperate tone.

"Don't, Mom."

"You can't fix your father, sweetheart." She looks like she might cry.

"I noticed! But what am I supposed to do? Just sit here and watch it all come crashing down?"

She just stands there rubbing the goose bumps off her arms. "Of course not."

"Exactly. You don't have a good answer. That's because there isn't one."

"Asher," she says, almost in a whisper.

"Is that all you can say?"

She's out of words. I've run her dry.

"I hate this day, and if history tells me anything, it's only going to get worse. I'm going to bed. Wake me up when this nightmare is over."

SUNDAY, FUN DAY

There are only two things that make me happily jump out of bed in the morning: The first is Disneyland. I've never jumped out of bed with that much instant energy before. Fishing is a close second, though. If I know I'm going fishing, I have no problem waking up. The instant my alarm goes off, I'm up and I don't even feel tired. Usually.

This morning is an exception. I couldn't fall asleep last night, so I stayed up until I passed out, looking through all the information we dug out of Grandpa's box.

I know Dad took Grandpa's death especially hard, but I'm not sure what I thought I could do about it. What was I hoping to find in this jumble of information? I can't go back and change the fact that Grandpa got cancer from living downwind of nuclear reactors. I can't make it all okay because it's not okay. It's messed up.

I made it through less than half the pile of papers, but I found some crazy stuff.

Hanford was part of the Manhattan Project, which was a government research-and-development program. Essentially, they were figuring out how to build nuclear bombs. They looked around the country and decided that Hanford, Washington, was perfect for what they needed. There was plenty of space, and the chilly waters of the Columbia River could keep their precious machines from overheating. So, they just kicked any farmers that were there off the land.

Dad sometimes calls the government a necessary evil. I think I'm starting to understand what he means. Two of the farmers that lost their land were my great-grandparents, Fred and Irma. The government forced them to sell, decided what the land was worth, and sent them packing. I understand that life isn't fair, but that's just not right. They didn't even pay them for their house or the crops they had to leave behind.

I did read that the Hanford employees who lived on the property had asparagus growing up through their floorboards for years. That was the only part that wasn't horrifying.

I also found some genealogy paperwork detailing our family history. My great-grandparents and their son, baby Grandpa, were kicked off their farm. They moved about twenty miles downriver and started a new farm there. From what I understand, this was where Grandpa became what's called a Downwinder and was exposed to whatever gave him cancer. I didn't know cancer could take so long to kill somebody, but I'm glad it took its time. He lived in Pasco until he was twenty-something. Then he and Grandma got married and moved up here, to Prosser, where they had my dad.

I still have plenty more to read, but after learning all this stuff, I don't feel like I'm any closer to helping Dad. I mean, after reading it, I'm angrier than ever. They made a bomb that killed something like seventy-thousand people in a place called Nagasaki, which I learned is in Japan. One bomb killed that many people! And on top of that, our government was giving cancer to its own people that lived near these nuclear reactors. It wasn't just Hanford. There were other places around the country too. It's just so wrong that a government can *accidentally* do this and not be held accountable. Now I know why Dad is always complaining about the government. I get it. The government is the one that decides if the government did anything wrong. There's no way to get justice.

So yeah, I know more about *why* he's angry, but I still have no idea how to fix it.

As if that weren't enough stress, Mari still wants to help find workers for the harvest. I want to help, but I'm at the point where I don't know if I can even think straight around her. Ever since I hit my head on the wall and she ran her hand through my hair, my brain keeps spinning in circles, and she's in the middle. I was honestly considering hitting my head again. I'd have to make it look like an accident, of course. Most people would call that crazy. So I guess I might be going crazy. Honestly, though, I wouldn't be that shocked.

I'll go see if she's busy. Maybe I'll bring an ice pack . . . just in case.

YOU CAN SAY THAT AGAIN

I throw an ice pack and a juice box into the cooler, then shove five chocolate-chip granola bars into my back pocket and fill up my water bottles. My exit is pretty stealthy. Boots, fishing pole, tackle box, and I'm on my way.

I pause just a few steps away from the house, realizing that Mari will need a pole too, so I backtrack and grab an extra. It's nice. Must be new.

My walk down the driveway is chilly, but I try to enjoy it. The fresh air and low morning light renew my energy and sanity.

When I finally make it to the end of the driveway, I set my stuff down off to the side. I'll have to come back this way after I get Mari, so I'll pick it up then.

I walk the short distance from our driveway to their house, feeling pretty good. But when I set foot on their front lawn, my stomach starts to churn.

I unwrap a granola bar and shove the whole thing into my mouth.

That was probably too much.

I chew and chew and chew. Progress is slow. I keep chewing and chewing and—

Mari opens the front door and slips out quietly. She tip-toe-runs down the steps and over to me.

I'm still chewing.

I hold up one finger and make some noises that I hope sound like, "Just a second."

My jaw hurts, but I finally finish and return her greeting. "Hi! Sorry about that. How did you know I was here?"

"I have this magical hole in my house. It's called a window and—"

"All right, all right, all right. I got it. Thanks."

She flashes me a big smile. She's so proud of herself when she's funny.

"You think you're so hilarious, don't you?" I ask her. "Do you want to come fishing? I brought an extra pole."

"That's my pole," she says.

"Your pole?"

"Yeah. Grandpa bought it for me. He said he got me a nice one because he wanted it to last a long time."

"Well, mine is lucky," I tell her.

"Is this a competition?"

"No! Of course not. But if it was, I'd win."

"Uh-huh. Then good thing it's not."

"Yeah, good thing. Now let's go. Do you need to tell your dad?"

"I left a note. It's his only day to sleep in, so our instructions are to not wake him up unless there's one of the four B's."

She says it as though I should know what that means. "The four B's?" I ask.

"Bones, barfing, blood, or burning," she explains. "If there are broken bones, someone is barfing, there's lots of blood, or the house is burning, then we can wake him up. Other than that, we're supposed to let him sleep."

"Okay then. Since none of those apply to us, let's go!"

We head back down the road. I spend the time trying to watch for oncoming cars, but since Mari's there, I don't notice many.

For some reason, she decides to talk about more problems. "I think my dad's kind of frustrated with your dad."

My stride stops. "What? No! Please, no more drama. I don't have any room in my life for something new."

A car comes out of nowhere. We jump into the ditch. When it passes, we climb back up and continue on our way.

"I don't think it's a new problem," she says. "I think it's the same problem, but things aren't getting any better."

"So, no help for the harvest, huh?"

She nods.

"Do you know any details? Is there any progress at all?"

"I could only hear my father's side of the phone call, but he said that it's not exactly his job to find more workers, and that he will try to help, but he doesn't think there's much he can do."

"Car!" I interrupt. We jump in the ditch again, pause for a few seconds as the car passes, then hop back out.

"Then your dad talked for a long time. I could hear his voice, but I couldn't understand him. Then my dad just said, again, how he would keep trying to help, but that they will have to come up with something creative."

"Something creative, huh?"

"Yeah. Got any ideas?"

She looks at me with hope on her face.

I really don't.

"I was hoping you had solved it already," I joke.

"Wow. No pressure."

"Yeah. You can say that again."

"Wow. No pressure."

She tries to hold in her laughter. It looks like her face is about to explode.

There are some things in life I wish I could record and watch whenever I need a pick-me-up. I think Mari's laughter is one of them. She's a good excuse to smile. Other people in my life make it difficult to be happy. She makes it difficult to be sad.

YELLING AT THE STARS

"**A**sher. Did you really bring a cooler and an ice pack just to keep your juice cold?" Mari stares down into the nearly empty ice chest.

"Yes. I mean, no. It's for the fish."

"Just one ice pack, then?"

"More room for fish."

I'm proud of my quick thinking.

Today we're fishing the bend. The water comes around the turn in the river and erodes the bank, making little shelves for the catfish to hide under. They just hang out there, not really doing anything, until you put a piece of food in front of them.

"This should be a place we can catch some big ones," I tell her. "I could save multiple chickens today."

She stares at me blankly.

"Save the chickens!"

She continues to stare.

"Why are you looking at me like that?"

"Save the chickens?" she says. "From what?"

"From my parents."

"Ohhhh," she says, understanding the farm life. "You guys

just got here, and you're already eating the chickens?"

"Hey. Don't judge. Besides, I'm trying to save them, not eat them."

"I didn't realize you were so compassionate."

Huh?

Oh!

"Of course," I say. "Very compassionate. I have compassion for lots of things. So much compassion."

She stares at me briefly, then breaks into laughter.

"I'm sure you do, Asher McCovey. I'm sure you do."

"Hold on tight, chickens! I'm gonna save you!"

I bait the hooks, hang the tips of the poles over the ledge, and let out the line. Then I take a seat with my feet dangling over the water.

When I turn around, Mari isn't there. I look back a little farther and see her in a small patch of white flowers. She's busy making a daisy chain. I don't interrupt. Peaceful moments are hard to come by for everyone these days, and I'm sure she could use a few minutes to just enjoy life. When all else fails, turn to flowers, trees, and rushing water to rejuvenate you.

I keep an eye on both of our poles in case there's any action. It's not long before Mari sits down next to me. I pull my eyes away from my job for a second to say something to her, but I immediately forget what it was.

She's wearing a crown of daisies; just a simple circle of flowers on her head. But I can't stop looking at her.

I try to pull my face away, but it won't budge. It lasts long enough that I'm pretty sure I've made it awkward for both of us.

She finally speaks. "Asher? Are you okay?"

"I really like your daisy crown," flies out of my mouth, in a weak attempt to save myself.

"Thanks," she says. Then, after a long pause, she continues, "But are you sure you're okay? That was kind of weird."

"You can say that again," I blurt out. Then I realize what I just said. "But don't. Don't say it again."

She tilts her head sideways. "I think something's wrong with you."

Duh.

"Maybe you're sick. Let me feel your forehead."

She leans in close.

Wait, what? I can't handle this. Breathe. Breathe. Breathe.

She puts the back of her hand on my forehead.

How is her skin so soft? She must moisturize.

"You feel fine," she says.

You feel soft is the first thought that comes to mind. Luckily, I have enough brains to stop myself.

"Oh good. I think I was just distracted or something. I feel fine, though."

"If you say so," she says, clearly not convinced.

"Okay! Let's fish!" I announce, eager to move on from the conversation.

"So," she says, "while we fish, could we come up with some ideas for finding workers?"

I pause and try to organize my thoughts.

"We probably need to come up with some pretty original ideas to find something our dads haven't tried," I suggest.

"Sounds difficult, but possible," she says. "You first." She shoots me a cheesy smile.

"Um. Okay . . ."

I take a minute, thinking as hard as I can.

"How about we call Mexico and see if they can help?" I suggest. "They probably want their citizens to have jobs too, right?"

"Call . . . Mexico?" she says.

It sounds like she's considering the idea. It could work.

"I don't think Mexico has a specific phone number," she says, bursting my bubble. "And even if it did, I don't think governments work like that."

"Oh. Okay," I reply. "I'm gonna write it down, just in case. You know. It's good to get something down on paper."

I pull my notebook out of my backpack, find a pencil, and write down our first idea. We're off to a good start.

"Okay, now, your turn," I say.

"Well. Maybe we could contact somebody who we know can be helpful, like a police officer or a teacher. They usually have connections, and teachers always have creative ideas."

"That has potential. Teachers are definitely helpful and police officers . . . um . . . maybe they could have prisoners come do it or something?"

That prisoner idea isn't horrible.

"Great. I'm going to write those down. Nice work."

She smiles, which makes me smile.

"Okay. Your turn," she says.

"All right, I feel like this one has some good potential. Hear me out. We hire Canadians!"

I can see it in her eyes. She knows this could be a game changer.

"Okay," she says. "Can we even do that?"

"Of course! It's less than five hours away from here! It's the perfect plan!"

"Don't you think we're going to have some of the same problems?"

"What do you mean?" I ask, surprised at the pushback.

"Well. There's still the immigration issue, for one," she points out.

"Yeah, but they're just right there!"

I point north.

"There's not even a wall or fence or anything. They could basically walk here. Or at least hitchhike."

"I don't think that's going to be as easy as you think," she tells me. "It might be possible, but I don't think it's going to happen anytime soon."

"Okay," I concede. "Well, what else do you have?"

"We could hire homeless people," she says. "You know. It would give them a job and some money for things they need."

I nod my head.

"Yeah, totally. That's a great idea!" I encourage her, with bonus excitement, so I can see her smile again. "We've got some winners here."

I move the poles about twenty feet downriver. These catfish don't move a whole lot, so if they're not here now, they're probably not going to be here anytime soon.

"Can we get a few ideas down on paper for our other big problem?" I ask.

I guess this is really *my* big problem, but I feel like we're a team.

"Sure. I'll do my best, " she replies.

"All right. How do we stop my dad from hating everything that has ever existed in the world, and maybe even things out of this world?"

"Wow," she says, "that's not a gigantic task at all."

I ignore her sarcasm since I have plenty of my own. "I can even picture him," I say, "so angry at every little thing on Earth that there's nothing left to hate. So he stands out in the middle of the field, cursing at the moon and yelling at the stars."

ANSWERS AND QUESTIONS

"Jeez. Does he yell at puppies and kittens too?" she asks.

"It depends on if they get in his way."

"Grandpa was angry about what he learned," she says, "but your dad's taking it to the next level."

There's no denying that.

"I guess we have some work to do," she continues. "Where should we start?"

"I honestly don't know. I'm realizing that he really does have a lot to be angry about. None of it has to do with me, Rory, or Mom, but we're the ones who have to deal with it."

Mari looks at me as though I'm a poor puppy with big, sad eyes.

"Looking ahead," she says, "if we're not able to hold the government accountable, what are some of the other problems that might actually be fixable?"

"The biggest problem other than the government?" I wonder out loud. "Probably that he lost his job, which made us lose our house."

"Okay," she says, encouraging me to continue. "So, is there anything we can do to help there?"

"It just ties right back into wasting all his time trying to get back at the government. He probably deserved to get fired, and I don't think he's done much to change in that area."

"So he got fired for researching the government at work?"

"Well. I'm not one hundred percent sure, but it sounded like he let the investigating become his full-time job, and the job that paid him became less and less important. Researching payback doesn't pay back the money you owe the bank."

"I see what you did there, Mr. punny." She gives me a small golf clap. "Felicito!"

"Gracias. Gracias." I accept her applause and allow myself to smile temporarily.

"That sounds pretty painful," she says, "for all of you. Do you think anything's gotten better since you moved here? Does he enjoy farming at all?"

I stare at her. "Uh. No. He grew up on a farm, but he's no farmer. And it doesn't even seem like he wants a job, unless he can find something where he gets paid to research things he hates. Do you think there are any jobs where he can work to outlaw Christmas lights before Thanksgiving, loud noises, or brussels sprouts?"

"Ha!" Mari laugh-snorts. "If you find a job that works to outlaw silent letters and stupid words that make no sense, like *colonel* or *rural*, count me in."

"For sure. I hate those."

We aren't having any luck, so I move down the bank another twenty feet. I make sure the tips of the poles are just barely hanging over the edge, in case any fish grab the bait and run with it. I don't want to lose a pole.

"Okay, so he doesn't really want a job, but he's stuck doing something he doesn't like. I'm not an expert on adults, but that sounds pretty normal. I don't think most people like their jobs."

"Yeah, maybe," I concede. "I hope he can eventually find something he likes again."

"Do you know what kind of things he *does* like?"

"He doesn't like much of anything right now, but he used to like his job as an engineer."

Mari perks up. "Oh, that's fun! Did you get to ride with him?"

"Like to work? A few times. Why?"

"Did you go fast?" she asks excitedly, as if it's a normal question.

"What? I'm not sure what you mean."

"Did you go fast? On the train?"

"The train?" I stare at her blankly.

"Yes. Choo-choo. The train! You said he was an engineer."

"Ooooohhh. No. The kind of engineer that helps plan buildings." I laugh, not sure if it's at her or myself. "Anyway, there's one idea for our list," I confirm. "Maybe Dad can be a train engineer. He'd be good at sitting up front alone."

"What else did he like?" she asks, moving the conversation along.

"He liked to do lots of stuff: bowling, hiking, watching baseball, golfing, LEGO, and going on walks. Or, as he called it, urban hiking."

"Did you say LEGOs?"

"No. LEGO. Dad's a purist. They're officially called LEGO, no S, so don't let him hear you say otherwise."

"So your dad plays with LEGO, no S?"

"It's not playing. He says it's essentially miniature engineering and totally acceptable for an adult to enjoy. One time, I asked him why he felt like he needed to 'engineer' so many Star Wars spacecraft. In his best Darth Vader voice, he answered, 'Ash, I am your father. Be quiet.'"

As if triggered by the force, I jump up, run and grab a long stick, then start an imaginary fight with Darth Dad.

"Asher, your pole!"

"It's called a light saber," I say, as I wave my imaginary weapon. "Duh."

"No! Your fishing pole! You have a bite!"

I drop my light saber and run to set the hook. My foot hits something hidden in the tall grass. I fall, and my knee bashes against a rock. Then my left side lands hard on the ground.

I hobble over to the pole. The tip is moving up and down, left and right. The fish has clearly set the hook on itself. I sit down, grab the pole, take a deep breath, and yank the tip up.

"Oh, God! Ow! Ow, ow, ow, ow, ow! Mari, please take the pole. I dislocated my shoulder again."

I hand her the pole with my good arm.

"Again?" she asks. "How many times has this happened?"

She reels in a few rotations, then pauses as the fish tries to dart away.

"I don't know," I say. "Two? Three? Twelve times?"

"Twelve? How did it happen the first time?"

"I don't really like to talk about it."

She reels in slow and steady, keeping the tip up. "Well, now you have to tell me," she jokes.

"But do I? Do I, really?"

"Yes! Come on, it's me, your best friend!"

"I don't think that's actually a rule of friendship. I'm pretty sure embarrassing things can stay private."

"It's embarrassing?" She sounds too excited for anything good to come out of this. "Pleeeeeeeeaaaaaaaase!" she begs, "I won't tell anybody." Then she flashes me a big smile.

And of course I give in.

"All right. But you can't make fun of me."

"Of course. Why would I do that?"

You'll see.

I try to keep the story short. "So I was on second base and my friend hit a line drive to left field. I started running, looked at the third-base coach, and saw him waving me toward home." I pause, because I don't really want to continue.

"Okay," she says. "Keep going!"

"I did. That was the problem."

"Huh?"

"When I got close to third, my coach changed his mind and signaled for me to stop, but it was too late. Before I knew it, I was tripping over third base."

"Oooooooohhhhhh," she says. "No bueno."

"Yeah. No bueno is right. It gets even less bueno."

"It keeps going?" she asks in a way that makes me wonder if she feels bad for me or loves that there's more.

"I flew into my coach, bounced off him, and landed on my shoulder. And if that wasn't bad enough, my coach came tumbling down on top of me."

"Ohhh," she says, "Wow. "

"Yeah, so now that you know, if you can forget it, that would be great."

"Forget what?" she says.

"Thank you."

A minute later, Mari has the fish up next to us and has already put it out of its misery. She even guts it, without me asking, and throws it into the cooler with my ice pack. It's okay, though. There aren't enough ice packs in this whole town to cover all the injuries I've given myself, so it might as well be put to good use.

"Do you need to go home?" she asks.

"I'll be fine. The doctor taught me a trick. Do you want me

to rebait the hook for you?"

"I can do it," she says. "Then afterward you can show me your trick."

"Okay. Yes, ma'am."

I breathe so deeply that I feel like an over-inflated balloon. I let the air escape slowly and it joins the breeze, then I repeat it three more times.

"Asher?"

I hear my name and roll over to see Mari looking down at me.

It takes a few seconds for me to come back to reality. I must have zoned out.

"Yeah?"

"Do you want to do your trick now?"

"Oh sure," I say, struggling to get up. "I'm going to need your help."

I walk over to a boulder and lie face down on it.

"Uh," she laughs. "Is this a magic rock?"

"No. Anything big enough will do, really. I just have to hang my arm straight down over the edge."

I drape my injured arm over the side of the rock and ask Mari to come sit at the base.

"All right. What I need you to do is pretty simple," I tell her. "I just need you to hold on to my hand and pull down on it gently for twenty minutes."

"Twenty minutes?" she exclaims.

"You don't need to pull hard or anything, and you can switch hands if you want, but the doctor said twenty minutes."

He actually said fifteen, but we'll do twenty to make sure everything is good.

"Okay, let me move into a good position," she says, trying to get comfortable. Before she's ready, she asks a question.

"Wait. How are we going to time this?"

"Just use your fingers," I tell her.

"My fingers? How am I supposed to do that if I'm holding your hand?"

"No. I mean, to measure the sun. Hold your hand out with your palm facing toward you and your thumb tucked in."

She does it.

"Each of the four fingers you see there is worth about fifteen minutes. To test it out, just count how many fingers the sun has moved from where it rose to where it is now."

She stacks finger upon finger. "Twelve," she says. "I think twelve."

"Okay, so if you multiply twelve by fifteen minutes, you get three hours."

"That's amazing!" she says. "That's pretty accurate!"

"So once the sun has moved one and a third fingers, you know it's been about twenty minutes."

"But one of my hands will still be holding yours."

I see no problem with that.

"You can just do your best with one hand. You'll get pretty close. Okay? All ready?"

"All ready!" she says, excited to use her newfound knowledge. "Here goes nothin'!"

AY, DIOS MIO!

"It's been a little over one finger," she tells me.

"Oh yeah? Okay. It feels a lot better. Thanks for the hand."

"I give that pun an eight for timing but a two on originality," she says with a big grin. "And no, that does not equal a ten."

I lie there for a second, collecting my thoughts.

"And you're welcome," she adds.

I hear her words, but I'm mostly focused on the fact that she held onto my hand for the whole time . . . even though it got sweaty.

These thoughts keep popping up everywhere. I feel like a large portion of the last couple days has been spent thinking about her. I don't try to.

How do people live their lives like this and get anything else done?

To distract myself, I get up, move the poles again, then open my bag and dump the papers out on the grass.

"If we can help my dad not be so angry at the government," I tell her, "all the other things could fall back into place. But from what I've read, it sounds like it's almost impossible to get them to own up to anything. Only two people received anything from cases like this, and both got less money than it took to sue the stupid government."

"What? How could you end up with less? How does that fix anything? How can you pay the doctor if you have less money?"

"Exactly. I think that's the point. If you do that to a few people, then the others will stop trying to sue."

"That's horrible!" she says as she digs her fists into her hips. I'm not sure why, but it's really cute.

Stop it, Asher. Focus.

"I know my dad is right about one thing," I continue. "The government isn't here to help or protect us. They're here to pretend like everything is okay, then punish us if we question them."

"It does seem that way," she agrees, "but can we really do anything about it?"

"They had the workers at Hanford building a bomb and they weren't even told what they were making. How is that okay? Then they used the bomb to kill tens of thousands of innocent people in Nagasaki. And before that they killed over a hundred thousand people with a bomb in a place called Hiroshima!"

I can see her doing the math in her head.

"And as we know," I continue, "people that lived close to Hanford ended up dying of cancer because the government cut corners."

"Ay, Dios mío," she exclaims. "That's horrible. It sounds like maybe we should try focusing on helping your dad be happier instead of helping him get payback. It doesn't even sound like we have a chance if we keep going the government route."

"And just let them get away with killing Grandpa?" I say, sounding more defensive than I thought I would.

"I'm not saying that you should be okay with what happened. I'm just trying to think about what you really want from this. If you and your father spend all your time being angry and trying to get back at the government, then they will have just taken two more lives, and still nothing will be fixed."

I sit there for a minute, trying to wrap my head around that.

"I *have* to do something," I say.

"And I want to help. Let's try some things that leave the government out of it, though. They sound like a waste of time."

"Standing up for what's right isn't a waste of time."

"No, but if you focus on all the things behind you that make you angry, you might miss out on the things ahead of you that could make you happy."

She pulls at her sleeves.

"Did you get that out of a fortune cookie?" I joke.

She laughs and breaks the tension.

"I've just been through something kind of like this, and my dad helped me. I'll never stop missing my mom, and it's not fair that she probably would have lived if she had the same medical care as Americans, but I'm not going to let that ruin the rest of my life. Yes, I get angry when I think about it, but I'm going to let myself be happy, because that's what she wanted for me."

"She'd really be alive if she was in the United States?"

"There's no telling for sure, but women are over three hundred percent more likely to die during pregnancy in Mexico than in the United States."

"Wow. That's crazy!"

"And that's not even the worst of it. If you're born in Africa, you're four thousand percent more likely to die giving birth than you are in rich countries."

"What? That's ridiculous!"

"Yeah," she agrees. "I may have done some research of my own, so I know what it's like to be angry about things you can't fix. At least, can't fix yet."

"I hear you," I tell her. "So you probably know how hard it is to let it go."

"I don't know if I'd say I 'let it go.' I just haven't let it control me."

Glancing down at my stack of papers, I come up with an idea. "I'll tell you what: If you help me go through this last pile, and we don't find anything helpful, like, actually helpful, then we'll focus our energy on other ideas. Deal?"

She looks unsure.

"If I can get through these, I'll feel better about moving on. Please?"

I come within seconds of begging before she gives in. "Okay, if you promise. Just these, and then we'll try something else."

"I promise," I assure her. "Pinkie swear?"

"Pinkie swear," she agrees.

I hold on for a few extra seconds, because why not?

SOY ESTUPIDO

I pick up an article.

"Hey, listen to this. It's called the Hanford Thyroid Disease Study.

"The iodine-131 exposure of children occurred mainly through the milk they drank and, to a lesser extent, through the leafy vegetables and fish they ate. Breathing contaminated air also exposed Hanford area residents and was included in the exposure calculations. The radiation exposures of the thyroid glands of small children were, on the average, much higher than those of adults because children's thyroids are much smaller than those of adults and children consume a lot of milk."

"Milk, vegetables, fish, and breathing? That's every kid that grew up in that area!" I point out. "How is there this much information about kids getting poisoned and nothing has been done?"

"That's a good question," she says. "It's probably not from lack of trying. My guess is that it's just too hard to get justice when the other side can make as much money as it wants and hire the best lawyers."

"True." She summed it up pretty well. "Let's move on."

"Look at this one," I show her. "It has to be the world's longest title. *Population exposures to I-131 releases from Hanford Nuclear Reservation and preterm birth, infant mortality, and fetal deaths.*"

"Oh no," she says sadly. "That means babies, right?"

"So sad. I only read through the first paragraph. The last couple sentences are full of science jargon, but I'm pretty sure I get the main idea . . . unfortunately."

I hand the paper to Mari and watch as she scans the page.

This study found that iodine-131 exposure was associated with increased risk of preterm birth . . . Hypothyroidism during pregnancy can increase a mother's risk of a preterm delivery.

Mari has her "deep in thought" face on. Before I can ask her what she's thinking, she tells me.

"Do you know where your grandma grew up?"

"Right next to Grandpa."

"No," she sighs. "I mean, like, when they were kids."

"Yeah, right next to Grandpa. I thought that meant around here, but now I know that's not the case."

"Do you know anything else?"

"I've been told things, but I'm not sure what's true anymore."

"What have you been told?"

"Her parents owned the dairy farm next door. Well, it was a little ways away since the farms were so big, but you can see the roof of their barn in the background of one of Grandpa's baby pictures. It's a cool story, if it's true."

"Hey. Come on now. Have some faith."

"Ha. Yeah, right."

She sends me a sad smile.

"Her parents would trade dairy products with his parents in exchange for their fruits and vegetables."

She looks concerned.

"What? Are you okay?"

"Do you know how your grandma died?"

"She had a stroke. Why?"

"Did she have cancer too?"

"No." I think for a moment. "Well, I don't know. That's not how she died. Where are you going with this?"

She doesn't answer my question. "Your grandpa didn't get diagnosed until he was pretty old," she reminds me, as if I'd forgotten.

There's a brief pause while I collect my thoughts.

"You seriously think Grandma got atomic cancer too?"

"They grew up next to each other," she says, staring at me like she wants some kind of award.

"Okay?"

"They lived on farms." She talks slowly to me like I'm an idiot.

"Correct."

"They shared food."

"Well, crap!"

I take a second to let it sink in.

"This doesn't help at all. It makes things even worse. Why did you tell me?" I ask sarcastically.

"You wanted the truth!" she reminds me. "You asked for this!"

"I know, I know, but not that truth!" I laugh a little to let her know I'm joking.

"Do you think your dad knows?"

"I'm sure he's figured it out already, which gives him yet another reason to hate the government."

"Yeah," she agrees, "It's still piling up."

"He's had so much crap to deal with. I mean, if I were him, I'd probably be just as mad."

"But you wouldn't take it out on the people you love."

"But how do you know—"

"You wouldn't," she blurts out. "You know what it feels like. You wouldn't be the same."

I'd like to believe her, but if it can happen to Dad . . .

"As your best friend . . . ," she continues.

Is "best friend" closer to a girlfriend than "friend," or further away?

". . . I feel the need to point out that all we've done so far is make things worse."

I can tell she's worried. "It's fine. I just won't tell him. I'm not an idiot." Then I realize how sad it is that I have to convince her.

"Then let's move on to other ideas," she says. "This is a dead end."

"Is that a pun? Dead end?"

"No, it's not. And that's horrible."

"Actually, I thought it was pretty good."

"Seriously," she says. "Whatever we learn, we can't unlearn, and it seems like we're learning things we'd rather not know."

"Is there more? Do you know something I don't?"

"Yeah, lots of things." She smiles again.

"So I'm just supposed to trust you?"

"Yes," she says, as though it were a fact.

"Even though there's probably something you're hiding from me?"

"Asher, please?"

"Okay, okay. I guess I owe you that much."

"Really?"

"Really," I confirm. "Why do you sound so shocked?"

"Well, I . . . I didn't really think that would work."

"If I can't trust you, who can I trust?"

The tip of my pole bounces. I try to get up, but she puts her hand on my head and gently shoves me to the ground.

"I got this one," she says smugly. "I don't want you to hurt yourself again."

"Ouch. What about my pride? Apparently, you don't care about that."

"I'm not worried about it," she replies. "You have plenty to spare."

TAMALES AND VISAS

"**W**ant a juice box covered in fish slime?" I ask.

"Sure, after you rinse it off."

Dang it!

I throw the newest catfish into the cooler and take the juice box down to the river. *Maybe she's right. I wish I didn't know some of this stuff.*

I wash the slime off the juice box, then toss it up to her.

"Hey," I say. "What are you doing the rest of the day? Do you have chores or homework or anything?"

She tilts her head while she thinks. "I just have to help with dinner."

"What are you making?"

"Tamales," she says. "We make a huge batch all at once and then freeze them."

All I hear is: *We have extra tamales. You should come eat some.*

"Well, that sounds delicious," I say, hoping she picks up the hint. "I should probably get these fish in the fridge. We'll probably be having one for dinner tonight . . . again."

I pause, fishing for an invite.

Nothing.

"Do you think your dad will be home for dinner?" I ask.

"I'm pretty sure he will be. Why?"

"I thought maybe I could come over and run some of our ideas by him."

"Do you think they're good enough?" She looks doubtful.

"One or two, probably, but that's all we need. We can each try to come up with more before dinner if you think we need to."

"It couldn't hurt," she says, looking relieved.

"Okay, then. I'm officially inviting myself over for tamales." I play it cool, like it's totally normal.

She looks at me curiously. "I didn't know that was a thing."

"It is. Some people consider it rude, but luckily for you, I'm not one of them."

Okay, that sounded ridiculous, even for me.

"Lucky me," she says. "I guess I accept your invitation?"

"Great! I look forward to it."

She reels in the other line, tosses the old bait in the water, and attaches the hook to the cork handle. I secure Grandpa's old pole, close up the tackle box, and throw the cooler strap over my shoulder.

"Do you want me to walk you to your house?" I offer.

"Sure! Can you give me a piggyback ride?" Her face is dead serious.

Whoa. I did not see that one coming.

"Um. I think . . . sure." I get down on one knee. "I can just come back and get this stuff later."

"I'm kidding," she laughs. "I wouldn't do that to you."

"Oh. Right. I knew that."

Thank God.

"Can I at least walk you to the driveway?" I ask.

"Sure. You can protect me from the rattlesnakes."

"There are rattlesnakes here?" I check the ground around me.

"No. Not really," she laughs. "You're more likely to get hit by a car than bit by a snake out here."

"Hilarious," I say. "Ha, ha." *I'm never going to live that down.*

"Sorry. I couldn't help it." She cracks up.

"Uh-huh," I say, as if I'm actually annoyed. "I'm glad I could make you smile."

We make our way through the tall grass. It tickles our legs and we swat it away.

"What do you think your grandpa would tell you to do?" she asks.

"About what?" I joke, trying to keep things light. "The snakes?"

"No, goof. I mean your dad."

"What about him?"

"Why are you so weird?" she teases. "Answer the question. What would your grandpa tell you to do if he knew you guys couldn't let this stuff go?"

"You guys?" I say, feeling the need to defend myself. "When did I become part of the problem?"

"I'm sorry, I'm sorry, I'm sorry," she says, rapid fire. "It slipped out."

"Do you really think that?" I ask.

"No," she says. "It's just taking its toll on you. That's all."

"I thought I was doing a good job not letting things affect me. That's what I was shooting for, at least."

"I know you're doing your best."

"I mean, I might be a little angry sometimes, but at least I'm not as bad as my dad, right?"

"Sure. If that's who you compare yourself to, then yes, you're doing great."

I feel like I should be offended, but considering how gracious she is with me, I keep my mouth shut.

"So?" she asks.

"So?" I ask.

"What do you think Grandpa would say?"

"Oh right. Well, he'd probably tell me a random saying, and I'd have to figure out what it meant, like *Always drink upstream from the herd.*"

"Um. No," she says, clearly not impressed. "Try again."

"*If a task is once begun, never leave it till it's done. Be the labor great or small, do it well or not at all.*"

"Ah, yes," she says. "I've heard that one before. I'm not sure it fits what we're looking for, though. Got any more?"

"Lots," I say. "This one could apply to any difficult situation: *Do any small thing you can do. Step by step, you'll make it through.*"

We reach the driveway and pause.

"I think that one could work," she says. "Think about it on your walk home, and let me know what you come up with. Then you can tell me over tamales. Deal?"

"Okay," I respond, not yet feeling inspired. "See you soon, I guess."

"I'll be there!"

"I'm excited to try your tamales," I add.

"Me too," she says, then she laughs at herself and tries again. "I mean, I'm excited for you to try them. They're my mom's recipe. Her cookbook is one of the few things of hers we brought to America. That and some pictures, of course."

"Those must be really special," I say, stating the obvious.

"They are. We had to leave almost everything behind."

"What was it like coming to the United States?"

"Long," she jokes.

"Thanks. So informative."

She continues, adding more details to her description. "We had to wait at the border for our paperwork, and because we arrived at the border just after 9/11, everything was shut down. It took so long for it to open back up. We had no money and received help from strangers, which is dangerous because you never know who you can trust. Thankfully, they helped Papi get the money he needed and helped him fill out the papers required to become a worker in the US. After more than eleven months, Papi finally got his visa. We found out that we were going to be moving to Washington State and that the person who hired Papi was paying for our trip, a place to stay, and three meals a day. It sounded too good to be true. We knew Mama must have been looking down, taking care of us, just like she always has."

"I'm sure she was," I agree.

She continues. "After the first week, your grandpa helped Papi apply for a green card so he could stay and work here in the US permanently. They said they needed us and didn't want us to ever have to leave unless we wanted to. I couldn't see why we would want to leave our abuelos americanos."

Mari's family has been through a lot, and look at them: They're happier than we are by a long shot. We could definitely learn a thing or two.

"I'm going to get started on some more ideas," I tell her, "but I'll see you soon, okay?"

"Okay. Come over when you're ready. Maybe I can put you to work."

"I'll do my best to hurry, but you can't rush genius."

"Well, if you meet a genius . . . tell her to take her time, but you should get here faster."

I probably deserved that.

I clap slowly. "You think you're so funny, don't you?"

"Yes, I do," she responds matter-of-factly. "And you do too."

"Oh, do I?"

She's right.

"Whatever you say," I add. "See you soon!"

I begin the trek home, walking backward so I can say good-bye.

"Okay, see you soon!" she agrees.

She watches me for a few seconds. "Are you going to walk all the way home backward?"

"No. I was just admiring the view."

"Well, bye then, weirdo," she says.

"Bye!"

I turn and start up the driveway but look back briefly to see if she's still there. She's turned the other direction, her face pointed at the sun, arms outstretched wide.

How is she so happy? And how can I get that?

WAITING FOR A MIRACLE

On my way back to the house, I smell my dad before I see him. Well, it's actually the fertilizer he got from the guy down the road with a thousand cows. Maybe not that many, but I'm probably not far off.

He must be fertilizing the asparagus, which means they'll probably start popping up within the next week or two. Good to see that he's out getting stuff done.

There's nowhere to hide out here, so if he sees me, he sees me. Nothing much I can do about it. I doubt he'd come over, anyway.

I step into the house with my boots still on, thinking I might only stay for a second.

Mom quickly puts a stop to that by staring me down. From her seat at the table, she watches until I slide my boots off and put them by the door.

I sit down across from her.

"What are you doing?" I ask. Though I can clearly see she's reading the Bible. "Isn't there somewhere more comfortable you could do that?"

"I suppose," she says, "but I like to have a solid surface if I need to write down any ideas."

"Did he give you any good ideas?" I ask.

"Who?"

"God," I say, pointing up, though I'm pretty sure God isn't up.

"Oh. Just to trust Him with the details." She recites it to me like she always does; like I haven't heard it a thousand times before.

"That's not very helpful. How long does it take to get an actual, specific answer?"

"Unfortunately," she says, "there's not a simple answer to that. God doesn't work on our schedule."

"So, there's no timeline at all?"

"Not that we would understand," Mom parrots the preacher. "God knows what's best."

I facepalm. "Well, if it's going to take a while, can he at least tell us that much?"

"It could be a few minutes, weeks, months, or years. Our job is to keep trusting Him."

She says it with such conviction; it makes me want to believe it, but I can't. There's zero evidence to believe that the man upstairs is going to do anything to help us.

"How is that answer good enough for you? When did 'no answer' become an acceptable answer? If that's not allowed in school, it shouldn't be allowed from God. We need help now, not eventually."

Mom continues with her patented calm voice and prepackaged words. "I know that's what you want, sweetheart."

"No. It's not a want. It's a need. It's what we all need."

"I know, sweetheart."

Her calm-in-the-storm responses to my flood of frustrations isn't helping.

"I don't think you *do* know," I argue. "You're too busy reading the Bible and praying."

That one didn't feel good coming out of my mouth, but it's out there now. "Just forget it," I tell her. "I've got it covered."

She looks at me for a few seconds, trying to figure out what I'm up to.

"What do you mean, you have it covered?"

"I can't tell you. It's top secret."

"Asher. I need to know if you're up to something."

"No, Mom. You WANT to know," I say, enjoying the opportunity to use her own words against her.

"Asher. Are you angry at me?"

"I don't know!" I admit. "Maybe!" I fold my arms on the table and bury my head in them.

"I just wish you would put some actual effort into this," I confess. "Sitting and reading a two-thousand-year-old book isn't *actually* helping. Why won't you do something we can see, something that makes a difference?"

"Asher. I'm doing my best. I'm sorry it's not what you want me to do."

"I think you could do more if you weren't waiting for a miracle. It's almost as bad as Dad waiting for justice to come. It's not going to happen."

I head toward the stairs.

"Asher," she calls.

I turn to face her.

"Oh, and I'll be having dinner at Mari's tonight," I tell her. "So don't set a spot for me at the table."

I pivot and head upstairs.

"Prayers do work," she insists. "God gave us a new home exactly when we needed it."

I stop at the top of the stairs. There are so many things I want to yell.

"So he killed Grandpa?" I imagine saying. *"Cause I'm pretty*

sure Grandpa dying was the only way we got this house. And this is the job that God picked for Dad? Really? From an engineer to a farmer? Make sure to thank him for killing Grandma and Gabe too. Oh, and for letting Mari's mom die just because she lived in Mexico and not the US."

But instead, I concede. "Okay, Mom. Whatever."

I barricade myself in my room, crash on my bed, and cry until I pass out.

WEEDS

"I hate my life."

The words sound horrible as they come out of my mouth and soak into the pillow covering my face.

I yank the pillow off and rub my eyes, hoping it will help me think more clearly after my tear-induced nap.

I stare up at the old boards and try to focus on something useful.

"Concentrate. Be in the moment," I tell myself, trying to access my inner genius. "How the heck are we going to pull this off?"

We could hire kids and pay them with candy!

Or we could hire vegetarians and pay them with asparagus!

Maybe we can get a famous person to help. People always listen to celebrities.

Oh! Maybe people can come pick it themselves, like a berry farm or Christmas tree farm.

My brain literally hurts.

I close my eyes and try to collect my thoughts, but trying to force my brain to relax is like telling someone to *not* picture a purple spotted cow. It's impossible because trying to *not* think about something causes you to think about it!

I put the pillow back over my face and yell, "Stupid purple spotted cow!"

The heat from my breath warms the pillow. I pull it back a bit and let it rest just over my eyes and forehead. I take a deep breath of cool air and let it out slowly. Then I do it again, and again. My body calms a bit.

Why does taking deep breaths calm people down?

Mari pops up in my head because that's where she hangs out now. This time it's for a logical reason, though. I don't want her to think I'm like Dad . . . at all. Sure, I'm angry at times, but who isn't? Besides, I have good reason to be mad. I see Dad as the nuclear bomb and me as a firecracker. Sure, I might hurt somebody, but only if they're careless. Dad can take out half a small country and there's nothing you can do about it.

And when I get angry, it's not usually my fault. It's Dad that causes the problem. His anger is a weed that spreads to everyone else's gardens. It grows in mine, whether I want it to or not. When it goes to seed, the winds spread it far and wide, leaving it to sprout up yet again, invading new, previously pleasant places.

"I'm a freakin' weed garden!" I yell at the ceiling.

I wonder if anyone heard that.

Grandma hated weeds. She would cover her entire garden with weed block and cut little holes for her vegetables and flowers: tomatoes, peppers, eggplant, cabbage, broccoli, lettuce, kale, zucchini, dahlias, snapdragons, and my favorite: zinnias. The vegetables and flowers had enough space to grow, but the dirt around them was completely blocked off, so weeds never had the chance to invade.

I need human weed block. I need to keep out the bad and only let the good in.

I lie around for a few minutes, trying to convince myself that this isn't all my fault, when words from a poster in my dad's old office bathroom pop into my head: *A journey of a thousand miles begins with a single step.* It sounds kind of like Grandpa's old saying about doing *any small thing I can do.*

It seems kind of obvious, but it's true. Every journey starts with a single step . . . no matter how long it is or where it takes you. It's not just a cheesy saying. Going down the stairs starts with a single step. Going to the river? Single step. Up a mountain? Single step. Out of a flying plane? Single step . . . literally. If you ever want to get anywhere, you have to start with a single step. Otherwise there can't be a second, third, or nine hundred seventy-seventh.

It seems too obvious. And maybe it is, but I just never took the time to think about it.

What would my first step even be?

Maybe I could apologize for yelling at him? I don't think I can be the first to apologize. He yells at us all the time. That's on him.

Maybe I could buy him a present. What kind of present do you get for the man who has nothing and enjoys nothing?

Maybe I could do extra chores? Right. Not gonna happen.

Maybe I suck at coming up with ideas.

Then, as if to prove myself wrong, an idea pops into my head.

What if I just put the documents back in the box? It seems like it's too simple, but that's what a first step is supposed to be, right? The papers are just weeds; anger weeds, and I've been letting them grow in my garden.

Time to block some weeds.

WEED BLOCK

When I was a little kid, I snuck into my parents' room and stole some change off of my dad's nightstand. But just a couple minutes later, I felt so guilty that I had to sneak back in and return the money. This is how I feel right now.

I'm about 87 percent nervous and 13 percent excited.

I slip the stack of papers into my bag, sling it over my shoulder, then head downstairs.

When I see Mom, my stomach churns like the eddies in the river. I'd like to think it's my excitement for tamales, but I'm 99 percent sure my insides know I'm a jerk.

There's no getting around it. It needs to be fixed. It's like a bad cut. Take care of it quickly, or it will start to fester.

"I'm sorry, Mom," I tell her. "I suck." I walk over and give her a hug. It won't fix everything, but it's a small step.

"You don't suck, sweetheart. It was hurtful, but I forgive you."

"Thanks."

Graciously, she changes the subject. "Are you on your way to Mari's?"

"I am."

With one quick stop along the way.

"Are you taking your schoolwork with you?" she asks, pointing to my bag.

Oops. I forgot about that little detail.

"Oh. Um. It's just a project Mari and I have been working on."

"For school?" she asks.

"It's been very educational," I tell her, not wanting to lie. "It's helped me decide what I don't want to be when I grow up."

"Don't want to be?" she asks. "Or did you mean, 'want to be'?"

"Both, I guess. I'm definitely learning a lot about myself."

"That's great, sweetheart. What do you two have planned for tonight?"

"Well, I'm going to help make tamales, then I will help eat tamales."

"That sounds like fun. Do you know when you'll be back?"

"I don't, really. But do you know what would get me home faster?"

"Running?" she says.

"Ha!"

I realize I'm going to have to be a bit more clever with how I go about this.

"That is on the board," I confirm, in my best game-show-host voice, "but not the number-one answer."

The only TV mom ever likes to watch is old game shows, so this reference to *Family Feud* goes straight to her heart.

She catches on quickly and continues, "I'm going to guess . . . a donkey?"

"No, I'm sorry. That did not make our list of top-five fastest ways up a driveway. You have one strike, so be careful now."

"I'll go with . . . your mother driving you?"

"Let's see what the survey says." I pause for dramatic flair. "That's our number-two answer!"

"Number two, huh? I can't imagine what number one would be."

"Think really hard. This is for no money at all."

She puts on her nervously excited game show contestant face. "I'm going to go with . . . riding a bike?"

"Is the answer . . . 'riding a bike'?" I pause again, this time pointing to a big, imaginary answer board on the wall.

"Oh no! Sorry. So close. You needed to add two more wheels."

Then she does the simplest of math equations. "The four-wheeler? Ha! Right. Like your father would let you do that."

"I'm not talking to Dad. I'm talking to you," I say, all businesslike.

"And my answer is the same as your father's would be," she replies, just as businesslike.

"So I have to go ask him?" I say, setting aside my game-show-host persona.

"Yes."

I don't see any conversation with Dad going well . . . especially one about the quad.

"Or you said you'll come pick me up, right?"

"Yes. That is an option," she confirms. "Which will you pick? Door number one," she gestures toward an imaginary door, "which requires a conversation with your father? Or door number two," she gestures the other direction, "which is guaranteed to be better than walking?"

"I'll go with door number two. I don't even want to see what's behind door number one. It seems like it could be dangerous."

"Okay. Just call when you're ready to be picked up."

"Thanks, Mom."

"You're welcome, sweetie."

"Gotta run," I say, as I again head toward the door.

Once I get outside, I glance around. The coast is clear. I run over to the barn, say hi to Winston, and make my way over to the ladder.

As I place my hand on the first rung, a memory pops up. Dad built us a tree fort at our old house. The rungs of the ladder were just nailed to the tree, but they led to a trapdoor. That door made the fort so cool. I was amazed that my dad could build something like that.

I never know how to feel when good memories come up. Should I be happy because we had fun times together, or should I be sad 'cause there aren't any new memories being made? Good ones, at least.

I climb up the ladder, hoist myself over the top, then stand up.

There it is: the box. I feel like dramatic music should be playing, but all I hear are chickens and a goat. It's amazing how warm it stays up here throughout the year. It's probably animal farts, since hot air rises.

I take the bag off my shoulder and walk over to the chest. After pulling out the papers, I let the bag fall to the floor. My free hand opens the chest, then I drop to my knees and peer in. There are more papers than I remember. It would take weeks, if not months, to go through it all.

There has to be something in here that could help.

I look at the small collection of papers in my hand and think about everything I've discovered already. I've learned a lot . . . and if I'm honest with myself, it's gotten me nowhere. Maybe even made things worse.

I set my stack down on the ground and pick up a few more articles out of the chest. They're just more of the same. Hanford this, cancer that, jury, Downwinder, thyroid. There must be thousands of papers, and it's probably all the same useless information.

I rummage around a little more, begging for there to be something helpful. Then I realize I don't even know what something helpful would look like, if it even exists. It's just a collection of things that make me angrier and nothing that will make things better.

Why did Grandpa even save these? Are they just here to tell his story, or did he think they might actually be useful some day?

Having no reason to believe he can hear me, I still can't help but talk to him.

"Come on, Grandpa. You knew I was gonna find these. What were you thinking? I tried to learn your story. I tried to help our family, but I just can't seem to do it. What do I do now?

A NOTE

I hold the tears back because there's no use in crying.

After picking my papers up off the ground, I place them in the chest, gently, like a burial.

My eyes get blurry, so I rest my arms on the edge of the open box and bury my face in them.

Don't cry. It won't do you any good.

I lift my head, rub my eyes, and yawn deep and long. My body isn't listening to me.

Once I give myself permission to let it out, it comes hard. My head lands on my arms again, and I give in to a loud-sobbing, hard-to-breathe, nose-running, tears-flowing cry.

My eyes hurt. I'm so tired. I just want to go to sleep and wake up when this is all over, if that day ever comes.

After resting for a few minutes, I massage my temples, take deep breaths, and ask why over and over again, knowing very well that no one will answer. I somehow hold back the tears long enough for my eyes to dry a bit and the world around me becomes a little clearer.

I can't let Dad see this chest. What if there are things in here he doesn't know about yet? I'll just keep making things worse.

I raise my head a bit and take a deep, deep breath. Then another, and another, and another. I'm calmer.

I raise my head all the way, and that's when I notice a pink birthday-card-size envelope duct-taped to the inside of the chest lid.

My name is on the front.

I rip it off, open the envelope, and slide the card out. It's a birthday card with an old man on the front. He's lying down on the ground, and the words read:

Here's a quick way to tell if you're old. If you fall down in front of people and they help you up, you're old. If you fall down in front of people and they laugh, you're still young. Happy birthday to some-one young at heart.

That's pretty funny, but why the heck would he give this card to me? Maybe he meant to give it to Dad?

On a folded piece of paper tucked inside the card, I find Grandpa's handwriting:

Hey, young man. It looks as though you've decided you're old enough to look in this box. I figured that might be the case, which is why I've left you this card. It was one that your grandmother bought for me before she passed away, so she never got a chance to give it to me. I thought I would make use of it.

Anyway. I'll get to the point. You probably wouldn't guess what's inside this box. These articles tell the story of how I got cancer some sixty years ago. You read that right. When I was diagnosed, I had already seen reports about Hanford and its radioactive waste. There were many stories like my own. Others hadn't had any luck winning their lawsuits, but I felt like I had to right this wrong. Later, I discov-ered that the government spent almost $60 million to prove that our illnesses weren't their fault. SIXTY MILLION! They should have just used that money to help the people who were affected.

Everything was a dead end (no pun intended). I spent all my time on this research and got nowhere. Finally, a wise soul helped me see that your grandmother and I only had a short time left together, and I was squandering it. Little did I know, we had almost no time left. Your grandma passed away two months later. I would have missed out on our last two months together. There is a cost to bitterness, Asher, and I almost paid an enormous price.

I feel you deserve a chance to read this part of our family history . . . since you asked about the chest a while back. I know you'll want to do something about it, but don't try to solve some mystery like I did. The only mystery is why I wasted so much time banging my head against a wall. I know you will make better decisions.

I'm sorry that I let your father get so invested in this. He's as stubborn as a mule. He gets it from your grandmother.

You are such an amazing young man, Asher. I bragged about you every chance I got. Just ask folks around town.

I'm so glad I got to spend these years with you, and I'm sorry that I have to leave so soon. I don't think you can miss people in heaven, but if you can, I'll miss you so much. If I can't handle it, I'll come back and visit.

Just kidding. I don't really think there are ghosts, but I'll let you know if I'm wrong.

I love you to the stars and back (the moon's too close),

Grandpa

PS Don't you think it's weird that they treated my leukemia with radiation? That's how I got cancer in the first place! Crazy world. Be safe out there.

"I love you too, Grandpa . . . to the stars and back."

WHEN YOU TELL YOUR STORY

"You said to come down whenever," I remind Mari as I walk through the door.

"But it's only been six fingers."

She laughs at her own joke, and I join in.

"I got all my stuff done," I explain.

"Wow. That was quick."

"I'm a genius, remember?"

She laughs again.

"Is your dad here?"

"No, not yet."

"Okay. No worries." I pause, forgetting what I was about to say. "Oh, I have something crazy to show you."

"It's not something out of that box, is it?"

"It is, actually. Good guess."

"Oh no. What did you find?"

"It's not about Grandpa's death. I mean, it is, but it's not bad. Well, it sucks that he died, of course, but . . ."

I could probably speak Spanish right now and make more sense.

I try again. "It isn't anything that will cause people to get angry."

She looks at me, still unsure.

"I just have to show you."

I take a seat, and she does the same. I pull the card out of my back pocket and toss it on the table.

Mari scoots closer to get a better look, then picks it up and begins poring over the words. One hand rises, covering her mouth, as if she's trying to hold something in. She brings the paper closer to her face and focuses on something important. Her head nods gently, and her hand drops from her mouth to cover her heart. She sniffles. Then she transitions to a slight smile, and that's when I know she's reached the end.

After giving her a minute to digest it, I speak up. "So? Crazy, right?"

"He was a smart man."

"You were right!" I admit. "How did I miss it?"

She throws her palms up, signaling that she doesn't have any great answers for me. "He wasn't advertising it," she says, "but after they told him about his cancer, he was pretty wrapped up in it. We couldn't blame him. That's a lot to have thrown at you. He needed answers. Luckily, he quickly figured out that he was wasting what little time he had left."

"How do you know all this?"

"I live here," she says, looking confused as to why I'd even ask that question. "He was my abuelo americano. I got to see him all the time . . . until he started doing his research. Then he spent most of his time at the library."

"That sounds just like my dad."

"You know how you feel about your dad?" she asks. "Like you're losing him?"

"Losing? He's already gone. I'm trying to find him again."

She sits quietly for a few seconds. "You know, even though

Grandpa was hurt and angry, there's one big difference between how he and your father responded."

"What's that?"

"I was never scared of Grandpa; just very sad for him, and myself, I guess. Your father causes fear in the ones he loves."

Good point.

She continues. "It seems like you can never be sure what he's going to do, but you can be sure that, whatever he does, someone will end up hurt."

"He doesn't *hurt* hurt us," I tell her, just to make sure that's clear.

"Some injuries aren't so easy to see," she says, "like a dislocated shoulder." She smiles, bringing some welcome humor to the moment.

"I guess you're right."

How does she notice these things?

"Are you like a detective or something?" I ask. "What have you figured out about me since I moved here?"

"About you? Lots of things, but I don't think you'd really be interested in them."

"Try me," I tell her, imagining all the things I'd like her to say. "But be kind," I add, fearing any deep, dark things she may have discovered.

"One of my favorite things about you is that you have a heart much like your grandpa."

"Gracias," I tell her. "I needed that."

"De nada."

"So," I say, slightly changing the subject, "since you seem to know a lot about our family, what exactly made Grandpa stop his investigating? Maybe it can help my dad too."

"I'm sure it would, but he'd need to be willing to listen first, like Grandpa, and like you."

"What do you mean? I'm not a great listener. In fact, I don't think I'd even qualify as a *good* listener. I really just kept talking to you until I figured some stuff out."

"Yep. That was pretty much it."

I feel like I'm trying to solve a riddle. "Does talking to you count as being a good listener?"

"I believe you did a good job listening. Better than Julia for sure."

"Gee. Thanks."

"I'm kidding. You're a great listener. I always feel like you care about what I'm saying." She stands there for a few seconds, looking at the ground, shuffling her feet.

"After we came to this country—"

"Is this another riddle?" I interrupt her.

"No. This is where you listen."

"Sorry. Go ahead."

"When we came to America, I became angry. I saw other kids with their moms and knew that it wasn't fair. They got to keep their moms because they were born in America, when other kids around the world, like me, lose their moms even though there are ways to stop it. It ate me up inside."

She looks to the sky for a few seconds, then back down at her feet.

"My father helped me see what I couldn't. Every minute I spent focusing on how unfair life was, was a minute I could have been spending with those who I still have. My mom lost her life, and I was so bitter about it that I was wasting my own." She sniffles once, twice, and then the back of her hand slowly wipes away the tears trickling down her cheeks.

"My mother." She pauses to catch her breath. "My mother would have wanted me to come here and go to school, make new friends, and live a happy life, and I was wasting my opportunity."

I stare at her, in awe of what she's been through and who she is.

"It became clear to me because of my dad. He loved me until I could see it."

I take a step toward her and pull her into a hug.

After a minute, I realize I need some clarification.

"So, I think I'm still a little confused. Are you saying that it was your dad that talked to Grandpa? Helped him see this, like he did for you?"

"Not exactly. The inspiration for his choice was like mine. He decided he didn't want to waste the time he had left, but he needed help to see what he was missing before he could make that decision for himself. And that's where my story came in."

"Your story? Like what you told me about your mom?"

"Yes. That one."

"So you're the one that helped Grandpa?"

"I just shared my story, and when kids share, sometimes adults listen. Our stories can be powerful."

"Is that why you told me about your life?"

"I told you because you're my best friend and I want you to know me. I want you to know how much I care about you and I want to help you see the things you might be missing out on."

"But I was barely angry," I argue, wishing I could take back the words as soon as they leave my lips.

"It was more obvious than you think," she says. "Besides, even if it was little, why give it the chance to get bigger? You know what they say about giants."

"No. I don't think I do," I confess. "Don't climb their beanstalks?"

"Ha!" She gives me a courtesy laugh. "No."

"Okay, then. What do *they* say?"

"The easiest time to kill a giant is before it gets big."

"Who says that? Who's killing baby giants?"

"Asher." She waves her hand dismissively. "You know what I mean."

"I think I do," I concede, "and thank you."

"You're welcome, but you know what I'm going to say."

"You'll probably say, '*I just told my story*' or '*Give me an abrazo.*'"

"Oh yeah? Is that kind of like inviting yourself over for tamales?" she asks. "Do you want a hug?"

Was I that obvious?

"You have me figured out, don't you?" I ask.

"Pretty smooth," she says, "but yes. You are found out."

I hug her before I say something stupid. She puts her arms around me and leans her head on my shoulder.

Good lord. How does her hair smell so good . . . and how long can a hug last before it gets awkward . . . and am I willing to test the limit?

"So can you tell your story to my dad?" I ask, mid hug.

She steps back. "Are you serious?"

I was. But now I'm not.

"Of course not. Totally joking."

"Good."

"Just out of curiosity, why not?"

"It's my story to share with the people I love. Your father and I aren't close. It wouldn't mean the same to him."

"Darn you. You make too much sense."

SKINNY TREES

Julia runs from her room to the now-open door. "Welcome home, Papi!"

"Gracias, mija. It's good to be here. It's been a long day of problem-solving, and we still have no problems solved."

"So no workers yet?" I chime in.

Manny scoops Julia up into a hug. He glances in my direction, surprised to see me. "Asher. Didn't know you were there. Glad to see you're still alive."

"Definitely still alive," I assure him.

"Mari tells me you guys have some thoughts about the harvest?"

"Oh! Yeah!" My energy picks up. "If you've got some time later, we came up with a few ideas. We can just give you a quick rundown of the best options."

"Sure." He pulls out a chair and takes a seat. "I'm all ears."

"No, you're not, Papi," says Julia. "You just have two ears, like us."

"It's just a saying, sweetheart. It means I'm listening." He turns back to Mari and me. "Go ahead, guys. Your ideas can't be any worse than what I've already tried."

"Oh. Like right now? Okay," I agree with anxious excitement.

"Sí. Por qué no?" asks Manny. "We don't have any time to waste."

"You can say that again."

"We don't have any time to waste."

I stare at him. He looks over at the girls, and they all crack up.

"Are you finished?" I say, trying to get us back on track.

"Oh. Yes, sir. Sorry, sir," jokes Manny. "Please. Continue."

"Idea number one: Call the government."

The room is silent for a few seconds.

"Can I ask a question?" Manny says, breaking the awkwardness.

"Sure. Of course," I say, then motion him to begin.

"Is that your best option? Because if it is, we might have a problem."

My mood immediately deflates. "What do you mean?"

"Calling the government is the first thing we did. They're in charge of who comes into the country. They were our only hope to get our friends from Mexico here in time, but they said it was impossible."

I try to look on the bright side. "So what I hear you saying," I respond, "is that I really came up with the best idea, but you already tried it."

He laughs at me. "I guess so. If that makes you feel better."

"Great," I say.

"Great," agrees Mari.

"Great!" adds Julia.

"Okay. Let's try this again. Are you ready for a few more?" I ask.

"Lay 'em on me."

"Are illegal border crossings off the table?"

"Yes. Next."

"Okay, then. How about we ask for the help of classmates, church people, homeless people, or prisoners . . . or all of the above? We can hire kids for pretty cheap, I've heard a person at church offer to help someone out for free, homeless people could probably use the money, and prisoners don't have anything else to do and would probably like the fresh air. And we could give them snacks. I'm sure they would love snacks."

Why are they just staring at me? Were those ideas that good, or that bad?

"Say something, people."

"Wow," says Manny. "You really put some thought into this, didn't you?"

I'm not sure if he's being sarcastic, so I pause before answering. "Do you think any of them could work?"

Manny gives me the look you get when you have to tell somebody their pet just died.

"For the sake of time," he says, "I'll just be blunt."

Uh-oh.

"Hiring kids is illegal; I don't think prisoners get let out of jail for jobs; the homeless idea isn't horrible, but I wouldn't even know where to begin; and the church idea seems logical, but most of the churchgoers around here are pretty old or have their own farms. I don't know how much help they would actually be."

Ouch.

"Are parents allowed to make their own kids work?" I ask.

"Yes."

"Dang it!"

We stare at the walls for a few seconds; nobody is sure what to do.

"Okay," says Manny, as he puts his hand on my shoulder. "Thank you for trying—"

"Wait!" I interrupt. "I have one more idea. I just thought of it before I came."

"Okay," he slaps my back. "One more. What do you got?"

"You know when people pay a lot of money to go to a U-cut Christmas tree farm so they can cut their own tree?"

Manny nods his head.

"They pay *more* money so they can do all the work themselves. Now, I know it's not exactly the same, but what if we became a U-cut asparagus farm? I've seen a place near Yakima that lets you come pick your own vegetables and pay by the pound."

"Does that place have lots of vegetables to choose from?" asks Manny.

"Yes," I admit, knowing what's coming next, "and I know we only have asparagus, but everyone loves asparagus."

"Do you?" Manny asks with a chuckle.

"I did until I moved here."

"Te gustan, mijas?" asks Manny

Mari responds first. "It's not that bad with lots of butter."

Julia adds her two cents. "It makes your pee stink!"

"Yes, it does, mija." He laughs some more. "We have all experienced that."

We nod like bobbleheads.

"Look," he says, taking a slightly more serious tone. "We're obviously not a great sample of your basic vegetable eaters, but coming all the way out here to buy a single vegetable that you can get at the store doesn't sound like it will work. I'm sorry, amigo."

"Can you at least tell me which idea is better? Homeless people and churchgoers . . . or the U-cut asparagus farm?"

"Well," he pauses and glances out the window. "The U-cut farm seems kind of crazy, but if it actually worked, that would be pretty amazing."

"Okay," I say, "so we need to do something, right?" They nod. "Can we say that if we don't have a better option by the end of Wednesday, we move ahead with the Christmas-tree farm idea?"

"You said Christmas-tree farm," Julia points out.

"Oops. Maybe U-cut asparagus farm?" I say, not sure what to call it.

"Booooooooooooooriiiiiiing!" Julia complains.

"I don't know," I admit. "What would you guys call it?"

"Smelly Pee Farm!" laughs Julia.

I give her a high five. "Nice! I like it."

Glancing around, I ask, "Anyone else?"

Mari chimes in, "I think U-cut asparagus farm is nice and simple."

"I don't think this is going to happen," says Manny, killing the vibe.

"That's a horrible name!" I joke.

He throws me a look.

I ask again, hoping it's not too pushy. I need him to buy into this. "But if it *did* happen, what would you name it?"

"Okay. Okay." He gives in. "I guess if it happened somehow, I would call it 'Skinny Trees.'"

"Skinny Trees?" I say, surprised at the thought that went into it. "I like it! It's creative."

Mari laughs. "Skinny Trees, huh? "

"Yeah," he says. "You know. I always thought they looked like super skinny, really tall trees, like if you were an ant or something."

"All right then," I say, trying to ride the momentum,

"Skinny Trees U-cut Asparagus Farm. That pretty much captures all of our ideas into one name."

"Not mine!" cries Julia. "What about my name?"

"Sorry Julia. I would have gone with yours, but your sister and dad like this one."

"Really?" she says with hope in her eyes.

"Totally."

PART-TIME COUNSELOR

"You think the school bus driver is still mad at you?" asks Rory, as the bus rolls up to our stop.

"Gee. Thanks."

With the craziness of the weekend, I had almost forgotten about it.

"You probably would have remembered when she opened the door. At least I gave you a few more seconds to prepare."

"Prepare?" I question her. "You think it's going to be that bad?"

I briefly consider hiding in the ditch, but it's too late.

The door opens, and staring down at me is the face of . . . a new school bus driver?

"Good morning!" I say as I start my way up the steps.

"Well, aren't you in a good mood for a Monday morning?" he says.

"Where's the old driver?" I ask.

"Oh. I don't really know her that well, but I heard her say she was retiring. It sounded weird for someone to retire in the middle of the school year. Did anything out of the ordinary happen on the bus?"

We look at each other, lips zipped shut.

He tries to take back his question. "No. Never mind," he says. "That's none of my business. My wife keeps telling me to mind my own business, and here I go again. Forget I said anything."

I plop down in the second seat, and Rory scoots in next to me.

"You don't think it has anything to do with us, do you ?" I ask Rory.

She doesn't answer. When I look over at her, she has a guilty-looking grin.

"Did you do something?"

"I just wanted her to learn her lesson, so I reported her."

"Good Lord. Justice runs deep in this family. You're eight, kiddo. Don't let this kind of stuff bug you. What she did was wrong, yes, but now it's our job to let it go."

"Okay. I didn't even remember I called them until the bus door opened."

"Sounds like you've already let it go," I note.

"Yep!"

———

In math, I sit quietly and draw while we're going over dividing fractions. If you already know how to multiply fractions, which is ridiculously easy, then you pretty much know how to divide fractions too. It's just three words: keep, change, flip. Once you know it, you know it. And, since I already know it, I decide to use my time more wisely.

I raise my hand.

Ms. Mitchell points to me. "What do you need, friend?"

Teachers calling their students "friends" has always seemed

weird to me. Friends go outside and play. They don't force each other to do meaningless reports about European explorers. It turns out that learning about Marco Polo isn't as fun as I thought it would be.

"Can I go to the bathroom?" I ask.

"I don't know," she answers. "Can you?"

At what age does a person begin to think grammar jokes are funny?

I give her what she wants. "MAY I go to the bathroom?"

"Absolutely. And I believe you CAN as well." She winks at me.

That's not awkward at all.

"Okay then," I say as I make a beeline toward the door.

After stopping at the urination station, I continue on to my actual destination: the counselor's office.

Last week, a kid named Marcus went up to Ms. Mitchell's desk and quietly asked if he could go see the counselor. Of course she said yes, but then she called the counselor to let her know Marcus was coming. I don't think teachers know that the class can hear them when they talk on the phone, but we can. In a matter of seconds, the entire class knew that Marcus had issues. I'm going to take a hard pass on that happening to me. It's not like I lied. I *did* go to the bathroom. I'm just going somewhere after it too. Besides, what teacher would get mad at a kid for going to see the school counselor?

I knock on the door that says MS. CARMONA in beautifully cut paper letters. On just the third knock, she opens the door.

Wow. She's fast.

"Hi! Welcome! Nice to meet you," she says. "I'm Ms. Carmona, or Ms. C., or even Annie if you'd like. We're pretty relaxed in here. It's just a place to come chat, be yourself and get some support, if you'd like."

Like it? More like need it.

"And whom do I have the pleasure of meeting?" she asks.

"Asher."

"Oh yes. The young Mr. McCovey. It's great to meet you. I heard your family was moving into town."

"Oh," I say, a bit surprised. "How do you know me?"

"Oops. Sorry about that." She puts on an apologetic grin. "Your grandpa always had lots of great things to say about you. I was hoping I'd get to meet you. We sure miss him around these parts."

"I miss him everywhere."

"I'm sorry for bringing it up," she says, "but you know what? I am so happy you reached out today. Why don't you grab a seat, and we can chat?"

She swings her arm open wide, as if she's revealing a prize on *The Price is Right*.

"I have a few options for you: stool, rocker, recliner, beanbag, and swing. Pick whichever one is calling your name."

I go with the beanbag, since the rest seem like they're for little kids or old geezers. I try to lower myself into it slowly, but I keep sinking and sinking. I worry that it's a never-ending abyss, but I finally reach the maximum butt depth and settle in.

"What can I help you with?" she asks, as she takes a seat. "School problems? Home problems? Girl problems?"

"Whoa! What?" I say, totally not expecting that.

"That's just what I say to see if kids are listening. You passed the test."

"There are tests in here?" I ask, ready to leave if she says yes.

"No. Not really. It's just a saying, I guess. But *is* there anything I can help with?"

"Well. I was just wondering if there are any small things a person can do to help someone stop being angry."

I glance around, trying not to make eye contact.

"Is this a friend of yours?" she asks.

"No. Not really."

"Is it an adult?"

My head swings back her way. "I don't want to get any-body in trouble or anything," I explain.

"There's nothing inherently wrong about being angry," she says reassuringly. "It's what you do with the anger that gets some people in hot water. Is this person doing anything I should be concerned about?"

"Like what?" I ask, wondering if any of my problems make her list.

"Things like abuse, neglect, or abandonment would be very concerning and would make me want to get you some extra support."

"Oh. I'm not sure exactly what those mean, but I don't think I have any of them. Maybe you can tell me if I do."

She laughs. "Okay. I'll let you know."

"Thanks."

"Can I just tell you . . . ," she says, "I love your question about anger. We always want to help people we love, and sometimes it's hard to do that. We really want to fix the prob-lem but—"

I interrupt her. "Is this where you tell me I can't fix any-body?"

"Well, yes, I guess," she says, as she folds her hands in her lap.

"I know I can't fix him, but is there any way to help the pro-cess along without it being called 'fixing'?" I plead with her, realizing that it probably sounds ridiculous.

"Well," she says, collecting her thoughts, "I don't know if it's a specific way, but it's really a combination of trying to love them and, at the same time, keep yourself safe and healthy."

At the moment, I'm not sure how I stack up in those areas.

"But what if you try to love them, and they can't show it back?" I ask.

"Well. That *does* happen sometimes. A lot, actually. If both people want to work on the relationship, then visiting a counselor together would be a great idea."

"What if only one of them goes to a counselor? Would that help?"

"It will definitely help, but mostly for the person who's choosing to work on themselves. You can't magically fix a relationship if the other person isn't willing to put in the work on their end."

"So what if the other person thinks they can't change?"

"Then they're mistaken. Everybody can change. It just takes the right catalyst; the right reason that makes you feel the *need* to change. If somebody is overweight, they might not change until something becomes wrong with their health. The thought of pain or death is the catalyst for them wanting to change. Or, in your case, maybe the catalyst for somebody wanting to work on their anger would be a loved one saying they're going to leave if they don't change, or some other sort of painful consequence. Does that make sense?"

"I think so. People just need the right reason to come along that demands they do something."

"Exactly!" Her hands shoot up like I just made a touchdown. "Your grandpa said you had a good head on your shoulders, but I just figured that all grandpas say that."

"Did you know my grandpa well?"

"Maybe not so well," she says, "but I loved it when he came

into the drugstore where I work. He could always make me smile with his stories and kind words."

"You work two jobs?"

"The state doesn't provide enough money for schools to have a counselor full-time, so I have to work at the drugstore Tuesdays and Thursdays, and most weekends. "

"You're not here all week?"

She shakes her head. "No. Unfortunately not. If you have a problem on Tuesdays or Thursdays, you'll have to talk to the kind folks in the office. Sorry, sweetheart. Government stuff."

"The government? Again? Jeez. What do they have against us?"

"You are an old soul, aren't you?"

"Maybe?" I shrug, not exactly sure what that means.

She smiles and laughs a little.

"I'm going to head back to class now," I tell her. "Thanks for your help. I've got a lot to think about."

I struggle to get out of the beanbag chair until Ms. Carmona comes to my rescue.

"Thanks," I say, "Now you've helped me twice already."

"I guess I have," she acknowledges. "Well, you know what they say: *Things often come in threes,* so maybe I'll be able to help you out again soon."

I hope I don't need it very soon.

My expression must reveal my thoughts since she backpedals a bit. "Not that I want something bad to happen to you. I'm just saying that I'll be here if it does." She flashes a big, nervous smile.

"Got it," I tell her. "Thanks for the clarification."

DON'T APOLOGIZE FOR BEING RIGHT

esides a bit of anxiety, Tuesday goes by without a hitch.

On Wednesday, I'm all jittery at school, excited about the possibility of my U-cut farm idea becoming a reality. I could actually succeed at something big. Maybe Dad would even be less stressed. Thoughts of skinny trees and happy families do their best to distract me from my work, and they succeed.

This could actually work.

I'm not sure if I really believe it or if I'm still trying to convince myself.

Already today, Ms. Mitchell caught me staring out the window. Now, it's social studies, but since I already know how horrible of a person Christopher Columbus was, I'm drawing a logo for our potential Skinny Trees U-cut Asparagus Farm: a row of asparagus sticking up out of a long mound of dirt. There are five of them, and they kind of look like a zombie's fingers. Not exactly what I was going for.

"Mr. McCovey? Are you with us?"

Crap. Not again.

"Yeah, I'm right here. You can't see me?"

"Very funny, Mr. McCovey." Something tells me she's being sarcastic. "Would you like to answer the question, or do you want to call on somebody for help?"

"Somebody for help?" I say, still not sure what I need help with.

"Okay, who would you like to help you?"

I look around as if I'm actually deciding who to call on.

"Mari."

"Again?" says a voice from behind me. "You have a crush or somethin', newbie? Why you always pickin' Mari?"

I turn to look at Jake in the back row.

Great. I thought these guys were going to leave me alone. I should have known better.

"Jake. Were you hoping he would pick you instead?" asks Ms. Mitchell.

Ha! That was epic!

"What? No! Of course not!"

"Then I suggest you zip your lips until you have an answer for one of my questions, or you think of something nice to say."

"Are those my only options?" he asks.

Duh.

"Yes," she verifies. "They are."

"I'll stop talking then."

"Great choice."

Ms. Mitchell turns her attention to Mari, whose cheeks are somewhere between red and bright red. "Mari, would you like to help Asher?"

"Sure," she says, keeping her eyes faced forward. "Indigenous people all over the world have their own historical narrative that can differ from mainstream historical accounts of the same event."

"Oh yeah. I knew that. I just couldn't remember the first part."

"Very well said, Mari."

"Thank you. I just took notes, though," she says. "I didn't actually memorize it."

"Don't apologize for being correct, dear. You did what it took to remember it. I wish everybody did that."

Mari smiles a bit and looks proud, as she should be.

The phone rings, giving us a welcome rest from the lesson.

"Pizza Hut!" Sometimes Ms. Mitchell likes to answer the phone like she works at a restaurant. It was funny the first time. "No, we don't have anchovies. Uh-huh. No. Sure. Of course. He'll be right down."

Somebody's in trouble.

"Asher, Ms. Carmona would like you to stop by her room. I'll have Mari fill you in later."

"Oooohhhh," Jake teases again. "Like on a date?"

"Jake. Can I see you out in the hall, please?" asks Ms. Mitchell.

"Is there another option?"

"No," she tells him, before ushering me out the door.

She turns her attention toward me. "You know, crushes are a totally normal thing in sixth grade, Asher."

No. This is not happening.

"I had my first crush in sixth grade: Brian Robeson." She looks off into the distance for a moment, then returns to reality. "He didn't even know I existed, though. But that doesn't matter. I'm married to my job now, and I love it."

I look anywhere but her eyes.

"Can I go to Ms. Carmona's now? Please?" I try to not sound impatient.

"Sure!" she says. "I'm so glad you're meeting with her.

She is such a special human being. You know, she is a great resource if you have any questions about relationships. I'm not implying that you and Mari—"

"Gotta go! Thanks, friend!"

Jake comes out into the hall right as I'm leaving.

On the short walk to Ms. Carmona's, I keep wondering why the heck she called me to her office. Doesn't she know that can damage a kid's reputation? Jeez.

As soon as I knock on her door, it shoots open.

"Asher! Great to see you!"

Wow. Overexcited much?

I can't believe she outed me by calling the room.

"Sorry to call you in to my office," she continues. "I hope that was okay."

"Sure. Fine. No problem."

Definitely a problem.

"Great. I have two little reasons for asking you to come. I figured together they make a big enough reason to have you stop by."

"Okay," I say, unsure of how to respond.

"Great! First, I wanted to see if you have any more thoughts about our discussion. Sometimes we leave a conversation and then we think of something after it's too late. That happens to me a lot."

"Um. I think I'm okay."

She seems oddly disappointed.

"Okay. I just wanted to let you know that if you or your family need anything, please reach out."

"I'll make sure to let my parents know in case something happens."

"And that leads me to the second thing. Your grandpa sent some pictures into the drugstore before he passed away. I was wondering if your parents might come pick them up. I've called a few times, but nobody's answered. We'll have to throw them away soon, so I just thought I'd check with you."

"I'll try to remember to tell them."

"Great! Thank you, kindly."

She heads back over to her desk while I wonder if I'm supposed to stay or go. Before I can decide, an idea shoves its way to the front of my jumbled-up brain and explodes out of my mouth. "Actually, I *do* need help."

She pauses, trying to make sense of the quick switch.

"That's great!" she says, "I mean, great that I can help. Not great that you have a need. I mean . . ." She fumbles over her words, "I mean, it's fine to have a need. Normal even. I have needs, we all have needs. Some are big, some small, some the same, some different." She finally stops talking.

After we sit there for a few seconds, she starts over. "What can I help you with?"

"Well, my family doesn't have anybody to help harvest our asparagus. I was wondering if you might know anybody who wants some extra work."

Her eyebrows jump high up her forehead. "That's a new one."

"It's okay if you don't. I just thought it was worth a shot."

I head toward the door.

"Hold on. Hold on," she tells me. "While it's true that I don't know anyone off the top of my head, I can definitely check around."

That's better than nothing, I guess.

"There are lots of great people in our little town. Maybe we'll find the one that's perfect for this opportunity."

"Or four?" I add . . . *Making this four times less likely that this is going to happen.*

"Five?" she clears her throat. "Well . . . I will certainly do what I can."

"Okay. Thank you."

I don't want to get my hopes up, but why not try . . . just in case *Skinny Trees* doesn't work out?

"Well, then. Come see me again if there's anything else you need. No pressure, of course. I just like to help." She smiles, and I know she really means it.

"Sounds good," I say. "Will you let me know if you figure anything out?"

"Absolutely. I can't promise anything except that I will do my best."

And that's all I can really hope for, I guess.

When I get back to class, Ms. Mitchell and Jake are still talking in the hall. That's what my mom would call a "Come to Jesus" moment. It's when you have a difficult conversation that's supposed to change your behaviors or life or something. I'm sure he could use it.

I take a seat back in the classroom, where the other kids are reading their nonfiction books. I pull out my book about bass. So far, I've learned that bass don't have any eyelids, the oldest bass was twenty-three years old, and the longest one was twenty-nine and a half inches.

I come to the section on mating habits, so I start to turn the page, but then I see the word *dad*. I stop to read the section and learn that I have a lot to be grateful for. Bass dads start out as good fathers, protecting their offspring until they hatch. But when there are only a few stragglers left behind, the dads eat their own children to replenish all the energy they spent keeping the babies alive.

I guess, if I look on the bright side, at least my dad doesn't eat me.

ADULTS CAN BE LOGICAL

The new bus driver lets me off at Mari's house. I love when adults can be logical.

It takes a while for Manny to get back from his never-ending search for workers, but maybe he's figured something out this time. I mean, I wouldn't be opposed to another good idea.

When he walks in the door, he throws his coat over a chair, kicks off his shoes, and grabs a beer out of the fridge. He falls back onto the couch, pulls off his socks, and throws them onto the floor.

"Good day, Papi?" says Julia.

I can't tell if she's being sarcastic or if she's just hopelessly positive.

"Well, I'm alive, mija, so I've got that going for me." He takes a long drink.

"I already knew that, Papi. You don't look dead."

"That's good. I feel like I'm closer to it than I'd like to be."

"So, you didn't find a solution?" I say, just clarifying the obvious.

He looks over at me, straight-faced. "No. I didn't. I tried everything I could think of. Even some of the . . . well . . . very original ideas you guys came up with. Nothing clicked."

"What did you try?" asks Mari.

"I called the homeless shelters in Yakima. They said that if I send fliers, they can post them on their bulletin boards."

"Well, that's something," I say.

"It's not nothing!" adds Julia.

"Did you try anything else?" I ask.

Manny takes another drink. "I called the jail."

"And?"

"And they laughed at me. They said if I need someone to pick up trash on the side of a road, they can help. Otherwise, I should look somewhere else."

I want to know what else he tried, but I decide to steer the conversation in another direction.

"Well, I asked the counselor at school if she knows anybody that can help."

"You did?" asks Mari.

"I did. She said she would see what she can do. So . . ."

"Well, that's something!" says Julia.

"It's not nothing," I agree.

Manny sighs. "I also called your mom's church, and the receptionist said they can ask around, but most of the congregation is 'getting on in years,' as she called it."

"Well," I look around the group, "are you guys thinking what I'm thinking?"

"That beer and feet kind of smell the same?" says Julia.

"Yes. Exactly!" I agree.

"Really?"

"Of course! And I'm thinking about the Skinny Tree U-cut Asparagus Farm too!"

"Woo-hoo! Skinny trees!" cheers Julia. "What's a skinny tree again?"

"Asparagus," I remind her, holding in a laugh. "People are going to come cut their own asparagus and pay us so they can do all our work. It's genius. A foolproof plan."

"Hold on there, bromigo," says Manny. "We still need to ask your dad about it. It's his farm."

"Thanks for the buzzkill. Life would be so much easier if adults stopped ruining everything."

"Sorry, muchacho. Your dad owns it, so he makes the big decisions. Maybe it will be yours someday, but right now, he's in charge."

"Well, crap. Do you want to ask him?"

Manny lets out a single laugh. "No. Do you?"

"Maybe it would be best if we all did this together," suggests Mari, "to show him how much support there is behind the idea."

I really have no desire to attempt a conversation with my dad, but something in me won't stay quiet. I feel like he needs to know how much I want to help; need to help.

"I'll do it," I blurt out unexpectedly.

"I'll go too!" adds Julia.

"You're the best, kiddo."

"Hey!" Mari chimes in. "Am I being replaced?"

"Never. Not even possible," I assure her.

Mari gives her nod of approval. "I'm going too. Asher, you can do the talking, and we'll be there for support."

"Okay then," I say. "I guess this is happening."

"I guess it is!" agrees Mari.

"Woo-hoo! Let's do this!" says Julia as she jumps into the air. "Here we go!"

Julia heads for the door, but Manny stops her. "Hold on, hold on, mija. We need a plan. Let me think about it tonight, and then we'll make it happen tomorrow. Okay?"

"Okay, Papi. You're the boss!"

"I can't believe we're really trying to make a U-cut asparagus farm," says Manny. "Never in a million years would I have imagined people paying me so they can do my job. What a country we live in."

LOST

We're having fish and chips for dinner, minus the chips and minus any and all flavor.

The look on Dad's face tells me he doesn't want to hear my thoughts on eating fish again, so I keep my mouth shut. It works extremely well when I can pull it off.

If we can all make it to bed without starting any arguments, I'll consider it a success.

When Mom, Dad, and I are almost finished, Rory has only eaten the breading off her fish. Dad keeps eyeing her plate. I can tell he wants to say something, but he manages to keep it to himself.

Before long, though, he's had enough.

"Rory!" he barks, "Eat your food!"

She looks over at Dad, then down at her plate.

"It smells," she whispers, probably hoping the quieter she says it, the quieter he'll respond. That's not the case with him. It doesn't matter how you disagree. If you disagree at all, it's game over.

"Then plug your nose!" he shouts.

He grabs a napkin and throws it at her. "Here," he says

with disdain, "shove these up your nose and eat your food."

Rory looks at the napkin, then at Mom, then back at the napkin.

"Mac," Mom says. "Is that necessary?"

"She needs to eat, doesn't she?" he points out. "If she doesn't eat, she's going to whine about being hungry all night, and I'm not about to put up with that."

"It's not about 'putting up' with your children, Mac. You're supposed to treat them with kindness."

"I realize that, but she doesn't listen to you when you baby her. She needs to know what's okay and what isn't, and wasting food is not okay."

"So . . ." Mom says.

I can tell she's choosing her words carefully.

". . . would you say that treating her this way is okay?"

Oh crap. I mean, go, Mom! But oh crap.

"What way?" he shouts. "You mean holding her accountable for once in her life? I wouldn't have to do it if you would do your job. Why do you let them get away with this stuff, making me be the bad guy?"

Bite your tongue. Bite your tongue.

"I would like Rory to eat her food," says Mom, "but I'm not going to let that get in the way of treating her kindly."

"Congratulations," he mocks. "Sorry I can't be as good as you."

"I didn't say I was better. I'm just reminding you that she's your daughter and you should treat her as though you love her."

"Are you saying I don't care about my own child?" he yells. "Would I be trying to make things work if I didn't care about my kids? No! I would have given up by now."

"I know you're trying, Mac. I'm just pointing out that you're behaving in a way that could hurt your relationship with your daughter. Is that what you want?"

Dad slams his hands down on the table and jumps to his feet.

"Of course I don't want that!" he rages. "Why would you ask a question like that?"

The sound is so loud that Rory hits the floor, and within a few seconds, she's on the move.

She bypasses her shoes and crawls right out the back door.

"Rory!" Dad yells, before realizing that raising his voice isn't helping. "Rory. Come on," he says in his best fake calm voice.

He walks to the door and **GRUUUUNTS** like a rhinoceros. Rory left it cracked, so it opens easily when dad lowers his shoulder into it.

He stands on the porch for a minute, looking for any sign of where she went. Once he's done a thorough search, as thorough as you can do without moving, he yells one more time.

"Rory! You can come back now!"

He doesn't offer any assurance that things will be better. I wouldn't come back if I were her. Not with a lame invitation like that.

When Dad turns around, Mom is staring straight at him.

"I know. I know," he says. "I'll go look for her. I'm not going to leave her alone out there. She's afraid of the dark. I'm not a monster."

And yet she chose to run out into the dark . . . alone . . . to get away from you.

FOUND

We throw on our coats and boots. I'm pretty sure I know where she is, but I don't want my parents following me. I search with them for a few minutes, then break away while they're busy looking in the shed.

After sprinting to the barn, I scale the ladder and hoist myself into the loft.

Slowly, I make my way over to the chest and peek over the top. Sure enough, she's huddled up on the other side.

She doesn't notice me, and I don't want to scare her more, so I back away slowly before I whisper her name.

"Rory. Are you up here?"

She doesn't respond, so I try again.

"Rory. It's just me."

I wait a few seconds before I make my way over to her. She's still huddled there. I slowly take a seat next to her.

"You okay?" I whisper.

She sniffles and shifts her body.

I'll take that as a no.

Unsure if there's really anything I can say that will help, I put my arm around her and pull her in close. She buries her head into my shoulder and lets it all out.

Knowing the clarity that comes after a good cry, I keep my mouth shut and continue to be a stable shoulder to lean on.

After a few minutes of tears and boogers, Rory raises her head and stares at the wall.

"What did I do to Daddy?" she asks as she chokes back tears. "Why is he so mad at me?"

How do I answer that? There's no real reason. He's just mad at everybody and everything.

"You didn't do anything wrong," I assure her. "This has nothing to do with how good you are or what you did or didn't do. This is just about Dad being an angry person and taking it out on us because we're easy targets. Even if Jesus himself was here, Dad would be mean to him too."

This elicits a small laugh out of her.

"I'm serious, though," I add. "I'm your brother. If there was something wrong with you, I'd be the first to let you know. So if I say you're good, then you're good."

"Thanks," she says. "I think."

"You're welcome," I laugh. "Any time."

After a few seconds of silence, we hear Mom and Dad coming toward the barn.

"What do we do now?" asks Rory.

"Well, since we're partners, how about we go down together? That way, we've got each other and neither one of us has to be scared."

"You're scared?" asks Rory.

"You promise you won't tell anybody?"

"I promise."

"I get scared," I tell her. "I'm scared of Dad, snakes, heights, dying, and plenty of other things. You and I aren't too different, you know? So we can be there for each other whenever we're scared."

"Deal," she agrees. "I'll help you when you're scared too."

"I appreciate that."

Mom and Dad enter the barn, checking the stalls one by one.

"She's not with Winston," Mom calls.

"She's not with the goats," says Dad.

I whisper to Rory. "Now, should we get out of here? Together?"

"Sure," she says semi confidently. "We don't need to hide, right?"

"Right. Let's go."

I offer to go first, acting as a shield for her exit.

"Mom. Dad. We're up here. I found her."

I walk over to the ladder, put one foot on the top rung, and steady myself before I commit to the next step. Slowly, I make my way down until I'm standing next to Mom and Dad. We look up, waiting for Rory to make her appearance. She doesn't show.

"Come on, Rory," I call to her. "I'm right here."

"I'm scared," she says.

"It's just a ladder," says Dad. "You can do it."

I look at him, wondering if he really thinks she's scared of the ladder.

"We're in this together," I tell her. "We're a team, and I won't let anything happen to you."

"Are you sure?" she asks. "Sure, sure?"

"As sure as sure can be," I tell her.

"Okay," she agrees.

She backs up to the ladder and descends with ease, even skipping the last few rungs as she jumps to the ground.

"See now?" Dad says. "That wasn't so hard, was it?"

Rory hides behind me, placing me between her and Dad.

"She needs a little space right now," I tell them, not wanting to single Dad out.

"Of course," agrees Mom. "That's understandable."

Mom checks on Rory. Dad turns around and walks a few yards away. He throws his hands on top of his head and sighs long and hard. I assume he's frustrated with Rory for running away, but when I listen more closely, he's not mad at her . . . or any of us. He's cursing at himself.

"Stupid, Mac. Stupid, stupid, stupid," he says, barely audible. "You idiot. What the hell were you thinking?"

He swears at himself a few times before pounding his fist on his forehead.

Mom turns to see what's going on. She puts her hand on his shoulder, then rubs his back.

What is going on? Who's the one that needs comforting here?

"Let's go back inside," Mom says. "I hid some ice cream in the freezer for emergencies. I think this would be a good time to bring it out. What do you guys think?"

"What flavor?" I ask, hoping for mint chocolate chip.

"Does it really matter?" asks Rory. "Is there a kind you're going to say *no* to?"

"Good point."

"All right. Everybody in the house," announces Mom.

We make our way back, but when we get to the door, Mom turns to see that Dad hasn't moved.

"Honey? Are you coming?"

"I'm going to stay out here for a while," he says. "I don't want to scare anybody."

I can't tell if he's being sarcastic or heartfelt, but at this point, I don't really care. If Dad's volunteering to stay outside so the rest of us can relax, I'm all about that.

"Okay then," I say. "Dibs on Dad's ice cream!"

"Nuh-uh!" cries Rory. "I'm the reason we get to have ice cream. I should get to have extra."

"Nobody gets extra," Mom tells us. "You know we can just save some of the ice cream for later, right?"

I give Mom a confused look, because I never expected to hear those words come out of her mouth.

"Do you want me to remind you of that next time you're finishing off a carton, Mom?"

"No. I would not like that," she says. "Would you like to watch me finish off this carton?"

"No. I would not," I confirm.

"Then let's be grateful for what we have and go stuff our faces with sugar, okay?"

"Deal!" says Rory.

"Sounds good to me," I agree.

Dad turns around in silence and disappears into the barn.

THE RIGHT REASON

On the way home from school Thursday, I try to pick Mari's brain to see if she has any details.

"So have you heard anything about his plan?"

She shakes her head. "He didn't say a word to us last night besides his normal '*Buenas noches. Dulces sueños, mis amores.*'"

"That's it, huh?" I ask disappointedly. I was hoping for something a little more helpful.

"That's all I need," she says.

She's right, I guess. If my dad said something like that to me, my problems would be solved.

Rory and I get off at Mari and Julia's stop again, and again I wait anxiously to see if we're moving forward with the plan.

When Manny finally gets home, he tosses his phone on the table and himself into a chair. He looks exhausted. His face isn't smiling, which isn't a good sign. He might even be angry.

"What's wrong, Papi?" asks Mari.

"Yeah, Papi, what's wrong?" echoes Julia.

"It's been a tough day, girls."

I can hear it in his voice.

He looks over at Rory and me. "Your father fired me."

At first, I can't get any words out.

A few seconds later, they come, and they come loudly.

"What? No!"

I'm boiling inside.

"Tell me you're joking," I beg him.

"No joke, amigocho. No joke."

"Why?" asks Mari, near tears. "Did he tell you why?"

"Because I haven't found any helpers."

"And firing you is going to fix that?" I yell through gritted teeth. "What the hell is wrong with him? Doesn't he realize this affects your whole family? And that we'll lose our best friends?"

"This is what anger does," says Mari, with tears racing down her cheeks, like raindrops on a bus window. "Anger makes you hurt people. Even people you love."

"Does this mean you have to move?" asks Rory.

Manny looks down at his phone. "I already called a cousin in Oregon. They're having the same problems we are, so they can use me for a couple months."

"This is stupid," I protest. "This place can't exist without you. You guys are more important to this farm than we are!"

This can't be happening. We're so close!

"Come on!" I yell, as I pound the wall with my fist. "We can't let this stop us. If the U-cut farm works, maybe my dad will change his mind."

Mari stares at the spot on the wall where I left an indent.

I take a deep breath. Then another. Then another.

"So, now what?" asks Mari, before blowing her cry boogers into a tissue.

"Ms. Carmona said that people need the right reason to make a change," I tell them. "She said that it's usually about discovering what they've been missing out on . . . or what they might miss out on in the future."

As I'm saying this, my own words hurt. *Why am I not a good enough reason for him to change? And Rory? How come missing out on time with us isn't enough to give him the strength he needs? When did he choose to hold on to his bitterness instead of holding on to us?*

I feel an energy rising: a churning in my stomach, tying it into knots. It feels like a mixture of determination and wanting to puke.

He needs to know what he's lost. He needs to see what he'll be missing.

I break the silence. "I'm going to talk to him."

Within a second, I'm up, out of the chair and headed toward the door.

"Asher, wait!" calls Mari. "Maybe you should wait until tomorrow, after he calms down."

"It could be days, or even weeks, before he's *ready* to talk," I remind them. "We don't have that kind of time."

I grab my backpack and head out the door. Rory runs after me and takes my hand.

"Are you scared?" she asks.

"Yeah, actually. I am."

"Then I'm coming with you, and I won't take no for an answer."

"Thanks, partner. I appreciate the support."

We walk across the lawn and down the road, hand in hand.

MISSION IMPROBABLE

We get up to the house, and the truck isn't even there.

I take a seat on the rocker, and Rory sits down on the porch swing. I lean all the way back and close my eyes. I tune in to the beating pulse I feel in my body. The chilling fingers of the wind tickle my skin. I grip the worn-down, wooden arms of the chair and squeeze as hard as I can, for as long as I can, and then release. My muscles go weak, and I give in to the exhaustion. My mind follows my body and relaxes. For a few seconds, I imagine that everything's going to be okay, and allow myself to fall asleep.

When I wake up, Rory's gone, and Dad's walking from the truck toward the house. He has a small bag in his hand. He must have done some shopping, which is rare. I let him get a little bit ahead, then stand up and follow behind. I try to pick up any subtle signals so I know what I'm dealing with. His walk is slow, and his head is low.

As I round the corner, the door shuts behind him. It closes at a normal speed; no slamming. He didn't bother to take his boots off outside, but that's pretty normal, I guess. The rules don't apply to him.

I stop before the first step and take a deep breath. This doesn't have to be an all-or-nothing, last-chance moment, but it sure feels like it. If Dad doesn't at least attempt some sort of change tonight, there are going to be gigantic problems. First and foremost, Manny and the girls will have to move. If Dad makes Mari leave, that will be the end of our relationship. No loving dad would do that to his son. And if he doesn't hire Manny back, the farm will go under, and we'll all be out on the streets.

My legs feel heavy as I walk up the steps. Grabbing the doorknob, I turn it, breathe deeply again, then step inside.

Rory is sitting on the couch, watching cartoons. No surprise there. She saw her opportunity and took it. Smart girl.

Dad sets his bag on the table and walks over to his chair. He grabs the remote from Rory's lap, falls hard into his recliner, and changes the channel to the Mariners' game.

Rory slinks off the couch and crawls along the floor, away from Dad. Once she's out of sight, she stands up slowly and makes her way over to the stairs.

"Rory," I say in a loud whisper. "Come here."

She looks back at Dad and then at me, then hesitantly comes my way.

"What?" she mouths.

"I need you."

"You need me? For what?"

"I can't do this without you. This is our most important mission yet. Will you help?"

"Do I have to talk to Dad?"

I nod my head.

She shakes hers and turns to walk away.

"Please?" I beg.

"I just came to encourage you," she yell-whispers. "I didn't know I would actually have to do something! I'll just mess it up."

"No, you won't," I reassure her. "I can't do it alone."

"Right," she says. "What can I do that you can't?"

"You can be cute," I tell her, knowing that she can't deny it.

"Oh. Yeah, I guess you're right. I really am better at that. But how is being cute going to help anything?"

"All I need you to do is be sweet to Dad for a few minutes to see if we can soften him up. If it doesn't work, we'll have to bail out and come up with another plan."

"So you need me to be adorable and talk to him about happy things?"

"Yes. Can you do that?" I ask, already knowing the answer.

"Can I do that? If you had to describe me in two words, it would be cute and talks a lot."

"That's more than two words," I say. I can't help myself. "But that's okay. You're right. I would describe you like that. You're perfect for the job!"

"Okay. I'll give it a shot, but if anything goes wrong, you have to rescue me."

"Okay. Deal," I agree.

I was planning on it, anyway.

"So what do you need me to do, exactly?" she asks.

"There are three steps," I tell her. "Are you ready?"

"I'm as ready as . . . as ready as . . . as a race car at the starting line."

"Ooh. Nice simile!" I point out, trying to send some encouragement her way. "You must be learning about those in school."

"Yep. I'm real good at it."

"I can tell."

She smiles a big, cheesy grin.

"Okay," I continue. "Let's go outside and get on the same page."

"Why would we stand on a page?" she asks.

I'm not sure if she's joking or if she really doesn't know what that means. "It's an idiom," I tell her.

"What did you just call me?"

"Nothing! Never mind. Let's just go outside and talk."

"Okay," she agrees. "I don't think we would even fit on the same page, anyway, unless it's a really ginormous book!"

SUCH A GOOD SPY

We step outside and quietly close the door behind us. The porch light shines on half her face, leaving the other side in the dark.

"First, you need to ask Dad who his favorite Mariners player is."

"What?" she asks, crossing her arms. "Why?"

"We just need to get him talking about something he likes," I tell her. "Something that makes him happy."

"Does he even like anything anymore?"

"He likes watching baseball, and he likes to talk about the details of the game. You don't have to understand it. Just look like you're listening."

"So, like I do with you?"

"Ouch! Nice one."

"Thank you. Thank you," she says, as she takes a bow. "What's next?"

"This might sound weird, but I need you to ask Dad if you can snuggle with him while you watch the game."

"That's not weird. I love snuggling! I just normally do it with stuffies."

"Well, yeah." I pause, trying to find the right words. "Exactly. It's been a while since you've cuddled with Dad, and I wasn't sure if that's something you still want to do."

"I can ask, but what if he says no?"

That's what I'm afraid of. I don't want to put her in a position where she can get hurt.

"He might, but no matter what he says, it's going to give us the information we need for the next step."

"This is kind of scary," she says. "I don't want him to say no."

That's understandable.

"I don't want him to say it, either. But if he does, I have a plan."

"Okay. So what is it?"

"If he says yes, then your job is done. You can just chill out and watch some baseball."

"I hope I get to snuggle," she says, crossing her fingers and looking to the sky.

"Me too," I tell her, wishing I could make it happen for her, *"but sometimes things don't go smoothly. It's the cost of being such a good spy."*

"You think I'm a good spy?" she asks, with a mix of shock and joy.

"No." I pause for just a second. "I KNOW you're a good spy."

"Ahhhhh. Thanks!" she says. "I do my best." She puffs her chest out, digs her fists into her hips, and strikes a superhero pose.

Pretty quickly, concern spreads across her face. "So what if he does say no? Then what do I do?"

"This is where things might get tricky." I cringe a bit. "If he says no, do you think you can cry? We have to find some way to soften him up a bit."

"Like, make myself cry?" She bites her lip and looks doubtful. "Maybe?"

"Oh, come on," I pester her. "Don't pretend like you've never fake-cried before."

She shakes her head. "I can't admit to that. It's against the girl code."

"So you have," I say bluntly.

"I cannot admit to it, whether it has or hasn't happened."

"Okay, then." I roll my eyes. "Either way, can you do it?"

"Okay," she says.

She takes a deep breath and lets it out like a horse flapping its lips.

"I'll give it my best shot."

"All right, partner!" I try to get her psyched up. "Let's do this!"

I can see that she still looks a little uneasy.

"Are you sure this is going to work?" she asks, wavering in her confidence.

I want to tell her I'm sure, but that would be a lie.

"I don't know," I tell her honestly. "I can't predict how he'll respond, but I know that there's nobody I'd rather team up with than you."

Okay, maybe Mari.

"You'll do awesome, Rory. I love ya. Thanks for being a great partner."

"Ahhhhhh," she sighs. "I love you too. Thanks for being a great big brother."

She quietly makes her way over to the couch.

"Dad, would you like anything to drink?" she asks in her sweetest voice.

She's going off script already?

"Oh," he says, sounding surprised. "Um, sure. I guess I

would take a Coke since you offered, but you don't have to."

"I know. I just want to," she adds.

Holy cow. How is she so good at this stuff? She's like some sort of crazy genius.

She grabs a cold can from the fridge, sits at the end of the couch closest to Dad, and hands him his Coke.

"Here you go."

"Thanks," Dad says without taking his eyes off the TV.

"Hey, Dad?" she says. "Who's your favoritest Mariners player? Is it Jay Buhner?"

How does she know who Jay Buhner is?

He sits up in his chair. She has clearly piqued his interest.

"What do you know about Jay Buhner?" he asks, turning his face toward her.

Yeah, what does she know?

"I know he played baseball for the Mariners and that he's on a TV commercial for trucks," she answers matter-of-factly.

"Well, that's a start," he says.

More than I would have guessed she knew.

"Jay Buhner was our right fielder," Dad adds, "until 2001. That was the year we got one hundred sixteen wins and tied the record for the most wins in a season. Unfortunately, like all the other years, we stunk it up in the playoffs."

"Bummer."

"Yeah. But Jay Buhner isn't my favorite player, although he would probably be top five."

We got him talking. A promising start.

"It's probably cliché," he continues, "but I'd have to say my favorite Mariner of all time is Ken Griffey Jr., with Edgar Martínez being a close second."

"Ken Griffey, huh?" she says.

"Ken Griffey Jr.," he corrects her. "His dad played baseball too. He was the original Ken Griffey. They both played on the Mariners at the same time." His eyes gaze off into nowhere as he relives the era. "I remember watching them, thinking how cool it was. They were the first father and son to do that. You know what's even cooler?"

"What?" Rory asks eagerly.

"In one game, they hit home runs back-to-back."

"What's back-to-back?" she asks. "Like their backs were touching?"

He lets out a one-syllable chuckle. "No. It means one of them hit a home run and then the other one hit a home run right after that." I can hear the antique excitement in his voice.

"Whoa!"

This girl needs an Oscar.

She makes her next move. "Daddy, can I sit on your lap and watch the game with you?" She asks so sweetly, so adoringly.

There's no way he can say no to that. He's going to be ready for a real conversation in no time.

He looks at her, brushes some food off his lap, then levels his verdict. "I'm kind of hot and sweaty from working today. I'd like some space to just cool down and relax."

What? What happened? Now we need a quick transition to phase three. I feel like crap for asking her to do this.

Rory brings her legs up to her chest and lays her head on her knees. She sits there for a minute, and I wonder if she's having a hard time or just taking her time.

Pretty soon, I hear a sniffle. A few more seconds pass, and there's another one. Her breathing gets heavy, and she draws in air quickly. She rubs her eyes. She might just be amazing at this, but if I'm honest with myself, I know she's actually hurting. As bad of a brother as that makes me, this could be good for her. She can finally let it out after all those times she had to hold it in.

Dad is pretty engaged in the game, but I see him look over at her. This will show us how far gone he is. Does he comfort his crying daughter, who just got him a Coke and talked baseball with him? Or does he ignore her because he's too tired from battling his own demons?

After a minute, he seems committed to ignoring her. Maybe he's hoping it will stop and he won't have to do anything about it.

If this goes on for much longer, I'll have to go in.

He leans forward in his chair, hangs his head, and folds his hands. I know he's not praying, but he must be thinking about something. Is it about Rory? Me? Our family? Or just himself?

RAW TALENT

*C*rap.

I don't know how he does it, but he finds a way to ignore her. Somehow, deep inside, he reasons that it's not important to comfort his crying daughter. This is so messed up.

"Rory, you okay?" I ask as I make my way over to her. "Did you get hurt?"

I know full well that she's not hurt . . . physically.

What is Dad even thinking right now?

"Do you need a hug?" I ask quietly.

She nods her head oh so slightly, and I put my arm around her, pulling her in tight. The plan was fake crying, but this pain is too real. I shouldn't have put her in this situation. I got her hopes up.

Her tears bring out mine, but I hide them well. I don't want Dad to see.

We sit there for a few minutes, in the most ridiculous situation. Two kids cry next to their father while he watches grown men hit balls with a piece of wood and run around a diamond. In a painful irony, he watches these men mostly swing and miss, while he strikes out with his own children, and we all lose.

When I finally compose myself, I think about what we have to lose at this point, and all there is to gain. My determination surges. It's time for the un-cute version.

"I like Griffey too," I blurt out, "but Edgar Martínez had a way better batting average."

It's the bottom of the ninth inning. We're down by three runs and the bases are loaded. Two outs, full count, and I'm at the plate. This has to work.

Dad looks over. He can't force himself to smile, but he gives a little nod, which is at least an acknowledgment. He drops his head.

"Griffey's still my favorite, of course. There's just no denying how beautiful that swing is. Best in baseball."

He lifts his head back up and stares at the wall in front of him.

"Follow-up question," I add. "This one's local. Who's your all-time favorite player from the Yakima Bears?"

His face contorts. It's as if he's looking so far back in his memory that he's traveling through space-time to get there and retrieve the piece of information.

"Shane Victorino," he says.

"What? No. You have to be kidding me."

"Nope."

"Why?" I ask, just to keep him talking.

"Easy." He looks my way. "Raw talent."

"Raw talent like a batting average under two fifty? The whopping twenty RBIs he had?"

This gets him going.

"Number one," he says, "he was only nineteen years old. Number two: It was only his second year in baseball. He scored thirty-two runs, which was second highest on the team, and over twenty stolen bases. He was a great, young, up-and-coming player who went on to the big leagues and played there for twelve years. Twelve years! That's as long as you've been alive. He won three Gold Glove Awards, was an All-Star twice, and won the World Series . . . which reminds me, he was also a member of the 2000 Yakima Bears championship team."

"Yeah. I remember. It was a great series. The last game, we were in the first-base bleachers, and I got a foul ball off the bat of—"

"Shane Victorino," he says, putting the pieces of the puzzle together.

"Yup. And after the final out, we all went nuts, and you threw me over your shoulder and started jumping up and down and spinning around. I almost puked up my hot dog, but it was totally worth it."

And there it is. My best memory with Dad. I know I can't change him. But if he wants to change himself, maybe that will be his spark.

We sit there in silence for a minute, and all I can do is hope that something got through.

Rory has turned off the waterworks. She's one amazing kid. Her head rests on my shoulder now. A lot of stuff has gone wrong lately, but if I ever become an optimist, I could look back and view this time getting to know Rory better as time well spent.

She gets up, walks into the kitchen, and blows her nose on a paper towel. It's so loud, I'm surprised geese don't fly into the windows. She grabs a plastic cup off the bottom shelf of the cupboard and downs a whole cup of water.

She takes the leftovers out of the fridge and fixes herself a plate, then fills the cup up again and takes it to the table.

After a few bites, her curiosity gets the better of her.

"Asher, what's in this bag? Can I look?"

Apparently, she didn't see Dad come in with it.

"I don't know, kiddo. It's not mine."

"It's some pictures, I guess," Dad adds. "A lady from the drugstore called and asked me to pick them up. Sounds like Grandpa sent in some photos before he died and never had a chance to get them."

Oh yeah. Those. Oops.

"What are they of?" asks Rory.

"Don't know," says Dad. "I didn't really want to get all emotional at the drugstore if they were pictures of Grandma and Grandpa."

"Can I look?"

"Rory!" I shush her.

"As long as you don't show me any pictures of Grandma and Grandpa. I don't think I can take it right now. Other than that, knock your socks off."

She looks confused.

"Why?"

"Can you just do what I said?" he demand-asks. "If not, then just don't look."

"Okay," she says. She obediently takes her socks off. Once she's barefoot, she has another bite of food and starts digging into the bag. She pulls out a red-and-yellow envelope, unseals it, then slides the photos into her hand.

"Don't get grease on them," I say.

"I'm not," she replies as she wipes her hands on her pants. She looks at the first picture for a few seconds, then starts flipping through them a little more rapidly.

A dozen or so pictures in, she pauses. "Hey! I remember that!"

I'm not in a mood for conversation, so I ignore her. They must be of Grandpa or Grandma, cause she's not saying much about them and not offering Dad a look.

"Oh my gosh!" she blurts out. "I forgot about that."

Don't engage. Just ignore.

She giggles. "Asher! Remember when you got that haircut that made you look like a hedgehog?"

She wins. Now I have to see what the heck she's talking about.

A THOUSAND WORDS

I stand behind her chair, palms resting on the top of it. Looking over her shoulder, I see myself. Or should I say, a hedgehog?

"Why does this picture even exist?" I ask. "And why would he want it?"

"Maybe he didn't want it because you were in it," says Rory. "Maybe he wanted a cute picture of me, and you and Dad were just in it too."

"I'm in it?" asks Dad.

"Yep," she confirms as she stays glued to the picture. "You don't look as bad as Asher, but I'm definitely the star."

"Bring those over here, will ya?" he demands, as if politeness has gone out of style.

"But I just started looking at them," complains Rory.

I nudge her shoulder, not wanting her to cause any problems.

"And you can finish looking at them over my shoulder," Dad remarks. "You're driving me nuts over there talking about it when I can't see it."

Rory takes a swig of water and then a quick bite of food.

She taps the stack of pictures on the table to make sure they're all straight, backs her chair into me, then makes her way over to Dad. I quickly follow.

When we get close, Dad blurts out, "Lemme see 'em," with his hand outstretched, expecting a speedy delivery.

It's shocking that Rory and I have any manners at all.

She hands them over to Dad and we each take a spot standing at the back corners of the recliner, staring over his dusty shoulders.

"You're right," he says, glancing back at me. "Totally a hedgehog."

Rory tries to hold in a chuckle but fails.

He flips to the next picture, and it's me, Rory, and him when we were at the farm for Christmas a few years ago. Grandpa had hooked up a sled to the back of the quad, and we were all squished in. Rory is sitting in my lap. She couldn't have been more than five years old. Dad's behind me, and he has his arms around us, probably trying to keep us safe, but I don't think there was much safe about it. I notice that Mom's not in the picture.

"Oh my gosh!" says Rory. "That was so much fun! Remember when we turned, and we went shooting out to the side, and then we flipped over and went rolling and rolling and rolling? That was awesome."

"You guys didn't tell Mom about that, did you?" he asks.

"Nope. Sure didn't," says Rory.

"I didn't say anything," I assure him.

The times we couldn't tell Mom about were the best we ever had.

I see a guilty little smile crawl across his face.

He flips to the next picture. It looks like it was taken at the hospital when Rory was born. Mom is lying on the bed, and

Dad is sitting next to her, holding Rory. Grandma is holding me up next to Dad so I can see my new baby sister. Dad looks so happy. He used to tell us we were his king's pair. I guess that means when you get a boy, then a girl, and then stop having kids. I think the boy is because a king needs an heir, but I'm not sure why he needs a girl. Maybe to marry her off to a prince in exchange for land or livestock.

The next picture is Rory and me on her first-ever day of school. We're dressed up nice and fancy. She's holding a sign that says FIRST DAY OF KINDERGARTEN and I'm holding mine that says FIRST DAY OF THIRD GRADE.

Next is a photo of Dad and me at fifth-grade camp.

How the heck did Grandpa get that? Did Mom send it to him?

"Wow," says Dad. "That feels like it was so long ago."

"A lot has happened since then," I say.

Some of these pictures, I've never even seen before. I can't figure out why Grandpa would have them.

Next is a picture of our whole family at Disneyland. Then there's a picture of Dad and me at a baseball game with me holding up a big foam finger that says #1. There's one of Rory and me in the tree house Dad built for us. There's one of our whole family next to the eighteenth hole at the Yakima Family Putt-Putt Center. They're mainly of Rory, Dad, and me. There are a few with Mom. We're doing everything from swimming in Bumping Lake, hiking White Pass, doing a paper mache art project, biking in our neighborhood, picking apples in Wenatchee, visiting a train exhibit, and touring the flight museum.

After a few minutes, Dad comes to the end of the stack. I expect him to hand them back to one of us and go about his business, or lack thereof, but he doesn't. He just sits there, holding the pile, staring at the last picture. It's of me and him.

We're at the Yakima County Stadium. I must have been five or six. It looks like it was Little League night at the ballpark 'cause I'm all dressed up in my baseball uniform. I've got my glove just in case there's a foul ball. I'm holding a tiny wooden bat in my hand; a souvenir that Dad got me that's still displayed in my room. I'm holding it out to the camera to make sure everyone can see what my dad bought me, like it's the most amazing thing in the world.

Some random fan was nice enough to take a picture for us. I wish I could tell them how much this picture means to me at this very moment. It captures a moment of pure joy. Dad's not looking at the camera; he's looking at me. In this picture, I am enough to make him smile. It's just me being me, and Dad finding joy out of watching me be happy.

"Here's the remote," he says, as he hands it off to Rory.

He sets the pictures on the arm of his recliner, places a hand on each knee, and pushes himself up. Old-man noises escape as he rises; deep groans and cracking bones. He stands up tall; takes a big, deep breath; and blows it out slowly and loudly. He picks up the pictures again.

"You guys watch whatever you want," he says. "I'll be out in the barn for a while. Mom should be home soon."

He walks over to the back door and exits quietly.

I look up to where heaven might be and give recognition where it's due.

"Thanks for the memories, Grandpa."

I should probably thank Mom for her role too. Quiet, but effective.

AGAINST MY BETTER JUDGMENT

It's Friday.

Everyone loves the weekend, except for kids who have more problems at home than they do on a math test. For Rory and me, school is the place we look forward to. Today is tough all around, though.

Mari and Julia get on the bus like they normally do, but the joy is gone from their faces. Obviously, they couldn't have moved away overnight, but it's still comforting to see them. Mari reads a book all the way to school. When I sit next to her at lunch, she says she doesn't want to talk about it in front of other people. After school, she reads a book all the way home.

After the exhaust from the bus clears, she turns to me with misty eyes. "How could he fire my dad when he knows exactly how it feels? And my dad didn't even do anything wrong!"

She's right.

"Where are we going to move?" she cries, looking for an answer I can't give her.

"You're not moving anywhere. We'll get your dad his job back."

Her tears are spilling over now. "How are you so sure?"

"It's going to be okay," I say. "I'll take care of it."

"That's very sweet," she says, "but it's not that easy."

"You might be right, but I think I was able to get through to him. Well, maybe a little . . . hopefully. I don't really know how to explain it, but there was a slight change in him last night. He left before I could ask him about your dad."

Rory places her hand on my shoulder to let me know she needs to say something. I forgot she was there. "I'm going inside," she says, "to play with Julia before she moves."

"She's not moving!" I yell. "This is just a temporary issue. No moving."

"Okay. Okay. Jeez. I hope you're right," she says. "See you later, Mari."

"What am I? Chopped liver?" Snubbed by my own little sister.

"Dropped liver," Rory corrects me, then off she runs to the house.

I turn back to Mari.

"You didn't ask him about my dad yet?" she scolds me.

"No. I couldn't. He wasn't ready to hear it."

She looks a little unsteady.

"Asher," she says, "I don't know what we're going to do."

"I'll talk to him tonight and figure out what's going on."

"Tonight?" she says, with urgency in her voice. "Why wait til tonight? Just go now! Go, go, go, go, go."

She shoos me away like an unwelcome dog.

I walk backward while finishing our conversation so she can see that I'm trying to hurry. "All right, all right . . . but remember, I can't fix him."

"I know. I know," she agrees. "Just do something."

"I do have one idea," I tell her, almost yelling now. "It's kind of crazy, but I guess you'll have to trust me."

"I'm supposed to just trust you," she yells back, "after you tell me you have a crazy idea?"

"Yes," I tell her, hoping the confidence will convince her.

"Okay then," she responds. "If there's anybody I can trust, it's . . . well, my family, but you too!"

"I'll take it," I say. "I'll be back soon!"

———

While I was trying to fall asleep last night, I couldn't stop thinking about how lots of people *want* to change, but only some of us can get ourselves to do anything about it. What makes a person want to improve themselves, and then what makes a person actually start changing?

Apparently losing the farm isn't a big enough deal for Dad. I wonder if he even considered the fact that he's taking our best friends away. He probably didn't think about where Manny would get another job or if they could even find a place to stay. I don't think he considered anything, really. There are so many logical reasons for him to reverse course, but somehow he's blind to them all.

So, I'm going to have to do something crazy.

I came up with one idea that I think has potential. Dads love teasing their sons about girls. Last year, at camp, I showed my dad the girl I had a crush on. Big mistake. He didn't let me forget about it for months.

I warned my buddies to not tell their dads who they had crushes on. One of them didn't listen, then the rest of them did.

Against my better judgment, I've decided to let my dad know that I like Mari. It sounds crazy even considering it, but my theory is that sharing it with him might make him happier, and maybe he'll even want to tease me or joke around, which will lighten the mood. I can't believe I'm talking about these things like they're good.

Hopefully, this will make him realize why it's such a big deal that he fired Manny . . . as if displacing a whole family and losing the farm weren't bad enough. This is either genius or completely stupid. I guess I'll find out soon.

"Dad. I have a crush on Mari." *No. That's dumb.*

"Dad. You can't make Mari leave. I need her." *Jeez. Way too much drama.*

"Hey, Dad, did you hear Mari's leaving? Of course you did. 'Cause it's your fault! Please stop being stupid and ruining my life!"

Yeah. No.

Nearing the end of the driveway, I still haven't seen Dad out in the fields.

I pop my head into the barn and glance around. Nothing.

I guess he must be in the house.

I walk the few steps it takes to get to the back door and psych myself up. *You can do this, Asher. Just be kind and stay positive, but don't overreact if it doesn't go well.*

I walk up the first couple steps and then everything is in slow motion. Things get blurry. My heart sends vibrations through my chest. I feel light-headed, and my legs buckle a bit. I pause to regain my composure.

You're not trying to change him. You're letting him know what's important to you. It's his decision how he wants to respond.

I open the door. Nobody's there.

Where the heck is he?

I gather my courage. "Dad?"

From down the hall, he calls back, "Yeah?"

"I just wanted to see if we could talk for a minute."

"Just a second," he says. "What about?"

Oh, Lord. Here we go.

"I just . . . I heard you fired Manny, and I was hoping you would reconsider."

Doing well so far. Keep it up.

"I, uh . . . I think it's going to be hard to keep the farm running without him."

"You think so, huh?" he yells back.

Why won't he just come out?

"Yeah. And uh . . . I just wanted to let you know that . . ."

Here we go. You can do this, Asher. You can do this.

"I like Mari." I say it fast, as if that makes it less humiliating.

"Are you sure you want to talk about this now?" he asks. "I mean, I think she's a great kid too, but maybe this is a conversation for later."

That's just like him, trying to brush me off. Not today, Dad.

"I mean I *like* like her. She's pretty and smart and kind, and she's really helped me become a better person. I don't want to lose her." I let it all out. There's no point in holding back now.

"Oh ya?" he says. "That's very bold of you."

That's a good thing, right? I can't believe I'm doing this.

The toilet flushes.

Gross! Was he in the bathroom that whole time?

He washes his hands and opens the door, but he doesn't come down the hall right away. He's talking to himself. Or is he on the phone? It's so quiet, I can't hear any details.

"Maybe I *should* come back later," I offer, but he doesn't respond.

This is getting even weirder.

I stare at the opening to the hall, waiting for him to step out.

Then, as quick as a curveball, everything goes wrong; very, very wrong.

Out of the hall steps Manny.

ONE STEP AT A TIME

Dad follows Manny out of the hall, trying to hide the grin on his face. "Hey," he says, "Manny's here."

The heat radiating from my face tells me I'm probably as red as a radish.

"Thanks, Dad. You could've warned me."

"How was I supposed to know you were going to say that? Manny found out the same moment I did." He chuckles and looks over at Manny, who is also having trouble holding back his laughter.

I slap my hands over my horrified expression, press hard, and let out a loud groan.

How? Why? This can't be happening.

"Well, Asher," says Manny. "You're more than welcome to date my daughter."

"What? Really?"

This is too good to be true. This can't be real.

"When she turns sixteen and *if* she decides you're good enough for her."

I knew there was a catch.

"Sixteen?" I whine. "That's really far away."

"I know. That's the point."

"Besides," adds Dad, "You've got plenty of time to get to know her better before then, since she'll be around for a while."

It takes a second for my brain to register what he said.

"Can you clarify what you mean?" I ask, not wanting to make any assumptions.

"I mean, I hired Manny back."

Manny nods in agreement.

"But how? I mean, why did you change your mind?"

"I guess I got a clearer picture," he says.

"And with that," Manny jumps in, "I'm going to let you guys have some time to talk, just the two of you. Gracias, Mac. I'm glad we had the chance to get to know each other a little better."

"Same here," agrees Dad. "And I'm really sorry. Thank you for agreeing to come back. We can't do this without you."

"You're right," agrees Manny. "You can't." He laughs as he heads out the door.

Dad looks over at the coffee table where the pictures are sitting.

"After looking through those photos for a while," he says, "I got sick to my stomach. I'll spare you the details, but I knew I had to do something. And for the first time in a long time, I felt like I *could* do something."

"Wait. Why would pictures make you feel sick? Did you eat one?"

He laughs out loud, bringing life into the room.

"No. I did not eat any pictures. Honestly, I got so mad when I looked at them. All I saw was a failure; a man who couldn't pull himself together."

He sighs hard, then breathes in deep.

"I'm a failure," he says, eyes squinting to hold back any tears that might try to escape. "My own kids are scared of me."

My heart drops. It's true, but it hurts to hear him say it.

"I failed as a son, too," he says. "Grandpa told me to leave the government stuff alone, but I didn't listen. How could I? They took my dad away. A son doesn't just sit back and let something like that happen!"

I nod, knowing just how he feels.

"I realize now that I've wasted so much time. I don't have anything to show for the last year of my life."

Like Dad, I've been mad at myself plenty of times before, but I always keep it in my head. Hearing him get mad at himself out loud is hard to watch, but it also feels important to not miss.

He continues. "I had time left with my dad, but I blew it. I threw away my job, lost the house, and now I'm losing my family. Heck, I'm even messing up other people's families."

He's not wrong.

"When I saw all those pictures of us doing things together, like being baseball buddies, at first I was *so* mad at myself, thinking about what I had thrown away. But after looking at them for a while, I realized those pictures don't have to be the end of the story. It's not too late to turn things around and make more memories; take more pictures. I don't want to just be in the old, happy photos. I want to be in all the future ones too."

"But you always had access to those pictures," I point out, "and the memories are right there in your head. How come you couldn't think clearly before?"

"I knew there were good memories, yes, but the world has a way of using those things against you; making you feel like a failure for not being the happy-in-the-picture person every second of every day." He pauses, looking at the ground. "I guess it was like I got stuck in a huge rainstorm, and I felt like I was all alone. The world had beaten me down. Everything important to me got washed away, and all I could think about was how I was drowning." He raises his head and looks right into my eyes. "But you know what?"

"What?" I answer, not sure if I was actually supposed to.

"Amid every great storm, there are moments that shake your world and force you to see things in a new light. You can either run and hide, or let it bring you to life."

I feel like my future is hanging on his every word.

"Asher," he continues. "You and Rory are my lightning and thunder. Those memories with you were my wake-up call."

"What about Mom? You do realize that she was the one who sent those pictures to Grandpa, right? He had the idea, but he couldn't have done it without her."

"You're right," he agrees. "There's a lot we couldn't do without your mother."

A dose of reality hits me, and I don't feel like I can ignore it. "I don't like to think of myself as a pessimist. I'd say I'm more of a realist, but really, why should we believe this is going to last for more than a day or two? What if you wake up tomorrow and something bad happens, then you get all crazy angry again? I don't think people usually change very quickly, or at least not for long."

"That's fair. I get it. I would be wary if I were in your shoes, but it wasn't as fast as you think."

"What do you mean?" I ask. "Have you seen yourself in a mirror? You even look different. There's a pretty big contrast between yesterday and today."

"I know it doesn't seem like I've even been trying this last year, but I've been battling every day, just trying to keep going. Last night was the first battle where I felt like I actually won back some ground. I felt like I took a step forward, instead of just holding on for dear life."

"So what things are you going to change?" I press him.

"Well, there's Manny."

"You're going to change Manny?" I joke.

"I gave him his job back, so kind of, I guess."

"What made you decide to do that?"

"I knew I shouldn't have fired him the second I did it, but I couldn't admit it. So I stuck with it, but luckily not forever. With Manny, we might have a shot at saving the farm for at least another year. He was telling me about the idea you guys had about a U-cut asparagus farm. I think it's a great idea. I'm also glad I didn't ruin your relationship with your future girlfriend," he adds with a smile. "You never would have forgiven me."

"Yeah. I was pretty mad. What were you thinking?"

"I wasn't," he admits.

"Well, thank God you started."

He laughs, bringing back a flood of memories.

"Remember what you used to tell us every time we hiked the Autumn Ridge Loop?"

"Are you about to use my own words against me?" he asks, chuckling.

"Not against you; for you."

"So what were these wise words?"

"Every time the trail got steep, you would say, *'The only way to climb a mountain is one step at a time. Don't worry about anything but the next step.'*"

"I said that?" he jokes. "I'm smarter than I remember."

"You did. And now it's my turn to say it. One step at a time, Dad. Let's do this."

A MILLION THINGS

"There are literally a million things to do," Mom says as she walks by.

"Literally?" I ask her. "A million?"

She gives me a look. "Not now, Asher."

"Sorry," I say, needing to keep things positive.

Mari, Julia, Rory, and I are all making signs to put out by the road.

"Hey, guys," I tell them. "Those look great! Almost as good as mine." I flash a cheesy smile.

They all give me dirty looks, like they coordinated it.

"Whatever," says Mari, with a shake of her head.

"Yeah. Whatever," adds Julia. Then she sticks her tongue out for added effect.

My sign is the original logo I drew, with a couple of changes. There are five asparagus, all in a row, and a hand is reaching down to the base of one of them. Across the top of the sign is our new farm name that we all agreed on: SKINNY-TREE U-CUT ASPARAGUS FARM. Mari's sign says, U-CUT ASPARAGUS. THICK OR SMALL, WE GOT 'EM ALL. She's also going to make arrows that just say U-CUT ASPARAGUS FARM to show people where to turn. Julia is being super helpful, making a sign that says MAKE YOUR PEE SMELL FUNNY! I'm also gonna make signs showing people how to pick the asparagus so they don't waste any of it.

Dad took a crash course for advertising on the Internet. He joined a new website that just started last year, called You-Tube. You can make videos, put them on there, and then people all over the world will see them. I would settle for all of Washington. We put a video on there about what happened to our friends from Mexico and how this is our last chance to save the farm. Some people right here in Prosser commented on it, and they said they'd bring their friends. Lots of people from Yakima watched it and commented, and even some from Seattle. But probably the best thing that happened was on a brand-new website called Twitter. Dad put our story up there and the governor of Washington "retweeted" it to pretty much the whole state.

There really are more details to figure out than I could have imagined. Luckily, that's Mom's specialty. She has to get change for people who need it, rent a porta potty (hopefully one that has an air freshener that can handle asparagus pee), set up trash cans, go to the grocery stores to get empty boxes and recycled bags, and then help Rory with her last-minute idea: a bake sale. She wants to sell cookies, brownies, and stuff like that to raise more money.

Manny is setting up a small petting zoo. Winston seems excited. He's also figuring out the pricing for the asparagus so that it's not too expensive but still makes us a profit. Then he has to find places for people to park and block off places they're not supposed to go.

All day, we keep finding more things to do and end up working until it's almost dark. When we can't see enough to work anymore, we gather in the dining room. The men are dirty and sweaty. The girls end up covered in flour with chocolate smeared on their faces. Everyone is tired.

"Well, that's frustrating," says Dad, sounding completely exhausted.

"What is?" asks Mom.

"There's still so much to do. I don't know how we're going to pull this off."

"Well," she says, "whether we're ready or not, tomorrow's coming. We can choose to worry about it or make the best out of it."

"I choose to worry."

I jump in to change the subject. "I have a question."

"What is it?" Dad asks.

"Is anyone else hungry?"

A chorus of *meeeeeeeeeeeees* rings out.

I offer a solution. "How about a bonfire? We can roast some hot dogs and s'mores. We'll end the night on a high note."

"I don't know, Ash," says Dad. "It's pretty late and I'm exhausted."

I can't let this go that easily, so I try one more time. "Come on. It doesn't have to be long. Like, half an hour. Then you can go watch TV or go to bed or whatever."

Dad gives me a look that says, "*I really don't want to, but I'm trying.*"

Manny chimes in. "Julia should probably get to bed soon."

I look over at Mom with my best pleading look. She comes through. "I can drive you guys down to your house after the fire," she offers. "Would that work?"

I smile at Manny. "So?"

"I guess a ride would save us some time. I'll give you thirty minutes, then we're off to bed."

A burst of energy springs me into action.

"Rory. Go grab the fire starters."

She stands there looking at me.

"Please?" I add, hoping the magic word will do the trick.

She throws me a big thumbs-up. "You got it, partner!"

"Mari, can you grab the wood? And Julia, can you find some matches? I think they're in the drawer next to the fridge."

"I have big muscles," says Julia. "I can help with the wood too."

"Are you sure they're big enough? Can you prove it?"

She roles up her sleeve, bends her arm back toward her head, and makes a look with her face that's probably supposed to say, *"Look how hard I'm flexing!"* but comes across as, *"Look how hard I'm pooping."*

I squeeze her skinny little arm and feign amazement. "Holy cow! Have you been working out?"

"I got it from my mom," she states matter-of-factly. "My dad says she was the strongest woman ever."

"That's awesome. If she was anything like you and your sister, she must have been pretty amazing."

My family nods their heads in agreement. Even though none of us met her, she's left behind plenty of evidence that she was a strong and selfless mother.

Once we're all seated around the bonfire with warm faces and cold backsides, I excuse myself. "I'll be back in a minute."

I look across the fire at Rory, the orange glow lighting her joyful expression. "Hey, sidekick." She doesn't respond. "Hello? Earth to sidekick."

Still nothing.

I get up, walk around the pit, and position myself right behind her ear. "Rory!" I say, making her jump.

She turns to me with a glare on her face.

"Can you come be my sidekick for a minute? Please?"

She lights up. "Sure! Do we have another mission?"

"Absolutely. And I can't do it without you."

"I figured," she says humbly.

I roll my eyes but let her have her dream. "Let's go."

"Where are we going?" she asks.

"You'll see." I have to string her along. If she knows exactly where we're going, she'd probably turn back.

Once I get close to the ladder, she knows where we're headed.

"What are you doing?" she asks. "I thought you didn't want to look at that stuff anymore."

"I don't. That's why we're here."

"That doesn't make any sense, Asher William McCovey, and you know it."

"What do you mean?" I ask, pretending to be oblivious.

"What are we really doing?" She folds her arms in protest. "Tell me or I'm going back to the fire."

"By yourself in the dark? I doubt it."

She knows I'm right. She's stuck with me.

"Asher! That's mean!"

"Oh come on." I start up the ladder. "You won't regret it. I promise."

"Your promises don't mean anything any more. Remember the time you promised me that Winston would talk if I kissed him?"

I look down at her. "Well. He may not have talked to *you*, but he told me he's hoping to take you out for dinner."

"Ha, ha. Very funny. Focus on your own love life, mister."

"My love life? What do you know about my love life? I mean, my lack of a love life."

"Whatever," she says. "Everybody knows you love Mari."

"What? No, they don't!"

"Do too!" she pushes back.

"Dang it, Dad! Why did he have to tell everyone?" *I knew he would do something like that. Such a dad move.*

"He didn't say anything. I figured it out right after we moved here."

"Nuh-uh."

"Yup. You kicked me and Julia out of your room so you could be alone with her. Then, when we came back later, you were cuddling on the bed. It doesn't take a detective to figure that one out."

"Whoa, whoa, whoa. Knock it off," I tell her. "It wasn't like that. You wouldn't understand."

I don't even understand.

"You didn't say anything to Mari, did you?"

"No! How mean do you think I am?" She waves it off.

"Oh, thank God."

"I only told Julia. She said she would keep it a secret."

"You what? Why would you tell Julia? She's Mari's little sister and has a mouth the size of the Grand Canyon!"

"She's my best friend! Of course I'm going to tell her!"

"You know what?" I say, grasping for some way to get back at her. "I'm not sorry for making you kiss a donkey. In fact, I'm thrilled for you two and hope that you have a long and happy life together."

NO IFS, ANDS, OR BUTS

We walk out of the barn, working together to lug this massive, green chest toward the group. The fire is now reaching for the stars. We wiggle our way through the chairs and drop it down with a **THUNK** next to the firepit. The dust of the ground mixes with the dust from the chest and they dance together, catching the light of the fire.

Mom looks at me with her *"What are you up to?"* look.

"What? It's just a little extra fuel for the fire."

"What kind of fuel?" she asks.

"Some old papers that Grandpa told me to burn," I say, like it's totally normal.

Dad overhears us and jumps in. "Grandpa told you to burn them? Why didn't he just burn them himself?"

"He said he wanted me to have the chance to see them."

"Grandpa said that?" he asks, clearly suspicious.

"Well, kind of. He wrote it in a letter."

"A letter?" His eyes bounce from the chest to me and to the chest again.

"It's not like he sent it from the great beyond."

"It's called heaven," Rory clarifies.

"He left a note for me where he knew I would find it."

"And it has something to do with this chest?" Dad asks.

"It does. He wanted me to see what was in here because I asked him about it a while back."

"So what exactly is it?"

"I could tell you," I pause, adding unnecessary and unappreciated drama, "or we could just burn it."

"Why would we just burn it?" he asks.

"Because it holds dark knowledge of untold powers," I say with my best evil supervillain voice. "Mua-ha-ha-ha."

"Seriously?" says Rory. "Just tell him."

"Okay. But before I do, just remember that Grandpa asked us to burn it all, so no matter what you see in here, it's going in the fire." I lock eyes with Dad.

"Why are you looking at me?" he asks.

"I'm just worried you're going to want to keep it."

"What? Why would you say that?"

"You'll see . . . and hopefully you'll understand. So do you promise it's going in the fire tonight? No ifs, ands, or buts?"

"Ha!" says Julia. "Butts!"

I can't help but laugh.

"Dad?"

"All right. All right. No butts," he says.

"Or ifs or ands."

"Or ifs or ands," he agrees. "Now, are you gonna open it, or should we go to bed and come see if you're still talking in the morning?"

"Okay. Okay. Jeez. You don't like the dramatic flair?"

"I'm kind of burnt out, bud."

"Is that a fire pun?"

"Was yours?" he asks. "Now, either show me what's in there or make me a s'more."

"All right. Here we go."

Rory opens the box before I get a chance, grabs a handful of papers, and chucks them in the fire. "BURN!" she yells. "BURN!"

"Whoa!" yells Mom. "Scary. Where did that come from?"

"It's evil, Mom," she says. "Burn it all!"

Mari crumples them up one by one and throws them into the fire.

Julia makes a few balls and chucks them at me. "Snowball fight!"

One hits me square in the forehead. I pick it up to throw it back, then realize I'm about to throw a projectile at a six year old. Instead, I chuck it at Mari but miss.

"Manny?" I say. "Aren't you gonna get in on the action?"

"I already know what's in there," he says. "I'll let you guys enjoy it."

"You knew about the chest?" I ask, somewhat shocked.

"I live here, amigo. I was with your grandpa from the day he found out he had cancer to the day he died from it. There's not much that happened here over the last few years that I wasn't a part of."

I had never really thought about that. I mean, I knew they were here, but I didn't know how much they were like family.

I look over at Mom and Dad. Dad's reading a paper, and Mom is just staring at the fire. "Mom? Wanna toss some snowballs in the fire?"

"No thank you, sweetheart," she says.

"Dad? Don't you think we should get rid of this stuff? I know Grandpa would be proud of us."

He puts the paper down on his lap, leans his head back, and stares at the stars.

After a brief eternity, he lifts his head to speak. "I had to do *something*."

He stares at the flames for a few seconds.

"What else was I supposed to do?"

Wanting to fix things makes sense. You can't fault a guy for trying, but it's clearly not working. It's time to try something new.

"That's one of the things I love about you, Dad. You want to help people. But grandpa doesn't need your help anymore. He's gone. And as much as that sucks, you still have us. He let go of what happened to him so he could focus on what was really important, and I know he would want you to do the same. The dead don't need you. I need you. Rory needs you. We all need you.

Everything goes quiet except the crackling of the fire.

"We've got two good things going for us," I continue. "First, *you're* still alive, and second, you took the first step."

He glances over at me before turning back to the fire. He stares into the flames and I stare at him.

After a few seconds, he slowly rises from his seat, walks over to the chest, and puts his papers back in. I'm disappointed. I was hoping he would join us in the burning; show another sign that he's moving on in life. If the kids burn it all, he doesn't get to make a statement.

He looks at me, and for a second, he seems to smile. But then he glances over at Rory, then at Mom, and then to the sky before he heads inside.

We look at each other, not sure what to do.

"All righty," Mom finally says. "I guess it's time for bed. Manny, Mari, Julia: I'll drive you home."

I sit there, not ready to leave. Mom goes to get water to put out the fire, and the others start folding up chairs.

"Hey!" I hear Dad's voice from the doorway. "Don't put it out yet."

"We thought you went to bed," says Mom. "Where did you go?"

"I had to get something."

"What's that?" asks Rory, pointing to the bag in his hand.

"It's a bag," he tells her.

"Thanks, Captain Obvious. What's in it?"

Dad smirks, apparently in the mood for some teasing.

"Do you want me to show you?" he asks. "Or should we just burn it?"

He walks over to the fire and opens the chest up again. Then he grabs a huge pile of papers and hands them to me. "Pass these out, will ya?"

Then he pulls an enormous stack of papers out of his bag.

"Here's a big step for ya," Dad says. "On the count of three."

We follow his lead, and together we yell, "ONE! TWO! THREE!" Then we toss our worries into the flames.

THE ASPARAGUS BROKER

The next morning, Manny gathers everyone around and tells us he received a call from a New York produce broker.

"The guy said he had a grower back out on him," Manny tells us, "and he'll buy whatever we can get him in the next four weeks. I told him we can't get him a lot because we don't have any help, but he said to just get him what we can."

"That sounds great!" I say.

"You're right. It does *sound* great."

"Buuuuut," says Dad, knowing there's a catch.

"Well," Manny starts in, "Short US history lesson: when the United States joined NAFTA—"

"What's a NAFTA?" asks Rory.

"Essentially it's an agreement between the US, Canada, and Mexico. It's pretty much each country saying, '*I won't charge you tons of money to sell things in my country if you don't charge me tons of money to sell in yours.*'"

"That's great, right?" I ask. "Is the broker going to sell our asparagus to Mexico?"

"No, amigo. Unfortunately, it hasn't really worked out like that. In Mexico, it only costs sixty-four cents to grow a pound of asparagus. Here in Washington, it costs us a dollar seventy-five per pound. We don't sell to Mexico. Mexico sells to the US."

"How can they grow it that cheap?"

"Things cost less there. In Mexico, you can pay someone a third of what you would have to pay someone here. Cheap labor equals cheap asparagus."

"So what are we supposed to do? We can't sell it for dirt cheap."

"I know, amigo. Trust me, I know. The broker offered us a dollar sixty-five per pound."

"What?" says Dad. "How are we supposed to make any money if we're selling it for less than it costs?"

"Obviously that doesn't work for us," Manny confirms. "I didn't accept the offer. I did, however, tell him I would talk to the boss to see what *would* work for us."

"So what will work for us?" Dad asks.

"Hold on," says Manny. "Before he hung up, he told me he could go higher if we could get him twenty thousand pounds."

"Twenty thousand pounds?" I shout. "How the heck would we do that?"

"That's a great question. Thanks for asking. I did some math. In past years, we've needed one worker for every two acres to keep up with the harvest. If we want twenty thousand pounds, we would need to harvest ten acres. So about half our crop."

"But now we're just back to the same problem we had before," I argue. "Where the heck are we going to get workers?"

Dad's massaging his temples, trying to keep the stress headache away.

"So we need a couple more bodies," he says.

I don't know if he realizes how creepy that sounds.

"Keep in mind," adds Manny, "this only happens if he's willing to pay us what we need."

"Which is what?" asks Dad.

"I recommend we ask for two dollars and eighty-five cents a pound.

"Okay," says Dad, "so that's what we tell him."

"All right," agrees Manny. "I'll give him a call."

"Twenty thousand pounds," I blurt out. "We're going to need a miracle."

I wonder if it would be too forward to call Ms. Carmona. I don't want to seem impatient, but we're running out of time.

"Nobody get too worked up yet," Manny reminds us. "It could still fall through, but just so we all know what's riding on the line here, the contract could get us as much as forty-five thousand dollars profit and, even if we somehow sell just half of the U-pick asparagus, we would make another forty thousand there."

"Wow," I say, "That's a ton of money!"

"It is," Mom says, "and it isn't. Life requires a lot of money. That would be enough to make ends meet for our families, but it wouldn't give us much extra."

"Oh. That sucks."

"But remember," says Mari, taking an inspirational tone. "We've come this far. We're not turning back now. This is the land of opportunity, and this one is sitting right here, waiting for us to take it."

I nod and smile, but my mind is somewhere else. I have to see if Ms. Carmona's found anybody.

"You guys get ready for customers. I'll be right there, but first I want to check in with someone that might be able to help."

I head inside and open up the phone book. It's a giant dictionary-like book that has phone numbers and addresses and images of local businesses. It's like Google for people who don't have the Internet.

It's organized in alphabetical order, but unfortunately everything in Prosser starts with the word *Prosser*, so it takes a couple minutes to locate *Prosser Food and Drug. 509-555-DRUG.*

I dial the number and wait in anticipation. I jump up and down a few times to get the nervous jitters out. It rings and rings and rings. It doesn't go to an answering machine. I'm not sure what to do.

Do I keep waiting? Do I hang up and call back?

A split-second later, a woman picks up.

"Hello," she says, in a singsong voice. "Thank you for calling Prosser Food and Drug. Can you hold please?"

"But I just—" The music starts. "Yes, I'll hold . . . I guess."

At least the on-hold music keeps me entertained. *IIIII've haad the time of my liiiiiiiiiife, and I searrrrched through eeevvvery open dooooooor. Yes, I sweeaar, it's the truuuuuuth, and I owe it all to yooooouuuu.*

I feel like I recognize the song from a movie, but before I can figure it out, a different woman picks up the phone.

"Hi, there. Thanks for holding. What can I do for you?"

"Oh. Hi . . ." For a second, I forget where I called and what I was going to say. "Oh. Uh."

Think. Think. Think. Oh yeah. "Is Annie there?"

Her first name feels weird as it comes out.

"This is she."

HOW MAY I HELP YOU?

"Hi! Ms. Carmona?"

"Yes? Who's this?"

"It's me, Asher. I go to your school. I mean, the school you work at. Do you remember me?"

"Of course I remember you. I'm not *that* old!" she laughs.

"Oh. I didn't mean—"

"I'm just teasing you," she assures me. "I know you didn't mean anything by it."

"Okay, good. I was calling. I mean, I am calling, because I need to ask you something."

"Well, it must be important. I've never had a student call me on the weekend. There's a first time for everything, I guess. Ask away!"

"Um. You know how you said you would look for somebody to help my family?"

"I do. It was pretty recent, as I recall."

"Yeah. Well. I know you're super busy with two jobs, and you probably have an exciting life with friends and every- thing . . ."

"Ha!" she laughs unexpectedly. "I mean, yes. I do lots of

things . . . with my exciting friends . . . in my exciting life."

"I figured," I say, slightly bummed. "Well, I was wondering if you had found anybody yet. A guy in New York called and told us he would buy our asparagus, but we still need a couple of helpers. Like, literally just two."

"I called some folks I know that are sometimes looking for extra work," she says. "But they're busy for the season. It sounds like other farms are having similar problems."

"Oh. I understand."

I'm glad we're not face-to-face so she can't see my disappointment.

"Is there anything else you can think of?" I ask.

"Well, not at the moment . . . and I should probably focus on my work while I'm on the clock."

"I understand."

Ugh. Why did I get my hopes up?

"But—" she continues.

There's a but . . .

"I'll tell you what. After I get off work, I'll call a couple of other school-counselor friends and see if we can figure something out. We might have to look beyond the normal way of doing things, but I have a feeling that's quite all right with you."

"My family is nowhere close to normal, so that's perfect."

She laughs loudly. I yank the phone away to save my eardrum, then inch it back slowly as she continues. "You know there's no such thing as 'normal people,' right?"

I nod my head, and then remember that she can't see me.

"You might find it helpful to know that there are plenty of kids your age, even in our own school, who are dealing with struggles remarkably similar to yours."

"They have to save their family's asparagus farm?" I ask, half joking.

"I was thinking more like our first conversation," she says. "Anger, feeling helpless, being hurt by those we love."

Yeah. That sounds about right.

"You've got a lot on your shoulders, Asher, and you are doing phenomenal. You really are. I have some other kiddos that I'd like you to meet. They're overcoming obstacles every day, finding creative ways to solve problems, and supporting each other through it all. I think you would fit in marvelously. I buy pizza once a month, and we just hang out and chat about life. No pressure, of course."

I take a second to think. I don't want to be known as the kid that hangs out with the counselor all the time, but I *do* love pizza.

"It's not cafeteria pizza, is it?" I ask, just to make sure.

"No," she assures me, "It's from the Pizza Connection right down the street."

"Okay. I'll come on one condition."

"What's that?"

"That my friend, Mari, can come too. She's super marvelous, so it only makes sense to have her there."

"Of course!" she says. "I love Mari. We've had the chance to get to know each other over the years. She is more than welcome. And you're right, she is quite marvelous."

There's a brief pause in the conversation before she says, "Oh wow! I only have six minutes to get this order done."

"Oh okay. Thank you!" I say, feeling like she deserves more than just simple words.

"You're very welcome. Hopefully, we'll have more to celebrate soon. Now, maybe I should get your phone number just in case we come up with a marvelous plan."

"Oh. Good idea. It's 509-555-7282. We just have a house phone and sometimes we're all outside, so if you don't get a hold of someone, just keep trying. Or you can stop by the farm. That might be the easiest. Do you know where it is?"

"I do. Your grandpa could talk the ears off a donkey. I've heard all about the farm."

"Really? Did he come in a lot?"

"He came in quite a bit. He was so sweet. He'd stop by my corner of the store just to say hi."

"What do you do at the drugstore? And are there really drugs there?"

"There are drugs here, but it's the kind your doctor gives you to feel better. I don't work with those, though. I just print the pictures."

DOLLAR OR DOLL-HAIR?

Back outside, everybody is heading toward their stations. Mari and Julia are going to be roadside, waving signs. Rory is going to be "in charge" of the bake sale, but really Mom will keep an eye on her from just a few feet away, where she'll be collecting the money for the asparagus. Dad and Manny will be in the field, helping people if they need it and making sure people don't trample the crop. I'm in charge of the petting zoo because the animals like me the most.

We'll have pigs, goats, a donkey, and a bazillion chickens. I made little bags of food for people to buy if they want to feed the animals. I remember always wanting to do that before it became a chore, so I'm hoping that there are other people who like feeding animals as much as I do . . . or did.

More than anything, I love the idea that somebody will give me money to do my chores. This might be the single greatest idea of all time.

The day starts off slowly, with just a few people trickling in. From what I can see, people are only buying a couple bunches of asparagus at a time. I'm not sure what I was expecting, but I guess I hadn't considered the massive number of customers it would take to sell all this asparagus.

If we're trying to sell at least ten thousand pounds of asparagus and each visitor is only buying two bunches, which is about four pounds, that means we need . . . 2,500 people to come buy asparagus. I don't even know if that many people live within fifty miles of here!

If we stay open twenty-five days out of the next month . . . divide 2,500 by twenty-five . . . we would need one hundred people a day to come up that driveway. Whoa. Even if we're open for ten hours each day, we would need ten people per hour.

So far, I've had two kids come to the petting zoo. They bought a cup of food to feed the goats, so my grand total, so far, is two dollars and fifty cents.

Rory looks like she's having some success. She's either sold a few things, or she's eaten a bunch of sugar by herself.

"Rory! How's it going?" I yell. "You made any sales?"

She turns toward me with big chocolate stains around her lips.

"Yep! I did a buy-one-get-one-free sale. If they buy one, I get one free. So far, it's working great!"

"How much have you made?"

"Um . . ." She looks over at Mom.

Rory shakes her head, then Mom points to their notepad on the table.

Rory looks at it, then turns to me. "I made six dollars and fifty cents!"

"Wow! That's great! Keep up the good work!"

If Rory and I can pull off one hundred dollars a day, that

means that we would need ten less customers per day. That's pretty good when I think of it like that.

After a little while, I start to feel claustrophobic. I'm itching to get out and do something. With some quick thinking, a genius plan comes to mind.

"Hey, Rory!"

"Yeah?" she mumble-yells with a cookie halfway in her mouth.

"Can we switch spots for a bit?"

"No way! You're going to eat my bake sale!"

I'm going to eat your bake sale? Please. I think we all know who the problem is there.

"No," I holler back. "I promise I won't. I mean, I might, but if I do, I'll pay for it."

"I don't know! I like it over here!" she yells, as she leans her head on Mom.

"Please? I'll give you a dollar."

"Like, to buy a cookie or a dollar just for me to keep?"

"Just for you!"

"Really? You promise? You're not saying doll hair, are you, 'cause that won't work on me again."

"No. Dollar. D-O-L-L-A-R. Dollar."

She leans over and says something to Mom, probably checking to make sure I actually spelled *dollar* and not something like *dog poop*. Mom nods her head.

"How long would you want to switch for?" she asks, thinking ahead.

I think for a second, trying to figure out the best way to play this.

"Let's say . . . until I sell five things."

"Okay, but you better be as good a seller as me."

She's so humble. I know I can't promise what she wants, so

I generalize it. "I'll do the best I can, considering the circumstances." And that seems to do the trick.

"Okay. Let's do it," she agrees.

She asks Mom to watch her stuff for the twenty seconds it will take us to switch spots.

"One dollar for entrance, fifty cents for a cup of food," I say to her as we cross paths.

"One dollar for everything at the bake sale, except for the small cookies. Those are only fifty cents, but if the person looks rich, you can ask for more."

Before I get the chance to mention how that's not very ethical, she takes off toward her BFFs, best fried friends, yelling at the top of her lungs, "Hey chickens! Here comes mama! Did ya miss me?"

I walk right up to Mom. "Hey, can you watch my post while I take the quad down to talk to Mari really quick?"

"Asher, you just made a deal with your sister to switch."

"I know. And now I'm making a deal with you."

"That doesn't seem like much of a deal. I watch the bake sale, and you . . ."

"Give you a dollar?" I offer half seriously.

She laughs. "I wish a dollar meant more to me than it does, but it's been quite a few years since a dollar would do much more than buy a candy bar. Besides, you're just going to look around the house for money. That dollar would probably come from *my* dresser."

She has a good point there.

"I'll do an extra chore," I offer.

"Oh yeah? A chore of my choice?" She's smart enough to ask for clarification.

"Sure," I say in haste and reach out my hand for a promise-binding shake. She reaches out and, with a firm grasp, shakes my hand. And only then do I realize I hadn't considered all the possible chores.

"Great!" she says cheerfully. "Tonight, you can clean the bathroom."

"Crap!"

"Exactly," she says, getting in on the McCovey family bathroom puns.

"Mom. Are you serious? The bathroom?" I complain but receive no sympathy.

She rubs it in a little more. "I know how seriously you take promises, so I appreciate you sticking to your word."

"Totally. I am so committed to my word. Thanks a lot."

"Oh, and you better not flip the toilet paper roll over again. You know very well it's supposed to come over the top and not from underneath. We may live on a farm, but that doesn't mean we have to be uncivilized."

"Okay. Okay. Jeez. I never knew people were so passionate about their TP."

I realize I better take advantage of my newfound freedom before Mom adds any stipulations. She never set a time limit, and my time limit with Rory is when I sell five things, which will never happen, so I'm free to enjoy the day . . . until toilet time.

I roll the quad out of the barn, making sure to check the brakes.

"Don't forget to wear your helmet, sweetheart!"

As I give Mom a thumbs-up, I'm forced to do a double take. Rory already has four people at the petting zoo. Maybe cute *does* make a big difference.

MY BEST CHEERLEADER IMPRESSION

It takes me less than a minute to get down the driveway. There, I find Mari waving her sign and Julia lying on the grass with *her* sign over her face.

I come in fast and slam on my brakes . . . too late realizing that it's not funny, considering this is where I almost died.

Mari gives me a sour look and walks over to me. She lifts her sign high in the air for the oncoming traffic to see, then slams it down on my head. The helmet was a good idea.

"Asher! No seas estúpido!" demands Mari.

"Yeah!" I hear from under the sign on the ground. "Don't be stupid!"

"Thanks, Julia. Remember, I already figured that translation out?"

I keep my eyes on Mari for a few reasons but mostly to make sure she doesn't hit me again.

"Why are you down here?" she asks, "Don't you have a job to do?"

"Mom and Rory said they have things covered up there. I thought I'd come down and see how you guys are doing."

"I feel like a high-school cheerleader at a car wash," says

Mari, "except with more clothes on."

"In high school, you'll be sixteen," I say, absentmindedly.

"And when I'm in college, I'll be eighteen," she says. "Anything else obvious you want to point out?"

Soy estúpido.

"Just an observation, I guess. Doesn't high school seem so far away?"

"Only if you think about it a lot. Time seems slow when you feel stuck in it, and then you look back and realize how fast everything passed by. I don't want that to be me. I want to get the most out of every day so I can have a bunch of stories to tell when I'm old."

"Are you sure you're just twelve? You're too mature. Have you checked your birth certificate? Maybe you're like thirteen, or fourteen . . . or sixteen?"

"I'm twelve. It's just that boys are less mature than girls at this age, so that's probably why it seems that way."

I wish I had something to say back, but I've heard of this boy-versus-girl-maturity thing before. I just wish it wasn't being used against me at the moment.

I change the subject. "Okay, wise one. How do we pick up the pace here and get more folks through the gate?"

"There's not much more we can do down here," she says.

"We're doing all we can!" says the voice under the sign. "What do you want us to do? Ride around town yelling at people?"

"Would you be willing to do that?"

"No!" they say in unison.

Mari elaborates. "Then everyone will think we're crazy."

"And we want to be crazy in private!" adds Julia.

"Ha. I know how that feels," I say. "Hey. Do you guys know if the broker accepted our offer?"

Mari shakes her head. "No. Papi said he had to leave a message, and he's been out in the field since then."

"Do you think he would come tell us if he got a call?"

"Probably. Unless he's really busy, but from what I've seen so far, I doubt that's the case."

"I'm gonna go find him. I need to know."

I start the engine and slowly engage the throttle.

"Okay!" she yells. "Let us know if you find anything out!"

"Will do!" I call back. And I take off in search of Manny.

I find him a ways up the road. He's out in the field with a young family: a mother, a father, a young boy, and a little girl.

They look like our family five or six years ago.

I start my way toward him, walking at a brisk pace. He sees me fifty yards away and gives a single wave.

When I reach him, he introduces me to the family.

"Asher, this is Brandon and his wife, Rebeka. And these are their two kids, Judah and Poppy."

"Poppy like the flower?" I ask.

"Yep," the man says. "It's short for Penelope."

"And I know where Judah is from," I say, thinking my limited Bible knowledge is going to impress them. "Same place as mine."

I squat down to get at the boy's level. "Did you know that you and I were brothers in the Bible? Judah and Asher?"

"I think they were technically half brothers," he replies.

Brat.

"He knows his Bible, huh?" I say, turning toward the couple.

"I'm a pastor," says Brandon, "so I guess that's mostly my fault. We just moved here to lead the Messiah Lutheran Church, right down the road. I practice my sermons at home, and he picks up on things pretty quickly. I'm glad he loves scripture, but I realize that it's kind of odd for his age. We'll see what God does with it."

I nod my head and look down at Judah, then I remember what I came for.

"Hey. Sorry to interrupt. Manny, I was just wondering if you got a call back from the broker yet?"

"No, I haven't felt any vibrating on my butt."

"That's an interesting way to put it."

He reaches back and slaps his right butt cheek.

"Where's my flip phone?" he asks, slightly panicking. He looks around, trying to remember where he's been. "It could be anywhere out here."

Rebeka chimes in, "Do you remember the last place you had it?"

"I don't remember using it since this morning, but that doesn't mean I didn't have it out here."

"Wherever you used it this morning is definitely the best place to start," she says. "Then go from there."

"I don't have time for a wild-goose chase."

"I have a few minutes to spare," I offer. "I can help."

"Really? Could you go ask Mari to look next to my bed and see if it's there?"

"Sure. You bet. If he texted, can we read it?"

"Sure, if you can figure out my password." He winks at me.

"So that's pretty much a no," I say. Then I wink at him and race down the driveway.

This time, I come to a nice, gradual stop next to Mari and Julia.

"Hey!" I yell, then turn off the engine. "There. That's better. Your dad wants to know if you can look for his phone next to his bed. He can't find it, and he thinks he might have left it there."

"He hasn't had his phone this whole time?" she asks.

"I guess not."

"So the guy could have called already?"

"I guess so."

"Well then. I'll go look for it," she says, as she starts off toward her house.

"Great! Julia and I will hang out here."

"Don't leave me with him!" yells Julia.

"Hey, what did I ever do to you?"

"I've heard stories," she says, all mysteriously.

"What do you mean? I thought we were friends?"

"Rory said to expect the unexpected, so I'm expecting it."

"Don't believe half the things she says. She has quite the imagination."

"She said you would say that."

Her look of suspicion grows. She takes off up the road toward their house, and Mari is forced to chase after her.

"Okay then," I yell, as they run away.

Then I lower my voice. "I guess I'll just hang out by myself."

I pick up a sign and do my best high-school-cheerleader-at-a-car-wash impression. Who knew I could kick my foot up so high? I impress someone driving by so much that they honk their horn and whistle at me. I hold up the sign and wave some more.

They may not have turned down our driveway, but at least I feel better about myself.

I try to do a little sign spinning to drum up some more attention. I toss it up in the air just as a Suburban drives by. The wind takes hold of it, spins it around, then slams it into my face.

The taste of blood hits my tongue quick. I suck it up, figuratively and literally.

I'M WAITING

"He called! He called! He called!"

Julia comes running down the road, jumps in the ditch to escape a car, then hops back up and continues toward me. Mari is running but still a ways behind.

"He called, he called, he called!" Julia shouts as she runs right past me.

When Mari gets close enough to hear me, I yell to her, trying to find out what she knows. She waits until she gets closer to answer. "We just saw that there was a missed call from New York, and there was a message, but we can't get into his phone."

I jump on the quad. "I'll drive it up to him and then let you know what he says."

I find Manny on the road, heading my way. As I get closer, I hold up the phone so he knows we found it.

He stops and steps off to the side as I pull up.

He must still be having flashbacks of my run-in with death. Dang.

I hand him the phone and do my best to wait patiently as he unlocks it. He holds it to his ear, and I strain to hear the muffled voice on the other end.

I have so many emotions churning inside me that there's no point in trying to figure out which ones they are.

Manny shakes his head, and I freeze, wondering what he just heard.

Is it bad? What's happening?

Finally, he hangs up the phone. After sticking it in his back pocket, he takes off his hat and wipes his brow. Then he squats down, resting his arms on his thighs, and shakes his head again.

"Soooo?"

"Not to put any pressure on you or anything, but we really need you to find us some help, 'cause we have twenty thousand pounds of asparagus to deliver."

"We do?" I yell. "We got the contract?" I dance around crazier than a mating ostrich.

"We got the contract," he says. "We did. Now we just have to fill it."

"Woo-hoo!" I continue. "Something went right!"

"Let's not get ahead of ourselves. It could still go wrong unless we find some help quick. But again, no pressure."

He seems nervous. Maybe I should be more nervous.

"I'm going to go tell Mari and Julia. They wanted me to let them know."

When I relay the message, Julia is as excited as I am. Mari has to be like her dad and point out the obvious.

"We still need at least two workers. Do we know how that's going to happen?"

"I have a friend who told me I could ask for help whenever I need it, so I did."

"Asking for help is different than actually getting help," says Mari, trying to bring me back down to Earth.

"I know," I assure her . . . and I *do* know. I just want to ignore that minor detail for now.

I continue. "I really believe she'll come through for us. She's just busy until this afternoon."

"You have another friend that's a girl?" asks Mari, distracting me from the issue at hand.

"I guess so," I say, stretching the truth.

"Oh," she says.

"Is that okay?" I ask, knowing I won't get the answer I want.

"Of course. I just didn't know."

Then Julia has to add her input. "Is she your giiiiiiirrrrrrr-rrlfriend? Are you going to maaaaaaaaaarry her and kiiiiiiiiss her and looooooooooove her and—"

Mari cuts her off before I can. "Knock it off!"

"Wait a second," Julia continues as she stares me down. "I thought you liked—"

Mari cups her hands over Julia's giant mouth.

I look at Mari, who's giving Julia a wicked stare.

"No, Julia," I tell her. "She's a little too old for me. Besides, I'm waiting until I'm sixteen to date."

Mari whips her head around. "You are?"

"That's always been my plan. What's the rush, right?"

She looks at me suspiciously. "Right. What's the rush?"

Then Julia hijacks the moment with another one of her ridiculous questions. "What if nobody wants to be your girlfriend when you're sixteen?"

"Then I guess I'll keep waiting until she's ready."

HAPPY TO HELP

When you're arriving somewhere late, say, for example, your job after a couple hours of joyriding, there's no smooth way to come in unnoticed, especially if you're riding a loud machine.

I pull up, expecting an angry mom and sister, but to my surprise, Rory's back at the bake sale table and Mom is doing her cashier thing.

"Who's watching the petting zoo?" I ask.

"Nobody," says Mom.

Rory clarifies, "After you were gone for a long time, we realized you were useless and that we didn't really need anyone over there."

"Hey!" I say in protest.

Mom gently scolds Rory. "Rory, I didn't say he was useless. I said the job was unnecessary."

"Same thing." Rory rolls her eyes.

"No, that's very different," Mom tells her, then she turns to me.

"You're not useless, sweetheart. Far from it. I think we can handle the petting zoo from here, though. You can keep helping with whatever you were doing."

"Great! That reminds me. Has Manny come and talked to you?"

Mom shakes her head. "No. Was he supposed to?"

"I don't know. I can just tell you. Manny got a call back from the guy in New York, and we have a deal!"

Rory gets excited.

Mom gets spiritual.

"Wow," she says. "God must have a plan."

"I've got one too," I say. "Can you ask God to give me a chance first before you give him all the credit? Mine's already in the works."

"Oh really," she says. "When will we know if your plan is happening?"

"We should know by the end of the day."

"Wow. That soon?" she says.

"Yep!" I say confidently, feeling much less confident inside. "It could be any time now, really. In fact, I'm going to open the door to the house a little so you can hear the phone if it rings."

"Okay," says Mom. "Does that mean you're going somewhere again?"

"I'm going to help Dad and Manny. They're getting everything ready for us to start picking tomorrow."

Manny, Dad, and I spend the next couple of hours getting everything ready. Among other super exciting things, we section out the field, fix up the harvesting containers we'll carry on our backs, get the stacking bins ready to go on the tractor and, of course, finally fix the tractor engine. This consists of Dad handing Manny tools while he's under the tractor and me giving him water and a rag to clean off his face when he needs it. I'm so helpful.

I decide to go see if Ms. Carmona has called, but before I head over there, I rub some grease on my hands, cheeks, and forehead so it looks like I actually helped. Then I decide to throw on Grandpa's cowboy hat and his old coat to see if I can fool anybody.

I walk up to the bake sale table, stop next to a customer looking at the treats, and hang my head low so my brim covers my face. I change my voice to sound like an old man and, last second, randomly decide to pull the ends of my sleeves over my hands.

"Hello, ma'am," I say in my manliest voice. "I'd like some asparagus, but I don't have any hands."

I have a hard time not laughing at my stupidity.

"Well, sir," Mom says, "You are in luck. My daughter just picked a few bunches, and we'd be happy to sell you those."

"Oh really?" I say, finding it hard to keep the voice going. "That would be mighty fine of ya. Can you tell me what shade of green they are? I can only eat asparagus that is lime green. If it's too dark, it tears apart my insides, if you know what I mean."

"I think I do, sir. If my son were here, he could go get some, but I have a feeling he's out getting into trouble."

"Or smooching with his girlfriend," says Rory.

"Hey!" I break out of character and pull off the hat. "What the heck? Why would you say that? Why would you think I'm doing something wrong, Mom? And I don't even have a girlfriend! What the heck was that about?"

"Oh, Asher," Mom answers, trying not to laugh. "I can't believe it's you. You were so convincing."

Rory joins in with a weird, high-pitched old-fashioned drawl. "Oh yes, Asher. However, did you trick us? I'm so embarrassed."

A third voice joins in. "I knew it was you because I could see you from the side, so maybe that doesn't count. It was pretty funny, though."

I look up to see who's talking.

"Oh! Ms. Carmona! Hi! Wait, you saw that?"

She nods. "I did. It was great. You should consider joining the school play. I hear they're doing *Oklahoma!* this year. You could be a gun-slingin' cowboy falling in love with a beautiful farm girl."

"I'll pass," I say, slightly embarrassed. Then I crack that door back open just a little. "Although I might consider joining if any of my friends are doing it."

Like Mari.

"Well, great!" she says. "You know what else is amazing?"

"Sugaaarrrr!" yells Rory.

I look over at her. She's like a can of Coke somebody shook up: full of sugar and ready to explode.

"Sugar is definitely great," Ms. Carmona laughs, "in moderation. But this is even better."

"Did you find anybody to help?"

"I did!" she squeals.

"You did? Woo-hoo!" I rejoice, running around the barnyard. "Thank you, thank you, thank you, thank you!"

"You're quite welcome," she says. "I found a lot of helpers, in fact!"

"Wait, what? What does that mean? How many?"

"Maybe . . . like forty?"

My jaw drops.

"What are we going to do with forty people? And how did you find so many?"

"They're not all going to be here at the same time. Everybody in town loved your grandparents, so it ended up being relatively easy to find folks once I started asking them for just a day of their time."

"Works for me!"

Before I know it, I'm giving her a big hug. Rory better not tell anybody.

"So how exactly is this going to work?" I ask, taking a step back.

"It's the old divide-and-conquer method. You know . . . many hands make light work? Teamwork makes the dream work? That kind of stuff. We may not have a lot around here, but we always have each other's backs."

"Wow. Really? I didn't think this kind of thing happened except in books and movies!"

"Yeah," she says. "This place is pretty special."

"I'm starting to see that. No wonder Grandma and Grandpa loved it here."

"We hope you guys love it here too," she says with a humongous smile. "We're so happy to have you as part of our community."

"We're happy to be here!"

This is so crazy.

"Do I know anybody who's coming?" I'm curious to find out what type of person signs up for this kind of thing.

"Some you do, some you don't. Starting everything off tomorrow, Ms. Mitchell and I will be here in the morning and then a sweet young couple from the church down the street." She pulls a list from her bag to check the rest of the names.

"You and Ms. Mitchell are gonna come pick asparagus?" My eyes go wide just thinking about how my teacher is going to get down in the dirt to help my family.

She shrugs at my question. "Sure. Why not? We're quick learners."

"What the what?" I say, feeling grateful and confused at the same time. "But why?"

She looks at me like my question is ridiculous. "You asked for help, that's why. You'd be amazed at what a bunch of educators can do. When it comes to helping our students, there's not much that will stand in our way."

"Does that mean that there are other teachers coming too?"

"All the sixth-grade teachers, PE, music, me of course, the custodian, the principal, and vice principal. Oh, and a few PTSA members. That's just the middle school."

"Holy cow! All these people signed up to help us?"

"Your grandparents spent their whole lives doing exactly what these people are doing for you. They were always there for us, and we're happy to be here for you guys. This ain't our first rodeo, cowboy."

I look at Grandpa's cowboy hat and brush some hay off his jacket. My fingertips hang out of the too-long sleeves, and my small frame barely takes up any space where his strong shoulders used to fill.

IF YOU'RE INTO THAT SORT OF THING

After Ms. Carmona leaves, I look for Dad and Manny. I find them test-driving the tractor behind the barn. It seems to be working pretty well. I think all tractors smoke a bit.

I wave, signaling them to shut it down .

As soon as the sound dies off, I relay the good news. "We have helpers!" I finish it with a big "YEE-HAW!"

"That's amazing!" Dad celebrates with high fives.

"Way to go, bromigo! Nice work!"

"How many?" asks Dad.

"And who?" adds Manny.

"Like forty people," I tell them, "but I'm not sure who they all are."

This brings the celebration to a halt.

Dad delivers the obvious follow-up question: "So we have way too many workers, and we have no idea who they are."

"Well, I know who's coming tomorrow, but after that, it's, like, people from all over town. A few different people each day."

"Who's coming tomorrow?" Dad asks.

"My teacher and the school counselor are coming in the morning."

"Seriously? Why would they do that?"

"To get rich, of course," I say sarcastically.

His eyes widen, probably wondering what I promised them.

"How much do we have to pay these people?" he asks, looking like he's dreading the answer.

"I'm joking. They're not asking to be paid. It sounds like most of these people knew Grandma and Grandpa and just want to help," I assure him.

"Are you sure? Nobody helps just for the heck of it."

"We did just move here," I point out. "So we don't really know anything about these people besides that they're offering to help us when we need it the most. So maybe we should just be grateful and go with it."

"Sounds wise," says Manny.

"Dad?"

Manny and I look at him, waiting for his response.

"I just don't get it." He shakes his head.

"I don't think you have to," I tell him. "That's the beauty of people being kind just to be kind. It doesn't have to make sense!"

———

Later that night, we gather around for another bonfire. We sit back in the camping chairs and put our feet up on the rocks around the pit. I take my shoes off, and my socks steam as they warm. They smell amazing.

Mom counts the money for the day and gives us the total.

"We were hoping to make around sixteen hundred dollars today," she begins. "Now that's just an average we're shooting for. There might be days that are better and days that are worse."

That sounds like a setup for a letdown.

"With that said," she continues, "we sold one thousand and seventy dollars worth of asparagus."

"Ahhh, man," I moan. "That's it? All that work?"

"Now hold on, whiny-pants," she says. "That's just the asparagus. Don't forget that we had a couple other side projects going on. I'm not sure exactly how we're going to continue them at such a high level, but Rory's bake sale sold two hundred and twelve dollars and fifty cents worth of treats, and her idea to put a tip jar out got her another seventeen dollars and thirty-eight cents. And we can't forget the petting zoo, where Asher came up with a great idea to sell food so people can feed our animals for us."

"Some hit it was," I say, thinking of the two dollars and fifty cents I made this morning.

"Actually, once Rory got over there and wouldn't let people ignore her, we had quite a few folks visit the animals. And people weren't just buying one cup of food. Most of them were buying three, four, or five. People paid us so they could feed our animals the food we would feed them anyway. Really a creative idea, Asher."

"Well thanks, I guess." I'll take a compliment whenever I can get one.

"So from that, we pulled in a whopping two hundred and sixty dollars."

"What? Are you serious?" My head swivels between Mom and Rory. "You weren't even over there when I came back. How did you pull that off?"

"If you're cute enough," she says, "people will give you their money like they don't even want it. It's pretty great."

"That's weird, but at this point, I'll take it."

She smiles and tries to bat her eyelashes, but it ends up

looking like there's something stuck in her eye that she can't get out.

"So what's the total for the day, then?" I ask.

"Well," Mom says, "it's not exactly what we were shooting for, but it's pretty close. Our total comes out to one thousand five hundred and fifty-nine dollars and eight-eight cents."

"Wow!" I blurt out, "That's not bad! It's only our first day, and we're already that close to our daily goal?"

"Maybe I can charge a little more at my bake sale," says Rory.

"And we have our helpers starting tomorrow, which will get us going on that ten acres," I remind them.

"And we don't even have to pay them!" adds Dad. "How crazy is that?"

"I don't want to jinx it"—I knock on a piece of wood—"but this kind of looks like things are coming together. It's only the first day, sure, but even a 'realist' like myself can find a lot of reasons to be optimistic."

"Sure. If you're into that sort of positive thinking mumbo-jumbo," says Dad.

"None of that!" I tell him. "Good things are happening, and there's no denying it."

"Okay. Okay," says Dad, as he gives me a salute and a smile. "I was just joking. I'm totally on board. We will follow your lead, Captain Optimistic."

"Yeah. About that. If it's okay with you, maybe I could just go back to being your sidekick for a while."

He nods his head in thoughtful consideration.

"Okay then," he says. "I owe you that much. I'll work my butt off to be your superhero again."

Rory jumps up and down. "I love you, Super Daddy!" she blurts out in her high-pitched squeal. Her grin stretches from ear to ear.

"I love you too, sweetheart," he says, with a smile that warms better than the fire.

"Can we do this again next year?" she asks.

"What?" Mom responds. "Run a U-cut farm and rely on strangers to harvest our fields? I'm gonna go with a big NO on that one."

"But maybe we can hire people for half of it," suggests Rory, "and then do the U-cut farm by ourselves, so it's not *as* crazy!"

"I don't know, sweetheart. We'll have to talk about it more when the time comes."

"That means *no*, doesn't it?"

"It's not a *no*. It's a *wait and see*. Life has been a little crazy, and Mommy needs some time to think about other things, but I promise I will consider it if you let Mommy get through this next month first, okay?"

"Okay, Mommy. Pinkie swear?"

"Don't do it!" I yell. "She's a promise breaker!"

Rory holds out her pinkie. "No, I'm not!"

"Are too!"

"Mom cooked my chicken!"

"You promised you'd stay calm, but you freaked out!"

"Because they killed Sunshine!"

"We better call it a night," says Mom. "It's been a long day. And you . . . " She focuses her attention on me. "Speaking of promises. You still owe me a clean bathroom."

"Ha, ha!" laughs Rory.

"Whatever," I tell her. "At least I keep my promises."

"You guys ate Sunshine!" she yells.

"We did," I confirm. "And she was delicious."

EPILOGUE

After that, things took off! We met people from all around the area and heard heartwarming and hilarious stories from people who knew Grandpa and Grandma.

Ms. Mitchell and Ms. Carmona were amazing. If I worked as much as they do, I wouldn't want to spend my weekend cutting asparagus, but I guess that's why they're teachers. They think about others more than themselves.

The young couple that came to help the first day turned out to be Brandon and Rebeka, the pastors from Messiah Lutheran.

Then we had some guys from Grandpa's Kiwanis club, a couple of his fishing buddies, and folks from the drugstore, including Ms. Carmona again!

The sixth-grade teachers helped on Saturday and the principals, music, gym, and art teachers came on Sunday.

Members from Grandma and Grandpa's church came on Monday, Tuesday, and Wednesday, then the city council members came on Thursday.

Some of their farming friends came Friday.

That weekend, there were employees from Grandpa's

favorite bakery, Toasty Buns; the owner of his favorite restaurant, Rajeev's Chicken and Churros; and the folks from Dutch Brothers Coffee.

After that, the Fraternal Order of Downwinders came. They invited me to join them on their mission to remind people of the dangers of big government. I passed.

Then we had the Horse Heaven Sportsmen Society, Northwest Farm Supply, and the Chevy dealership where Grandpa bought his truck a million years ago.

That weekend, we had high-school football players and leaders from the Boys and Girls Club. Apparently Grandpa volunteered there. They quoted him as saying, "If I don't play young, I won't stay young." It worked as well as it could, I believe.

Monday and Tuesday, we had nurses from the hospital where Grandpa had his treatments. One was a guy named Graham. I don't think I've ever seen a man-nurse before. He said it's great for meeting the ladies. I told him I already had that covered.

Thursday was the last day, since we needed to let the rest of the asparagus go to seed for next year. The helpers were from Grandpa's bank. I guess he had a safe-deposit box with some interesting things in it. Among them there were four envelopes. Each had a kid's name on it and a handwritten note. Mine read:

Asher,

Your grandma and I wanted to leave you some money for college. I'm not gonna lie. Our treasure is in heaven, so we don't have much. I asked my friend at the bank to give me some stock ideas, and I just went with the one that was in Washington. Why not support the local economy, right? It's a win-win. Hold on to it for a while. Hope-

fully it helps when you're ready to head off to university. If it doesn't turn out to be worth much, please buy something to make yourself happy. Just know we tried.

Lots of love,
Grandpa and Grandma

All four envelopes had a stock certificate inside. Each one listed the purchase price as a dollar and fifty cents per share for fifty shares!

That would be seventy-five dollars for each of us, which is awesome, but not enough for college. Then my dad told me that's how much Grandpa paid for them and that I should look them up to see if they've grown in value. So I checked, and sure enough, now each share is worth thirty-four dollars! That's $1,700! We're rich!

He reminded me that the price could go down, but I choose to dream big. I've got no reason not to.

He also explained that when you own a stock, you actually own an itty-bitty piece of the company. So now I can tell people I'm a business owner. Unfortunately, it's a boring online bookstore in Seattle named after the Amazon river. Random. Why would you want to buy books from Seattle when you can get them for free at the library, right here in Prosser?

It doesn't seem like a business idea that'll work long term, but who knows? Crazier things have happened. Maybe in a few years, if my company does well, we'll all be college-bound bazillionaires.

I wonder where Mari wants to go to school. I can be flexible.

A NOTE ON THE REAL HANFORD

The newspaper articles used in this story are real but shortened for the flow of the book.

In 1943, the Manhattan Project chose Hanford, Washington, as the best location to build a nuclear reactor for manufacturing enough plutonium to build an atomic bomb. The government took the land from the farmers and tribal nations. Unfortunately, those who were forced to move downstream were unintentionally placing their families in a death trap.

Nearly forty-five thousand workers were brought in to work at Hanford but were never given any information about what they were doing. If I found out that I was misled into helping to kill or injure thousands of innocent people, I think that could have just as much of a devastating effect on a soul as Grandpa's cancer had on his bones.

The plutonium produced at Hanford was used to make a bomb, nicknamed Fat Man, that they dropped on Nagasaki, Japan on August 9, 1945. Just three days earlier, the US dropped the first nuclear bomb, nicknamed Little Boy, on Hiroshima, Japan. The bombs ended the war, but they also took the lives of nearly two-hundred-thousand people, including the elderly, women, and children.

Production of plutonium grew even more moving into the Cold War. There were eventually nine nuclear reactors along the Columbia River, all of which were decommissioned in the 1960s.

Downwinders are real. When thousands of them tried to sue, the government left them waiting for decades, delaying the trial repeatedly until many of the Downwinders ran out of money. The government paid lawyers $100 million in taxpayer dollars to deny any wrongdoing and keep these families from getting the help they needed. They spent another $40 million on studies to determine the effects of the fallout.

In 2000, the federal government agreed to pay Hanford *employees* between $2,500-$250,000 depending on how much they were affected. However, it was nearly impossible to claim the money and, by 2005, only five percent of employees had received any compensation. Additionally, the government still refused to settle with the Downwinders.

Later, the government granted $100 million to clean up the Hanford site but still offered nothing to Downwinders. That amount would turn out to be almost nothing, as government expenses for cleanup are now expected to reach $100 *billion*.

In 2005, one year before this fictional story takes place, one Downwinder with thyroid cancer was awarded $227,508, and another was awarded $317,251. These two victories opened up opportunities for other Downwinders and, based on the amounts of radiation they were exposed to, they were awarded between $10,000 and $150,000. Unfortunately, this amount doesn't come close to covering the costs of their medical and legal bills.

As of the writing of this book, there is still radioactive material leaking out of the Hanford nuclear plant. While state and federal laws say that leaking tanks must be pumped immediately, or as soon as possible, these tanks aren't scheduled to be cleaned out for another twenty years. Meanwhile, they leak approximately eight hundred gallons of nuclear waste every year. While nobody is in immediate danger, Hanford remains the most contaminated site in the western hemisphere and some spots will remain radioactive for *thousands* of years.

A FICTION STORY WITH VERY REAL PROBLEMS

One very real issue highlighted in this story is the inability of US farms to get US workers to do manual labor. Because these farmers can't find Americans to do the work, even for good money, they have to hire migrant workers. If you go through the correct route, it's legal, and it works out for most, even though there are still plenty of people abusing the system and migrants. If the government gets backed up and can't process the paperwork, it leaves farms, like the one in our story, with nobody to do the work. Part of my inspiration for this book came from a story I saw on YouTube called *Oregon Produce Farm Gives 5,000 People Free Asparagus*. I encourage you to look it up.

Did you know over 50 percent of the fruits and vegetables you eat are picked by legal migrant workers? Think about that next time you hear somebody complaining about immigrants.

As you can see from the example in this book, some of our government systems make it very difficult for farmers to turn a profit. Because we can get our produce cheaper from Mexico, our own government has "accidentally" put US farms in jeopardy.

Finally, I'd just like to speak to the idea of anger. Asher, his dad, and his grandpa don't really exist, but they all exist as different parts of who I am, and who I want my son and me to become. As I grow older, I admit I find myself more bitter about the world and everything I perceive as "wrong" with it. This book was a way to view anger from both angles of the father-son dynamic. This allowed me to look at complicated subjects from an outsider perspective, where I could see things more clearly than I ever have before. Take the time to look at life from other people's perspectives. You won't regret it.

That's all for now. Until next time, thank you for taking the time to read my book. I hoped it would reach you. I'm so glad it did.

Michael Hertzog

A NOTE ON CONTEXT CLUES

Authors want you to be able to read through a book smoothly, without the need for starting and stopping. When you come upon a word that you don't know, it interrupts this flow. Because of this, they often include information around a word that can help you figure it out. When you were younger, your books often included pictures to help you figure out the meaning of these words. As you begin to read larger, more challenging books, the pictures go away and you are left to figure out what these words mean on your own.

In the next chapter, I have provided a glossary for many of the words that I thought might be challenging for some readers. But I have left others for you to interpret through **context clues** as well, as this is a very important skill needed to read fluently and still know what's going on. Please do use the glossary whenever needed to help you fully understand the word choice in this book, but at the same time, push yourself to figure out what some of the words mean by the **clues**, such as the other words or events that are around it, also known as the **context**.

Example:

You may have already heard about this idea of context clues, but just in case you haven't or need a refresher, here's a clear example from chapter two. They won't always be this obvious, but I hope this will show you what I mean.

"Four easy payments of $19.95?" he complained. "Do they really expect people to fall for that hogwash?"

This was one of the rhetorical questions he liked to ask.

"*Rhetorical* means that you're not supposed to answer it," he informed me. "You're just supposed to think about it."

Here I used Grandpa's dialogue to explain what this complicated word, *rhetorical,* means. I did it this way so that you don't have to stop your flow of reading and you can continue enjoying the book, while also being informed of a new word for your ever-growing lexicon. Lexicon means your personal collection of vocabulary words you understand. See what I did there?

Like I said, not all of the context clues will be this obvious, but when there's a word you don't know, I implore you, or beg you, to take me up on this (See! I did it again! I can't stop!). It will push your reading to the next level.

Thanks for reading this and I hope it helps in some small way.

All the best,
Michael

GLOSSARY

Home Is Where the Hurt Is

assure (uh-SHOOR): let somebody know that things will be all right

muffled (MUFF-uhl): to cover something in order to quiet it

muster (MUSS-ter): to gather or collect something

scoff (skoff): to mock or speak to unkindly

We're Farmers Now

aurora borealis (uh-ROAR-uh bor-ee-AL-iss): swirls of red, green or purple lights in the sky, usually near the northern or southern poles of the Earth

contraption (kun-TRAP-shun): a gadget or device

hogwash (HAWG-wash): nonsense, worthless

harsh (harsh): physically or emotionally painful, uncomfortable

Another Reason to Whine

fundamentals (fun-duh-MEN-tulz): the essential or necessary parts

manure (muh-NOOR): poop, especially of animals

beeline (BEE-line): a direct route traveled quickly

<u>Nice Running Into You</u>

quad (kwod): a motorcycle with four big tires

throttle (THROT-l): a lever, pedal, or handle for controlling the speed of a vehicle

pelt (pelt): repeatedly hitting someone or something

instinct (IN-stingkt): a natural response to do something

demise (dih-MIZE): death or ending

contorted (kun-TOR-tid): twisted or bent

sheepish (SHEE-pish): embarrassed from having done something wrong or foolish

de nada (day-NAH-duh): Spanish for "you're welcome"

<u>A Warm-ish Welcome</u>

vivid (VIV-id): super bright and intense color or light

papi (PAW-pee): Spanish for "dad" or "daddy"

estúpido (ess-TOO-pee-doh): Spanish for "stupid"

abuelo (ah-BWAY-loh): Spanish for "grandpa"

amigocho (ah-mee-GO-choh): Spanish for "buddy"

obituary (oh-BICH-you-air-ee): a notice of the death of a person, often in a newspaper

thyroid (THAYH-roid): a gland near the windpipe and right below the Adam's apple

Downwinder (down-WIN-der): a person who is downwind of a smell or other airborne particles

displace (dis-PLAYS): push out of one's normal area

precede (pree-SEED): come before

acre (AY-ker): a common measurement of land area; one square mile is the same as 640 acres

fallout (FALL-out): particles that come from the atmosphere and land on the Earth, usually from explosions, eruptions, forest fires, or nuclear explosions

American Immigration Council (Uh-MAIR-uh-kin im-ih-GRAY-shun KOUN-sull): an organization that supports immigrants coming to the United States and opposes racist or closed-minded immigration policy

plaster (PLAS-ter): attach something to

abrazo (ah-BRAH-zoh): Spanish for "hug"

My Shadow-self

muy (MOO-wee): Spanish for "very"

adios, amiga (AH-dee-ohs ah-MEE-gah): Spanish for "bye, (female) friend"

hasta luego (AHS-tah luh-WAY-go): Spanish for "see you later"

muchacho (moo-CHAH-cho): a Spanish general term for "boy"

mounting (MOUN-ting): increasing or growing

intriguing (in-TREE-ging): interesting

Here Fishy Fishy

forearm (FOHR-arm): the part of the arm between the elbow and the wrist

tackle box (TAK-uhl bahx): a box where fishermen keep their lures and bait

genuine (JEN-yoo-in): real, true, original

dejected (dee-JEK-tid): sad or depressed

imprinting (IM-prin-ting): when something leaves a mark

skin tag (skin-tayg): a small growth of skin that hangs off the body

Father-Son Time

interrogate (in-TAIR-uh-gait): to ask questions forcefully

fifth amendment (FIFTH uh-MEND-ment): a part of the constitution that says one doesn't have to answer questions in court if they might get oneself in trouble

snark (snark): saying something rudely or with attitude

philosophical (fil-uh-SOF-i-kull): thinking and discussing truths about life and meaning

Sliver of the River

startling (STAR-tl-ing): surprising, sometimes in a scary way

execute (EK-si-kyoot): in this case, it means to accomplish something

Suppertime

pointedly (POIN-tid-lee): said in a very direct way

rafter (RAF-ter): board that holds up a roof

propping (PROP-ping): holding up so something doesn't fall

gritted (GRIT-ted): grinded

TGIF

unhinged (un-HINJD): out of control

sí, comprendo (see kom-PREN-doh): Spanish for "yes, I understand"

hasta la noche (ah-stuh la NO-chay): Spanish for "see you tonight"

<u>Baggage</u>

Finnish (FIN-ish): somebody from Finland

measly (MEE-zlee): a small amount, or not enough

inexplicable (in-ex-PLICK-uh-bull): not able to be explained

acknowledge (ak-NOL-ij): to admit that something is real or true

dormant (DOOR-munt): resting, like a volcano that hasn't erupted in a long time but can at any time

spewed (spyood): to throw up vomit or let angry words flow out of one's mouth

molten (MOLE-ten): something turned into liquid by super heating

engulf (en-GULF): to swallow up or surround

<u>Fragile</u>

convulsion (kun-VULL-shun): an uncontrollable shaking of the body

skeptical (SKEP-ti-kull): doubting that something is true

<u>Hide and Seek</u>

composure (kum-PO-zhur): self-controlled, calmness

strain (strayn): try your hardest

naïve (ny-eve): having a lack of experience or wisdom

chastise (CHAS-tize): to discipline with words or punish

Seek and Find

savore (SAY-vor): enjoy one's senses, usually a delicious taste

musty (MUS-tee): having an old, moldy smell

chipper (CHIP-per): a positive, energetic attitude

scold (skold): loudly or unkindly blaming someone for doing something wrong

cascading (kas-KAY-ding): pouring or flowing through or over something else

nuclear reactor (NEW-clee-er ree-ACT-er): a place where nuclear reactions are used to create heat, which is then used to create power

Information Overload

furrow (FER-row): scrunching up or wrinkling

carcass (KAR-kuss): a dead body

contemplate (kon-tem-play-ting): thinking deeply about something

Winner Winner

reverberation (re-verb-er-AY-shun): multiple echoes after a sound has stopped

pose (poze): to present something, such as a question

A Cuss Word

precise (pre-SISE): being exact

seizure (SEE-zhur): a sudden attack of a disease such as epilepsy, often includes shaking

Who's Ready for Secrets?

mimic (MIM-ic): copy

opt (opt): choose

Little Agents

jury (JUR-ee): a group of people in charge of deciding guilt or innocence in court

devise (dee-VIZE): come up with an idea

Secrets Make Friends

immigrant (IM-uh-grint): a person who has traveled to live in another country; oftentimes to find a better life than they had before

dillydally (DIL-lee-dal-lee): wasting time by not doing anything useful

reluctant (re -LUK-tunt): doing something even though you really don't want to

Truth Bomb

defendant (de-FEN-dent): in court, the person who is being charged in a case; they're being blamed for doing something wrong

publicity (pub-LISS-it-tee): telling the public about a product through advertisements, articles, etc.

oust (owst): to get rid of

plaintiff (PLAIN-tiff): in court, it's the person who is blaming somebody else for doing something wrong

emissions (ee-MISH-unz): the release of something, such as a sound, smell, liquid, or light

radioactive (ray-dee-oh-ACT-iv): a property of certain elements that sends off radiation due to changes in the atoms of the nuclei

iodine-131 (I-uh-dine 131): a radioactive isotope used in treatment of the thyroid gland

plutonium (ploo-TOH-nee-um): an element used to create nuclear power

byproduct (BI-prod-ukt): an additional, often accidental, result of something done

lodges (LAWD-jez): gets stuck in or stays somewhere

sufficient (suff-ISH-ent): good enough

glands (glandz): parts of the body that release chemicals

statute of limitations (STATCH-yoot uhv lim-it-AY-shuns): a period of time where one can take legal action; if one waits too long, they can't sue

alleged (uh-LEJD): claimed; said to have happened

fetus (FEE-tuss): the offspring of an animal or human while still in the womb or egg

<u>**Explosive News**</u>

contamination (kun—TAMi-nate): to make something unclean

Nagasaki (Nah-gah—SOCK-ee): a city in Japan that was bombed during WWII; it was only the second use of an atomic bomb

Mr. Nice Guy

rein (rain): bring closer, control

Whatever

illuminate (ill-oom-ih-nait): shines light on, brightens

Sunday, Fun Day

jumble (jum-bull): something that's mixed-up or confusing

genealogy (jee-nee–all-oh-jee): an ordered document detailing the history and ancestry of your family

You Can Say That Again

sanity (SAN-it-ee): having a healthy mind

stride (stride): long step

Yelling at the Stars

rejuvenate (re-JOOV-in-ate): to make someone feel younger and more energetic again

concede (kun-SEED): admitting that another person has a better idea than one's own

sarcasm (SAR-kaz-um): using bitter humor to point out someone's failings

Answers and Questions

felicito (feh-LEE-see-toh): Spanish for "congratulations!"

gracias (GRAH-see-us): Spanish for "thank you"

colonel (KER-null): a rank of officer in the military

rural (ROOR-ull): in the country, away from the city

purist (PYOOR-ist): a person who wants everything done the right way in a certain field, profession, or hobby

dislocate (dis-LOH-kayt): to knock out of place

no bueno (no BWEN-oh): Spanish for "no good"

Ay, Dios Mío!

ay, dios mío! (EYE, DEE-ohs MEE-oh): Spanish for "oh my God!"

Hiroshima (heer-OH-she-muh): A city in Japan where the first military use of an atomic bomb took place

Soy Estúpido

occurred (oh-KURD): when and where something happened

contaminate (kun-TAM-ih-nate): to make something unclean

exposure (ex-POH-zher): to be around something dangerous

mortality (mor-TAL-ih-tee): the fact that all living things will someday die

jargon (JAR-gun): confusing words, often having to do with a topic you know nothing about

associate (uh-SO-she-ait): connect to something else similar

preterm (PRE-term): in pregnancy, it's when something happens earlier than it should

smugly (SMUG-lee): confident in yourself, almost to the point of being rude or annoying

Tamales and Visas

visa (VEE-zuh): a mark in a passport showing that you're allowed to be in a certain country

abuelos americanos: (ah-BWEH-LOHS ah-mer-ee-CAHN-ohs): Spanish for "American grandparents"

Waiting for a Miracle

parrots (PAIR-utts): repeats or imitates without actually thinking about it

conviction (kun-VIK-shun): strong, powerful belief

patented (PAT-en-ted): in this case, it refers to a behavior that is unique and constant

pivot (PIV-uht): rotate in place

barricade (BAYR-uh-caid): making a barrier that stops something from getting through

Weeds

induced (in-DOOSD): caused unnaturally

invade (in-VAYD): to enter a place forcefully, like the country of an enemy

Weed Block

fester (FES-ter): to rot or form pus

persona (per-SOH-nuh): the personality and behaviors that someone is known for

gesture (JESS-choor): uses your body movements, usually your hands, to help express an idea, opinion, or emotion

<u>A Note</u>

temples (TEM-pulz): the flattened sides of the forehead

squander (SKWON-der): waste

<u>People Like Us</u>

Sí. Por qué no? (SEE, por-kay NO): Spanish for, "Yes. Why not?"

caca seca (kah-kah SAY-kuh): Spanish for "dried poop"

gracias, mija (GRAH-see-us mee-huh): Spanish for, "thank you, daughter"

<u>Skinny Trees</u>

momentum (moh-MEN-tum): the force of a moving object that makes it want to continue moving until another force stops it

uno (OO-no): Spanish for "one"

diez (dee-ACE): Spanish for "ten"

ocho (OH-choh): Spanish for "eight"

amigo (uh-MEE-go): Spanish for "friend"

<u>Part-time Counselor</u>

inherently (in-HAIR-ent-lee): the way something naturally is; example: Some would say that children are inherently good because they're born good

catalyst (KAT-uh-list): something that causes movement, action, or change

<u>Don't Apologize for Being Right</u>

indigenous: (in-DI-juh-nuss): the "original" or earliest known people to live in a certain area

straggler (STRAG-ler): a person who wanders away from a group or fall behind because they're going slower or getting distracted

replenish (re-PLEN-ish): to make something full or complete again

<u>Adults Can Be Logical</u>

congregation (con-gruh-GAY-shun): a group of people getting together, often for a religious reason

foolproof (FOOL-proof): having no risk of something going wrong

mija (MEE-huh): Spanish for "my daughter, darling"

bromigo (bro-MEE-go): a word that I made up; a cross between the English "brother" and the Spanish "amigo"

buzzkill (BUZ-kil): a person or thing that ruins the fun or the mood

muchacho (moo-CHAH-choh): Spanish for "boy" or "youngster"

<u>Lost</u>

disdain (diss-DAYN): to look at with contempt or scorn; thinking very lowly of someone or something to the point of despising them

by-pass (BI-pass): a way around something

Found

clarity (CLAIR-ih-tee): having a clear understanding of something

stable (STAY-bull): not easily moved

elicit (ih-liss-it): to evoke or bring out

descends (dee-SENDS): comes down

audible (AHH-dih-bull): able to be heard

The Right Reason

Buenas noches. Dulces sueños, mis amores (bweh-nahs noh-chays Dool-sais sway-nyohs mees ah-morr-es): Spanish for "Good night. Sweet dreams, my loves"

churning (CHER-ning): spinning and mixing

Mission Improbable

subtle (SUH-tull): not obvious; difficult to understand or notice

slinks (sleenks): to move in a slow, embarrassed way

idiom (id-ee-um): a saying that isn't easily understood easily without already knowing the meaning, such as, "It's raining cats and dogs"

Such a Good Spy

cringe (crinj): to shrink back due to an awkward or painful experience

psyched (siked): prepared and excited

piqued (peekd): excited or interested

cliché (clee-shay): a phrase or sentence that is used so often it's almost meaningless at this point

Raw Talent

irony (I-run-nee): the clear difference between what is said and what is done or expected

batting average (BAT-ting av–rij): a number that shows the percent of time a baseball player gets a hit

RBI (R-B-I): stands for Runs Batted In; this number represents the amount of runs that have scored due to the player's plate appearances

A Thousand Words

heir (air): a person who will inherit someone's wealth or power

souvenir (SOO-ven-EER): a keepsake brought back from a trip or special event with intent to keep as a way of remembering the special occasion

Against My Better Judgment

humiliate (hyoo-MILL-ee-ait): majorly embarrass

theory (THEER-ee): an explanation that has lots of evidence but can't be completely proven

One Step at a Time

radiate (RAY-dee-ait): shine bright like the sun

wary (WAIR-ee): watchful, being on guard

A Million Things

coordinate (KOR-dih-nayt): working together to plan something

plead (pleed): beg

feign (fain): fake or imitate

oblivious (oh-BLIV-ee-us): unaware and forgetful

No Ifs, Ands, or Buts

projectile (pro-JEK-tile): any object thrown or shot

squelch (skwelch): to snuff or put something out, such as a
fire

The Asparagus Broker

broker (BRO-ker): a person who help you buy and sell stock
when investing your money

anticipation (an-tiss-ih-PAY-shun): being excited or hopeful
for a future event

jitters (JIT-erz): a feeling of nervousness

How May I Help You?

phenomenal (fih-NOM-uh-null): amazing and extraordinary

marvelous (MAR-vuh-luss): superb, excellent, great

Dollar or Doll Hair?

claustrophobic (claw-struh-FOH-bick): fear of small places

ethical (ETH-ih-kull): follows a set of morals; if one is ethical,
they do the "right" thing

haste (hayst): fast, speedy

binding (BINE-ding): committing or connecting

uncivilized (un-SIV-uh-lized): a rude, uneducated person

stipulation (stip-yoo-LAY-shun): a need or demand in order
to make a deal or agreement happen

My Best Cheerleader

brisk (brisk): quick

sermon (SER-mun): a speech given by a religious leader during a religious ceremony

no seas estúpido (no SAY-ahs es-TOO-pee-doh): Spanish for "don't be stupid"

I'm Waiting

assure (UH-shoor): make someone feel confident about something, encourage

suspiciously (sus-PISH-us-lee): to question or wonder about someone's guilt or purpose for doing something

Happy to Help

drawl (drawl): speaking with an overly dramatic tone of voice to show a fake sense of surprise

relatively (REL-uh-tiv-lee): close to, almost

If You're Into That Sort of Thing

mumbo-jumbo (MUM-boh JUM-boh): meaningless, useless words

NEED HELP WITH THE THEME?

Note: do not read this before you finish the book.

Teachers always ask what you learned from a book. They say, "What was the theme?" or "What was the author's message?" Well, because I am a fifth-grade teacher, I'll lay it out for you right here so you can check and see if your thoughts match up with mine. They don't have to, of course. I invite you to take the lessons you have found as your own, whatever they are.

Anger comes from deep pain. If you're angry, like many of us, it's not the anger you need to begin with. Begin with focusing on whatever pain you've been through; the pain that has piled up and turned into anger.

You can't fix people. And even if you could, you're a kid. That's not your job. You can love people who have unhealthy habits, but keep yourself at a safe distance and find someone to support you.

Great wisdom often comes from great pain. Listen to the people who have dealt with similar issues before you. They can help guide your way. Then later, maybe you can do the same for someone else.

Don't do life alone. As Asher's family found out at the end of the book, there are more people out there wanting to help than you would ever imagine. Give them a chance. Reach out to your teachers, counselors, and other people you trust. Try it out. There's really nothing to lose and everything in the world to gain.

AUTHOR DEDICATIONS AND ACKNOWLEDGMENTS

I dedicate this book to my dad, Richard Hertzog, whose lost childhood set him up against a lifetime of pain and anger. After he nearly died when I was thirty-one, his whole perspective on life changed. Unfortunately, he only lasted three more years, but they were the best three years of my life. Thank you, Dad, for thinking more highly of me than I ever thought of myself. I will always remember that you believed.

And to my mom, Karen. Thanks for battling all your "chips" in hopes of providing a more stable childhood for your own kids. I think you did pretty well. And thank you for supporting me in my ongoing battles. You're the one I can always count on.

And to my wife, Lani. Thank you for all you've done to help me have time to write. I realize that, out of all the characters in the book, I'm a little too much Dad at times, with a propensity toward Julia's bathroom humor. You're intelligent, beautiful, and I love you. Thank you for your patience, as I've dealt with my personal "cancer" over the years.

And to my son, Gideon. I hope that you'll learn from your grandpa and dad and control any sort of frustrations that may come along . . . before they turn into debilitating anger. Remember to reach out when you need help. I'll always be there for you. Always.

And to my beautiful daughter, Lilly. Thank you for being so gracious with me. I've gotten frustrated more times than I'd like to admit, and you're always willing to love me no matter what. Your kisses, hugs, and cuddles have encouraged me more than you will ever know. I am so blessed to be your daddy.

And to all my students over the years. Thank you for your continued inspiration to read great books.

To those students who were the first to read this book with me and give their encouragement along the way: Thank you, Anjali, Ashrit, Austin, Carter, Chloe, Claira, Darina, Dylan, Elijah, Evan, Grace, Hiranmay, Jackson, Jake, Jayden, Kanak, Marcus, Max, Mckenzie, Nikhil, Nita, Nived, Rithika, Saanvi, Sanjana, Saveer, Tanishka, Tejas, and Vindhya.

To the real Annie Carmona and all the school counselors who go underpaid, over-extended, and underappreciated. When the world figures out how important you are, I hope you get the recognition you deserve.

To my school librarian, Nicole Randles, and the great people at the Mock Newbery Awards. Thank you for picking amazing books for me to love and share with my students.

To Mie-Mie Wu, of the King County Library System. You're amazing. Thank you for your love of books. It radiates from you, and it fuels me, and my students, to read more than we ever would have without you.

To my beta readers: Bonnie, Isla, Emma, Jack, Nicole, and Mom. Thank you for your time and valuable input.

To the many authors who have inspired me for years, specifically Lois Lowry, Linda Sue Park, Gary Paulsen, Sharon

Creech, and Lynda Mullaly Hunt. You are amazing, inspirational writers.

And finally, to my favorite local author, Stephanie Kallos. Stevie, you started it all when you gifted me *Broken for You* when I was Noah's school bus driver so many years ago. You showed me that authors were just normal people with the passion and patience to tell their stories, and that I could someday become one too. And look at me! I did it!

And to you, my reader, feel free to reach out and say hi. I'd love to hear what you thought about the book or if you have ideas for any more. You can reach me at: Michael@MichaelHertzog.com.

WORKS CITED

Dorn Steele, Karen, "Lawyers Say Hanford Lawsuit Is Too Late," The Spokesman-Review (Website), July 16, 2004, https://www.spokesman.com/stories/2004/jul/16/lawyers-say-hanford-lawsuit-is-too-late/

Camden, Jim, "Hanford Illness Claims Split Jury," The Spokesman-Review (Website), May 20, 2005, https://www.spokesman.com/stories/2005/may/20/hanford-illness-claims-split-jury/

"Senators Win Victory for Former Hanford Workers Trying to Receive Compensation for Illnesses." Press release, 10/08/2004. https://www.cantwell.senate.gov/news/press-releases/senators-win-victory-for-former-hanford-workers-trying-to-receive-compensation-for-illnesses

National Academy of Sciences (US) Committee on an Assessment of Centers for Disease Control and Prevention Radiation Studies from DOE Contractor Sites: Subcommittee to Review the Hanford Thyroid Disease Study Final Results and Report.

Review of the Hanford Thyroid Disease Study Draft Final Report. Washington (DC): National Academies Press (US); 2000. Public Summary. Available from: https://www.ncbi.nlm.nih.gov/books/NBK225225/

Tatham LM, Bove FJ, Kaye WE, Spengler RF. Population exposures to I-131 releases from Hanford Nuclear Reservation and preterm birth, infant mortality, and fetal deaths. Int J Hyg Environ Health. 2002 Mar;205(1-2):41-8. doi: 10.1078/1438-4639-00128. PMID: 12018015.